"WE MEET AGAIN, MARSHAL," BUTTS SAID GRIMLY . . .

Longarm glanced around at the other riders. There were six of them all told, including Butts. The ranchers were getting together, acting in concert against a common enemy.

"Don't make a play for your sixgun, Marshal." Butts said, as he rode past Longarm to reach the side of Wally Troy, Longarm's prisoner.

"How you doin', Wally?" Butts asked.

"Hell, Butts, I'm doing just fine. All I got's a slug in my shoulder. Just get that sonofabitch riding behind me off my back."

"Sure, Wally, sure."

Butts pulled up slightly and fell in beside Longarm, then reached out his right hand. "Let me have that weapon of yours, Marshal . . ."

*Also in the LONGARM series
from Jove/HBJ*

LONGARM

AND THE LOGGERS

TABOR EVANS

A JOVE/HBJ BOOK

Requests for permission to make copies of any part of the
work should be mailed to: Permissions, Jove Publications,
Inc., 757 Third Avenue, New York, NY 10017

Printed in the United States of America

Library of Congress Catalog Card Number: 78-71880

First Jove/HBJ edition published March 1979

Jove/HBJ books are published by Jove Publications, Inc.
(Harcourt Brace Jovanovich), 757 Third Avenue, New York,
NY 10017

Chapter 1

Longarm paid the barber and stepped out through the shop's open doorway onto the sidewalk. The big lawman was restless, his blue-gray eyes gloomy, as he looked across the crowded street at the recently completed Windsor Hotel.

By his own reckoning, he had tarried too long already in the Mile-High City and had spent too many evenings in the hotel's ornate taproom. Perhaps it was the gaudy floor—studded with three thousand silver dollars. The evening before, the son of one of Denver's wealthiest men had stayed in a game too long with nothing in his hand but two pair—seven high. The bluff had not worked. Longarm's full house had taken everything the man had—which was much more than he could afford, as it turned out. A few moments later there had been a scuffle in the gent's room. A shot rang out, and it soon became common knowledge that the young heir had tried to shoot himself.

The memory was not a pleasant one. Longarm didn't like playing poker with men who couldn't lose with dignity. He didn't like those flabby, suet-faced wastrels who had hung about that poker table, either. Longarm was still as lean and as hard as he had been at the end of the War, some fifteen years ago. If he hung around this place much longer, he was afraid he might soon come to resemble that crowd in the hotel. He was eating too much and was sure as hell smoking too much.

5

It was a simple matter to quit smoking, he reminded himself bleakly. He had done it countless times.

Longarm took out a cheroot and stuck it into the corner of his wide mouth, then turned up the street and headed for Colfax Avenue and the federal courthouse. It was almost eight o'clock. He knew it would be well past eight by the time he reached Marshal Vail's office. He didn't care. Let Billy blow his stack. Maybe it would goad the fellow into digging up an assignment for Longarm that would send him out of this Sodom. Wallace and Grenoble had been getting all the juicy assignments lately; now it was Longarm's turn.

As he strode along, he was a study in gunmetal blue and saddle-leather brown. His hair and his John L. Sullivan mustache were both brown, as was the Stetson he was wearing, whose crown was telescoped flat on top. Longarm's tweed suit and vest were also brown. His shirt was blue-gray. He wore a black shoestring tie knotted at his neck. His boots, fashioned of cordovan leather, were low-heeled army issue.

Longarm moved with a swift, catlike stride. Those who saw him coming made no effort to dispute his progress as he cut a path through the early-morning tide of humanity now surging along the sidewalk. The curbing was lined with unharnessed trucks. Hesitant, unhappy people peeked out from between them, awaiting their chance to make a dash for it across the traffic-clogged streets. In contrast, street urchins ducked swiftly across, weaving among the thundering carts and ducking deftly in front of the horsedrawn streetcars to burst with cheerful shouts onto the sidewalks.

Longarm was approaching one corner when a small lad—his begrimed face round and impudent with the energy of youth—ducked onto the sidewalk just in front of him and slammed full-tilt into a drummer, sending the salesman back against the wheel of a parked brew-

6

ery truck. As if on cue, one of the truck's huge stallions began to void a thick steaming gout of urine. The drummer found himself being spattered from head to toe as the heavy yellow stream pounded into the steaming mash of manure and mud swirling about the horse's fetlocks. Jumping quickly away from the horse, the drummer uttered a startled cry of dismay and took off after the urchin. He might as well have tried to overtake yesterday.

Smiling slightly at the sight of the two antagonists disappearing into the crowd, Longarm turned the next corner onto Colfax and started up the slight hill to the courthouse.

Ignoring the clerk playing on his typewriter in the outer office, Longarm pushed past him and stepped into Marshal Billy Vail's inner sanctum. His superior looked up at Longarm's entry. One bushy eyebrow was cocked upward. As usual, the pink-cheeked, balding official was making an effort to shovel his way out from under a blizzard of dodgers and official communiques from Washington.

"Sit down," he growled. "I'll be with you in a minute —as soon as I dig myself out of this mess. I'm not going to bother telling you you're late."

"You just did," Longarm said, slumping into the chief's red leather armchair. He chewed impatiently on his unlit cheroot, his eyes on Vail. As he watched Vail, he was reminded that here was a man who had ridden over half of the Southwest after assorted bandits and hoodlums in his time—but who was now reduced to the role of a flabby bureaucrat chasing paper over a desktop. The thought of all that lean muscle turning to fat troubled Longarm deeply.

At last Vail found the dodger he had been looking for. He pulled it toward him with a grunt and glanced up at Longarm. "I understand you got young Tobin be-

7

tween a rock and a hard place at the Windsor last night. What were you holding, to beat him?"

Longarm never revealed a hand when he didn't have to—but this was a little different. He took the cheroot out of his mouth. "Fours and tens, full house."

"Ten high!" Vail's eyes lit up.

Longarm nodded. "And three fours."

"What did Tobin's kid have?"

"Two pair. Sixes and sevens."

"Jesus." Vail spoke softly, shaking his head.

"The kid asked me to hold off on his IOUs. They'd better be good."

"Old man Tobin'll see to it," Vail assured him. "Hell, this isn't the first time. But you're not getting too popular in Denver, beating young Tobin like that. Don't forget, his old man's helping Flannigan to finance that new opera house. That makes him a big man in town."

"Opera house!" Longarm snorted, shaking his head.

"That's right, Longarm. Culture. It's on its way. Yes, it is. Hell, we're all going to have to start taking a bath once a month, whether we need one or not, I swear." He sobered, and glanced significantly at the banjo clock ticking on the oak-paneled wall. "What kept you? I've got some action here—what you've been howling for —but I almost gave it to Wallace."

"I'm here now. What action have you got?"

Vail tapped the dodger in his hand with a finger. "I want you to take Blackie Bolen to St. Louis. The extradition papers are on the way. You can leave with Blackie on the afternoon train. They'll be right pleased to get the sonofabitch, I can tell you."

Longarm nodded. Deputy Wallace had brought Bolen in a week ago, after the outlaw had messed up a bank job north of Colorado Springs. In St. Louis they wanted him for everything from murder to armed robbery to kidnaping. But Longarm did not want to go to

St. Louis. He was sick of traffic, smells, and the swarm of overfed townsmen. "Send Wallace," he said.

"I thought you wanted action. You've been grousing now for two weeks."

"Send Wallace. He brought Bolen in; I didn't."

"I was going to send him on another job—to Nevada."

Longarm nodded. "Nevada sounds fine. Send me."

Shrugging, Vail put down Blackie Bolen's dodger and poked into the pile of envelopes and folders on his desk. He pulled forth a new manila folder and opened it. Glancing through its contents silently for a minute or two, he looked up at Longarm. "Ever hear of Silver City, Nevada?"

Longarm shook his head.

"It's smack dab in the middle of nowhere—Digger land, the Great Basin, as hot and dry as Hades, only not nearly as interesting."

Longarm's eyes glinted. "Go on, Chief."

"The Silver City sheriff telegraphed the War Department about three weeks ago. It seems he spotted an army deserter in a logging town well up on the headwaters of the Humboldt. He was on other business at the time and couldn't chase him. Besides, he didn't have the authority."

"You know that area?" Longarm asked.

Vail nodded, arching his eyebrows demoniacally. "Like I said, it's high, dry, and dusty—a godforsaken patch of alkali basins and black rock populated by bush Indians and a few damn fool settlers. You'll have a long, miserable ride on a livery horse to get to that logging town north of Silver City—and after you get there, most likely you'll find out the poor bastard you're hunting is long gone. You still want the job?"

"I want out of Denver, Chief," Longarm replied wearily. "And St. Louis sounds like more of the same —only worse. Let Wallace have it."

Vail sighed. "Okay, Longarm. Here's the background. The fugitive is a Mountain Man, name of Ned Shortslef. He deserted to the enemy while he was scouting for the cavalry during the Rosebud campaign four years ago. He was married to a Cheyenne squaw and is known to have had a son by her. He's a big fellow, better than six feet—almost as tall as you, I reckon. Hair on his face—plenty of it, in fact. Blue eyes. That's all it has here. Whipsaw's the name of the logging town where the sheriff spotted him."

"That must mean the sheriff knows this jasper pretty well," Longarm guessed.

"He scouted with him during the Rosebud campaign. Yeah. He knows him very well."

"What's the sheriff's name?"

"Martin Tanner. See him first in Silver City. Maybe you can get a better description of the scout."

"I'll need it."

Vail closed the folder. "Be on that train for Silver City tonight. Get your expense vouchers and your railroad pass from my secretary on your way out." He grinned suddenly. "I'll send Wallace to the fleshpots of St. Louis. And I'll just let him think it was all my idea."

Longarm got up and walked to the door. As he pulled it open, he glanced back at Vail. "I've got to shake the smell of this city, Chief. Seems to me the West is filling up too damn fast."

Vail nodded, smiling slightly. "It's all that damn Greeley's fault."

Longarm left the office.

Two days and some seven hundred miles later, Longarm waited for the baggagemaster to drag his saddle across the baggage car floor to him. When he did, Longarm hefted the army-surplus McClellan saddle onto one shoulder, and with the rest of his gear draped over his other shoulder, he went looking for the hotel.

It didn't take him long to find it. There was only one in Silver City—an unpainted two-story building with the one word HOTEL painted across the front. The whitewash used to paint this message had almost faded away in the blistering sun. Flanking the hotel were the town's livery stable, a blacksmith shop, a barber shop, and a general store. The town's best saloon, the Silver City, sat facing the hotel from across the wide, dusty main street. After this, the false fronts petered out swiftly; the remaining frame shacks, small and nondescript, seemed to be cowering visibly under the merciless sun.

Longarm mounted the hotel's porch steps and entered the building. An ancient cowpoke came to his feet behind the front desk. A room off the lobby containing about six tables served as a dining room, Longarm noted as he put his saddle and gear down.

"Got a nice room on the second floor, front," said the desk clerk. "And Jim Powers next door in the barber shop has some tubs in back if you're wanting to wash off that railroad grime." The clerk looked hopefully past Longarm. "Anyone else get off the train with you?"

"Nope," Longarm replied, signing the register.

"We don't have a bellhop," the clerk told Longarm unhappily.

"That's all right," Longarm said. "Maybe you can tell me where I might find Sheriff Tanner?"

The old man glanced down at Longarm's signature. "The sheriff's office is four buildings down on the other side of the Silver City Saloon, Deputy Long," the clerk replied, dropping the room key and tag into Longarm's waiting hand.

"That's right. I'm Deputy Long," said Longarm, hefting his saddle and the rest of his gear onto his shoulders. "I hope you ain't a flannelmouth, mister."

11

"No, sir," the old man said with some pride. "I keep it shut as tight as a burro's ass, and that's a fact."

"That's fine, mister," Longarm said, starting for the narrow stairs to his room.

A small, pudgy fellow wearing a black derby hat and a dark brown suit was sitting on a kitchen chair on the board sidewalk in front of the sheriff's office. The chair was tipped back on its two rear legs, the back of the chair resting against the building, the man's crossed ankles resting on the hitch rail. He kept this position until Longarm reached him, then pulled his legs off the hitch rail and let the chair tilt forward.

"I'd like to see Sheriff Tanner," Longarm said.

"Who the hell are you, mister?" the fellow asked Longarm lazily, a slight smile on his round face.

"Deputy U.S. Marshal Custis Long. And just who the hell are you?"

"Oh, I'm Constable Seegar. Pete Seegar." The fellow was too ill-mannered to offer his hand. Longarm didn't mind at all.

"I asked you a question, Constable," Longarm reminded him. "How long before you expect the sheriff to return?"

"You planning on waiting for him?" the constable asked laconically.

Longarm nodded, his irritation growing.

"You better take that chair over there. You got a long wait, I'm thinking."

Longarm took the chair, then pulled out a cheroot and lit it. His bath had been a long, steaming delight—and he had treated himself to a shave and a haircut as well, since the prices in this lonely outpost were very reasonable—two bits for the shave *and* the bath. He hoped the smoke would restore his spirits to the even temper they had enjoyed before he had started this conversation.

"Sheriff Tanner left about a week ago," the constable finally said. "Told me it wouldn't take him long to get to Whipsaw and finish some business he had."

"Some business?"

The fellow nodded. Parts of him seemed to be trying to ooze out through the weak points in his vest and over his belt. His brown suit and vest were lightly checked. They were filthy. He wore no collar with his striped shirt, and his black bowler carried a thin patina of dust.

"That business he wired the government about," the constable went on, "and what you're here for, I suppose —that renegade Mountain Man what ran off in battle and joined his Indian buddies. That turncoat."

Longarm had half expected this. The sheriff had gotten tired of waiting for the government to send someone and had gone off to track the man before he got out of reach once again. This Tanner was not the usual sheriff, it seemed, one content to sit back and wait for the plums to fall into his lap. Longarm decided he liked the man. Still, there was one thing about all of this that bothered Longarm.

"Say there, Constable," Longarm said. "How is it that Tanner didn't send out his deputies? How come he's not back here tending to the paperwork, like most county sheriffs I know?"

"Tanner don't have no deputies. And he said I could handle the paperwork. He's right; there ain't nothing to it."

Longarm frowned. "No deputies, Constable?"

"You gotta have money to pay deputies. Now, ain't that so?"

"I can't argue with that."

"And this godforsaken pasture in hell ain't got no money, Deputy—at least not any it wants to spend lining the pockets of deputy sheriffs, not when the Western Lumber and Land Combine provides us with their

13

own company guard. Hell, we got all the law we need in this county provided free by them."

"You mean the Western Lumber and Land Combine *is* the law in this county."

"And there ain't nothing wrong with that, neither. Slade Desmond—he's the company manager—him and Bat Lawson keep the lid on things real nice."

"And Bat Lawson's the man in charge of the company guards, I guess."

The constable smiled his agreement. "You know what I was before I got appointed town constable?"

Longarm waited; he was certain the fellow would tell him.

"I was one of Slade's bookkeepers at the mill in Whipsaw." The fellow smiled, tipped his chair back against the wall, and stuck his feet back up onto the hitch rail. "But I hated that, so he let me try this job. I been doing fine. I always wanted to be a lawman. Hell, that's what I came out West for in the first place—for some adventure."

"Maybe you've been reading too many dime novels."

The man smiled. "Just got the latest adventure of Deadwood Dick back in the office—*Deadwood Dick's Home Base*. It's a corker. That Bob Wheeler is some writer. He sure knows a lot about Calamity Jane and how the West really is."

"You're sure of that, are you?"

The constable looked at Longarm with suspicion. "You're damn right I am."

Longarm didn't want to argue with the man, even though he knew Calamity Jane as Jane Canary, a broken-down old ex-whore. When Longarm had last heard, she was spending most of her time cadging drinks at whatever bars still let her inside. Longarm puffed on his cheroot, turning over in his mind what the constable had given him: this Tanner was sheriff only on the sufferance of that logging company operating out

14

of Whipsaw; the logging company's operation was under the control of Slade Desmond; one of Desmond's lieutenants was a man called Bat Lawson, who bossed the company's private guard; further, this Constable Seegar was here to keep tabs on Sheriff Tanner as well as on the town of Silver City and its new inhabitants. Not a sparrow fell to the ground, it appeared, without this Slade Desmond knowing all about it. He ran a tight ship.

Longarm glanced at Seegar. "You say Sheriff Tanner's been gone about a week?"

The fellow nodded and pushed his bowler down over his forehead to shield his eyes from the sun's glare.

"Just one thing more, Constable. What did the sheriff tell you about this deserter?"

"Not much. Said he was a big son of a bitch—favored a bushy beard and mustache." Seegar laughed suddenly as he remembered. "Said there was one time on the Snake when this Mountain Man came up to their camp at night and one of the Shoshone scouts thought he was a grizzly. Tanner said the Mountain Man was all dressed in his furs, and with that beard of his, the only things that looked human were them two blue eyes peering out from behind all that hair. After that, the Shoshone scouts called him 'Man Who Moves Like Bear.'" Seegar nodded again as he thought over what Tanner had told him. "A real big man, I guess. Like most of them Mountain Men."

"They weren't *all* that big," Longarm said quietly. He was thinking of Joe Meek, who had been just a little over five feet tall. The little Mountain Man had fought and killed grizzlies hand-to-hand. Once he had used a coup stick on one grizzly and killed another with his hatchet. He'd been in real close and had buried the hatchet's blade in the grizzly's brain.

"What do you mean?" the constable demanded. "They sure as hell *were* big men—*all* of 'em. What do

15

you think they called them *Mountain* Men for?" He squinted at Longarm suddenly, almost losing his bowler in the process. "How long you *been* out West, Deputy?"

"Long enough," Longarm replied.

The fellow grunted. "Don't sound like it. Don't sound like it a-*tall!*"

"Maybe so, Constable. Now, is that all the description of Shortslef you can give me? Is that all Tanner told you?"

"That's all. Tanner ain't all that chock-full of information—not when I'm around, that is. He's a little suspicious of me because I'm such a good friend of Slade."

"Thank you, Constable."

Longarm got up, touched the brim of his hat to Seegar, and started back to the hotel. He figured now might be a good time to catch some shut-eye before supper. He was still weary from his long train ride—and even wearier from talking to the town's well-read constable.

He was about to enter the hotel when the sound of hoofs and the jingle of harness caused him to pause and look down the street. Riding into town from the north were at least six horsemen and a small coach. The coach looked quite elegant, with red trim, red wheel spokes, and gilt edging around the two side windows. Three riders rode in front and three in the rear. For a county with the lid on nice and tight, this was a most formidable guard.

As the coach pulled up in front of the hotel, the six riders dismounted noisily, loudly proclaiming their thirst. They paid scant heed to their weary, lathered mounts, which they left at the hitch rails in front of the hotel, and crossed the street to the Silver City Saloon. All but one. This fellow went straight to the coach's door and pulled it open. A buxom, handsome woman got out—and one look at the lovely chestnut curls

16

coiled on her shoulders and the wide, generous portion of her neck and bosom open to view told Longarm all he needed to know about her. Perhaps she *was* worth this much protection.

The fellow who escorted the woman from the coach was a dark-visaged man with a hooked nose and a strong, prominent chin. His shirt was of crisp, white linen and he was wearing an immaculate black string tie. His black hat was flat-crowned, his sixgun gleaming, his expensive, finely tooled boots shining despite the dust. As the man escorted the woman past Longarm into the hotel, the lawman caught a flash of her brazen eyes and gleaming teeth as she saw him standing there.

Abruptly, she turned in the doorway and called back across the street to the other riders in a strident, brassy voice: "Don't you bozos get too tanked, now! That train's due in pretty soon and those girls are going to be mighty tired."

"Hell, Ruby," one of the men called out, his hand on the Silver City Saloon's batwing door, "we're just going to wet down all that alkali. Come on over and join us —less'n you got *other* business!"

The rest of the men with him roared at that, then followed him into the saloon. Ruby laughed, herself. "You heard what he said," she told her escort. "Is that the kind of discipline you have over those bohunks?"

"You want me to discipline them or take you up to your room?" the man asked in reply.

"Now what do *you* think, Bat?"

He reached down for her canvas gladstone and led her into the hotel lobby.

Following them into the hotel, Longarm looked over the man she had called Bat. This was the leader of Slade Desmond's company guard, and those men who had ridden in with him were part of that guard—what amounted to a private army. In this case, a small company delegated to make sure the shipment of new girls

17

arrived safe and sound. Those loggers in Whipsaw were waiting anxiously, no doubt.

As Ruby and her escort neared the desk, Longarm moved past them and up the stairs to his room. The matchstick he had left wedged between the door and the jamb was undisturbed. He unlocked his door and walked in, pocketing the matchstick for future use. He was taking off his hat when he heard the clatter of hooves and the rumble of a wagon's big wheels. He stepped to the window and looked down.

Loggers—evidently tardy members of the same party escorting the madam—were piling out of a wagon in front of the saloon, filling the air with the hearty shouts of big men intent on slaking prodigious thirsts. They had come to help Ruby greet the new girls.

Longarm turned from the window, carefully removed his Ingersoll pocket watch from his left-hand vest pocket, and placed it on the top of the dresser. The gold-washed chain attached to the watch was clipped to the butt of a double-barreled .44 derringer. A potentially fatal surprise for any of Longarm's enemies, it fit snugly into his right vest pocket, the bright chain dangling across the front of his vest between his derringer and his watch. Next, Longarm unholstered his double-action Colt Model T .44-40. The barrel had been cut down to five inches and the front sight filed off. Placing the Colt under his pillow, he removed his cross-draw holster and gunbelt and hung them over the bedpost, after which he unbuttoned his vest and shirt front and flopped onto the bed without bothering to kick off his boots.

Longarm had trained himself over the years to be able to sleep instantly anywhere—while at the same time retaining a catlike ability to awaken on a moment's notice. Longarm's hand snaked under his pillow and came to rest beside the butt of his Colt. He closed his eyes and was asleep almost at once.

Longarm awoke to the sound of booming laughter and the clash of silverware, coming from the dining room beneath his room. Swinging off the bed, he stood up and consulted his watch. It was a little after five.

Swiftly he buttoned up his shirt and vest, replaced his watch and derringer, and strapped on his rig. The holster was open-toed, fashioned of waxed and heat-hardened leather. He wore the rig high, adjusting the Cordovan belt to ride above his hip bones. Withdrawing the Colt from under the pillow, he swung it out over the bed and emptied the cylinder, then dry-fired a few times to check the action. After examining the five cartridges, he reloaded and dropped the revolver into the holster, resting the firing pin on an empty chamber.

He settled the snuff-brown Stetson onto his head and left the room, ducking slightly to clear the doorframe.

Entering the dining room a moment later, he considered himself lucky to spot an unoccupied table, and headed for it. The small room was crowded with loggers, all of whom had eyes only for the three fetching young ladies sitting at the table with Ruby. The girls had arrived safe and sound. As Longarm sat down, he noted with some amusement that Ruby's girls were doing their best not to show how pleased they were by all this attention.

Two of the three were pretty only in that they were young and fresh-looking and were neither too fat nor too slim. The third girl, however, was more than just youthful—she was very pretty. She had glanced up at Longarm when he had entered the dining room. She did not know Longarm, and he did not know her, yet an awareness had passed between them in that instant; a feeling both of them immediately responded to and understood. The girl had dark auburn hair. She wore it combed out boldly, in thick curls. Her face was not heavily rouged like the faces of the others, and her eyes

—a dark, emerald green—dominated her pale, freckled face.

As Longarm turned his attention to the menu, he could feel her eyes on him. After he gave the waitress his order, he glanced at her again. She was looking directly at him. As soon as their eyes met, she looked hastily back to the other girls at her table and launched into a highly animated conversation. It did not fool anyone, however. Longarm saw the madam turn curiously and look boldly at him. She smiled. Longarm nodded at her, returning the smile. Turning back around, the madam said something to the girls, causing them all to break into delighted laughter.

Longarm's meal arrived and he tore into it. It had been a long day and he was famished. He was reaching for his second cup of coffee when he heard tables scraping the floor and looked up to see three hulking loggers approaching the madam's table. The one in the lead had obviously been selected as their spokesman. He was the tallest and roughest-looking, with a patch over one eye and shoulders wide enough to use as a gallows. He cleared his throat while his huge hands twisted his stocking cap. The madam waited. He cleared his throat again. In exasperation, one of the men behind him prodded him angrily in the back.

"Ruby," the fellow faltered, " . . . we was wonderin' . . . I mean, what we was hopin' was that . . ."

From the other loggers in the room there arose a sudden howl of protest that shook the small dining room. These three loggers were jumping the gun, moving too soon! The uproar was terrific. Ruby waved the room to silence and then looked up at the logger wearing the eyepatch. She obviously knew him.

"Now, Gus," she told him, "you know full well what these girls here have been through—a long, hard ride all the way from San Francisco. Now, why don't you fine gentlemen give them a chance to rest up—at least one night?"

"Aw, Ruby!" the logger replied, no longer tongue-tied. "They been resting up since they got on that train!"

Ruby shook her head. "Gus, you are no gentleman."

"That's right, Ruby!" cried a logger standing beside Gus. "He ain't no gentleman. None of us is. And these here ain't no ladies!"

A roar of agreement seconded that assertion. With a massive shrug, Ruby turned to the girls as if to say *What can I do, girls? It's up to you!*

At once, the first three were joined by other loggers. Surrounding the table, they beamed down with grimy, bewhiskered faces at the young girls. It didn't take long for two of the girls to make their choices. The third girl—the auburn-haired one with the green eyes —seemed undecided. This was the girl Gus wanted.

He reached down, took the girl by the wrist, and pulled her gently but firmly toward him. The girl left her chair and moved around the table toward Gus, still obviously reluctant. Abruptly, she leaned down and whispered something in Ruby's ear. Ruby listened attentively.

"Never you mind about that, Alice," Ruby boomed when the girl had finished. "Why, Gus here will be real gentle with you. Won't you, Gus?"

"As gentle as I can be," admitted Gus, pulling the girl roughly against himself. The other loggers laughed. Evidently, Gus was not considered the gentlest of men. This laughter—and the girl's reluctance—angered Gus.

The girl saw this. At once, her tactics changed. She wrapped her arm around the big logger's arm and smiled up into his face. "That's all right," she told him. "I don't want no trouble. If you promise to be nice to me, Gus, I'll be nice to you. Real nice."

21

Gus's capitulation was awesomely complete, his anger vanishing instantly. With an almost grateful glance down at Ruby, Gus left the dining room with the girl—to the jealous hoots and ribald jibes of the loggers remaining behind.

Longarm finished his coffee. Leaving a silver dollar to cover his meal and a generous tip for the waitress, he stood up and started from the dining room. He was almost to the door when Constable Seegar entered, nodded curtly to Longarm, and went directly to the madam's table. Ruby made him warmly welcome. The two, it seemed, had business to discuss.

Longarm continued on out of the hotel and made directly for the livery, where he proceeded to examine the horses. Ordinarily, if Longarm needed a mount for field work, he would borrow one from the nearest army post or remount station. Neither accomodation existed within miles of Silver City, however, and Longarm had decided to leave for Whipsaw the next day.

The deputy was a keen judge of horseflesh. Though he appreciated a good horse, he was not a sentimentalist. A horse is just about as bright as a cat—no brighter. Its one mental ability is a good memory. Usually that was enough for Longarm. There was no sense in expecting anything more than that from a horse, and he didn't. Usually, Longarm preferred an army mount over a cow pony because of its size. A good bay gelding was what Longarm was looking for at the moment—until he spotted the Morgan.

She was a tough, long-winded, all-purpose saddle mare that still had some good miles left in her. Longarm listened closely to her breathing, then carefully checked all four feet. One hoof would need a fresh shoe; the frogs of all four hooves would have to be cleaned as well. Longarm went to find the owner of the livery.

"Yep, best saddle horse I got here," the old cowpoke

said, when Longarm told him of his choice. " 'Course, everyone complains because she's a mite old and not as sassy as the younger mounts. But she's a Morgan." He shook his head. "Some people just don't know nothin' about horses."

"She'll do fine," Longarm told the man. Then he mentioned the shoe and asked him to clean out the frogs thoroughly.

"You didn't have to tell me," the man protested. "I wouldn't let a horse leave my stable what wasn't in perfect condition."

Longarm smiled at that, and was about to go back to take another look at the Morgan, when he heard shouts erupting suddenly in the darkening street. He stepped out through the stable door and saw four mounted men dragging four Indians at the ends of ropes. The men were riding at such a brisk trot that the Indians were unable to keep their feet for any length of time. They were, in fact, almost totally exhausted. Their appearance was wretched. Their hair was matted with sweat-caked alkali and their knees and elbows were raw and bleeding.

The horsemen pulled up in front of the Silver City Saloon with guns thundering into the sky. The Indians collapsed forward onto their knees. Longarm shook his head in disgust as loggers and gunmen poured out of the saloon to dance in glee around the sullen, prostrate Indians. With some satisfaction, Longarm noted that not one of the Indians had uttered a single cry. They were as silent as vengeance as they lay sprawled in the dust, looking up at their tormenters.

"Now that's real excitement, ain't it?" the old man said, his tone betraying the contempt he felt for those four riders.

Longarm glanced down at the old cowpoke. His hair was almost gone, and what was left was fine-spun cotton. He had the squinting look of men who have spent

23

too many years looking long distances under a glaring sun—and the bulbous, cherry-red nose of the inebriate. The bulge of a flask was clearly visible on his hip.

"You don't approve?" Longarm asked him.

The man thrust his chin forward indignantly. "No, sir. I don't. After all, them Indians is just Diggers— poorest damn excuses I ever saw for a red man. They ain't no bother. All they do is kill jackrabbits and eat pine nuts." Then he shook his head. "But there ain't nothing I can do about it. If I was to go agin' that bunch, they wouldn't pay me no more heed than a steer does to a cobweb. I'd have as much chance as a wax cat in hell."

He turned and started back into the livery. Longarm looked back and watched as the four men dragged the Indians—still roped—into the saloon. Abruptly, Longarm started across the street. He worked for the federal government. These Digger Indians were wards of that government. It was part of his job to see to their safety.

Chapter 2

Only a few men paid attention as Longarm entered the saloon. He moved to the wall, well behind the circle of men, and slumped into a chair behind a small table. One logger was already standing on top of a table, dropping ropes over a beam that ran the length of the ceiling. Another logger was busy fashioning hangman's knots in the ropes, while others were cheerfully tying the hands of the four Diggers behind them.

Once the nooses were ready and the Indians were securely bound, they were unceremoniously lifted up onto the tables—each Digger standing on a separate table. Standing on a chair behind each one, the fellow who had made the hangman's knots dropped the nooses over the Diggers' heads, then pulled them snug. Stepping down at last, he surveyed his accomplishment with some satisfaction—if not outright glee.

Longarm took out his Colt and placed it on the table in front of him, resting his hand lightly on its grip. Those closest to Longarm's table became aware of the exposed gun almost instantly. In a matter of seconds, the word traveled. The place quieted ominously. All eyes turned to Longarm—and to the dark bore of his Colt yawning at them from the table.

Through the crowd toward Longarm bulled the same fellow who had escorted Ruby from the coach earlier that day—Bat Lawson. He planted himself firmly in front of Longarm and looked angrily, insolently down at him.

"My name's Bat Lawson, mister. This here business ain't none of your concern."

"Maybe it is," Longarm said quietly. "I'm Deputy U.S. Marshal Custis Long."

The man's hawklike face darkened. He did not appear surprised, however, at learning Longarm's identity. The constable must already have gotten word to him of Longarm's presence. "I don't care who you are, Long, or why you're here. I take my orders from Slade Desmond."

"And he wants you to hang these four Indians, does he?"

"That's right."

"Why?"

"As a warning to other Diggers. It's the only kind of warning they understand. They been giving us trouble lately. Now, you can watch if you want. But I advise you not to interfere."

While Lawson had been talking, Gus had entered the saloon. Out of the corner of his eye Longarm saw how dismayed—at least for an instant—the man was at the sight of the four Indians standing on the tables with nooses around their necks. Now Constable Seegar entered the saloon looking a mite winded. He slunk over to the bar and tried to become invisible. Longarm anticipated no help from that quarter.

He got up with his gun leveled at Bat and said, "Cut them down, Bat. Now."

He thrust the barrel of his Colt deeply and firmly into Lawson's midsection before the man had time to draw his own Colt from its holster. Longarm prodded him with such sudden violence that Bat almost stumbled in his haste to get back.

But Longarm kept after him, increasing the pressure. "Do it, Bat! If anything happens to any one of those

Indians, this gun is going to go off—and most likely it'll cut you in two at this range."

"Everyone stand back!" Lawson cried, his face ashen. "I'm doin' what this here crazy lawman says to do. We'll settle up with him later! Now get back! All of you!"

The men crowded hastily back. Longarm kept his Colt's barrel pressed into the small of Lawson's back while Lawson reached up and lifted the nooses off the shoulders of the four Diggers. Longarm stepped back a little as Bat untied their hands. Considering the sorry state of Lawson's nerves, the Indians were free in a surprisingly short time. As each one was freed, he jumped down and disappeared through the door. At last, the fourth Digger was gone, the sound of his bare feet pounding down the street, the batwings thumping slower and slower.

Bat turned to face Longarm. "You ain't heard the last of this, Long."

"Maybe neither of us have. Those Indians are wards of the federal government. I don't know just how big this lumber company of yours is, Lawson, but it sure as hell ain't big enough to outlaw the constitution, due process, and a few other such items."

"You'll see," the man said meanly, still confident. "We got friends in Washington. Big friends."

It was pointless to continue the debate. Holstering his gun, Longarm left the saloon and crossed to the hotel. He was weary. It was late. Men like Lawson made him sick to his stomach. He would be glad to shake the dust of this town the next morning, but he knew he would most likely have to deal with Bat Lawson one way or the other before he left these parts. *Men like that work awful hard not to learn,* he thought.

Nodding absently to the desk clerk, Longarm mounted the stairs and turned down the hall to his room. His practiced eye caught the absence of the

27

matchstick from its spot in the doorjamb. Someone was waiting inside. Longarm unholstered his Colt, slowed down, and placed his back gently against the door, then pushed slightly. The door gave just enough to tell Longarm that it was not shut tight.

Longarm stepped past the door and flattened himself against the wall. With the barrel of his Colt, he gently pushed open the door. As it began to swing into the room, he gave it a final shove. When he heard it slam into the wall, he sprang into the room, crouching low, his sixgun in front of him, waist-high, his elbow bent. Nothing. No flash of gunpowder lancing through the dark.

He heard the bedsprings creak—and a girl's voice, low and seductive, laughing softly. Waiting a moment for his eyes to adjust to the sudden darkness of the room, he saw something long and pale stir on the bed.

"My, my," the girl said. "You must be awful nervous to enter like that all the time."

Longarm straightened, feeling a mite foolish, and kicked the door shut. By this time, he was able to recognize the girl. She was Alice, the one who had caught his eye in the dining room. She was lying on his bed, wearing a long silken nightgown. He glanced swiftly around the room to make sure there were no other surprises, then holstered his Colt, chucked his hat back from his forehead, and started for the dresser.

"Don't do that too often, Alice," he told her, lighting the lamp on the dresser. "I almost blew a hole in your pretty face."

"Well, I *did* do it and I *am* here. So what are you going to do about it?"

"Do I have any choice?"

"No," she said, a devilish gleam in her eye. "You don't. And it won't cost you one penny."

"I don't usually pay for it, Alice," he said evenly.

"I didn't think you did."

Longarm looked down at the slim, lovely girl. He was not exactly in the mood for playing with her. His adrenalin was still kicking up a fuss from that business in the saloon—and the manner of his entry into his room had done little to quiet him down. He was tempted to slap the girl on her fanny and send her packing. But he didn't.

"Please," she said, "take off your boots. I know men don't usually do that in sporting houses—but I would appreciate it."

"Would you, now?" Longarm slipped out of his coat and vest, placing his watch and derringer carefully on the top of the dresser, working swiftly enough to keep the small gun hidden from her. As he unbuckled his gunbelt and hung it over the brass bedpost, he saw the girl shudder just a little. He withdrew the Colt from his rig and tucked it under the pillow.

She watched him with widening eyes. "Do you always make love with a gun under your pillow?"

He smiled at her without replying, sat down on the edge of the bed, and tugged off his boots.

"Thank you," she said softly.

Peeling off his shirt and longjohns, he turned to her —almost grimly.

"Could you—turn down the lamp some?" she asked. "There's . . . so much of you. It kind of unnerves a girl."

"You do it," Longarm told her quietly. "I like to watch you move. Besides, this was all your idea."

She looked at him for a long moment, her green eyes wide at his curt manner. He thought she might get up and leave. Finally, with a shrug, she got up and turned down the lamp. It was worth the wait. The sight of a woman's body moving under a silken nightgown was a rare one for Longarm, of late. He enjoyed himself very much as he watched her return to the bed and coil softly beside him.

The softer light was an improvement. She cuddled playfully for a moment, then rolled onto her back and began to unbutton all the buttons that ran down the front of her nightgown. He watched her. When she was finished, she rolled out of the nightgown like a large glowworm out of its cocoon, and thrust herself delightedly against him. She had been wearing nothing under the gown, not even a shift. This was unusual. Working whores almost never stripped. They plied their trade with their shifts on, and kept their long stockings and high-heeled footgear firmly in place, just as their customers traditionally retained their boots.

This young whore was evidently a new breed of cat. As he looked at her long figure beside him, the ugly feeling left over from that ruckus in the saloon slipped slowly from him.

"What are you up to, young lady?" he asked.

"The question," she replied, glancing significantly down at him, "is what are *you* up to? Is there something the matter?"

"Alice," Longarm said quietly, folding his arms under his head and gazing up at the ceiling, "if a man's been lost on a desert for a spell, you don't let him drink a gallon of water all at once. You let him work up to it. Do you get my meaning?"

"Oh, I see!" she laughed. "You've been deprived."

" 'Disciplined' might be a better word." He turned to look at her, allowing himself to enjoy the view.

The nicest thing about her—besides her catlike eyes —was her long, curling hair. It reached to her waist, and as she reclined beside him, she contrived to let the long tresses spill over her full breasts, all the way down her slim body to her thighs. She had the delicacy to keep the hip closest to Longarm slightly upraised, preserving that much mystery, at least. Longarm liked a little modesty on the part of the women he bedded—if only because it gave him pleasure to make it vanish in the heat of passion.

"Ah, Mr. Long," she said, "I see you are doing much better now."

"Who told you my name?"

"Ruby—when she warned me to stay away from you." She seemed delighted with herself.

"I'll ask you again. What are you up to, Alice?"

She looked at him, her face suddenly grave. "I am up to enjoying myself," she said simply. "Is that such a crime? Men do it all the time."

"You enjoy yourself, working for Ruby?"

"I didn't want to marry some clod and have to put up with his miserable lovemaking, his beatings, and his kids, for the rest of my life. I have been lucky to find out in time what loving a man—a *real* man—could be like." She smiled at him. "My parents had money. Too much perhaps. They hired a French violin teacher for my two sisters and me. He gave me private—very private—lessons."

"Is this the story you tell your customers?" he asked bluntly.

"Heavens, no! Most of them would be shocked to hear such a thing. I tell them what every whore tells them—what they want to hear. How I was destitute, miserable, and lonely after my fiance jilted me and left me penniless on the streets of San Francisco, where Madame du Roch found me—little better than a beggar—and took me in. I was a stray cat, grateful and willing to do anything to help my benefactress. Only too late did I learn the real business of Madame du Roch's salon—and what was expected of me in payment for her kindness. Alas! What was I to do? Return penniless to the streets?"

Longarm laughed. He could almost see her, bathed in the white, unnatural glow of footlights, declaiming

31

this melodramatic speech, with the back of her hand against her forehead.

Alice laughed too, then looked seriously at him. "I saw something in your eyes," she told him, "when you walked into the dining room. And you saw something in mine. Didn't you?"

He nodded.

She moved closer. He gave up trying to figure her out and let his hand drop lightly onto her bare shoulder. Suddenly, her lips were on his, her mouth opening, her tongue darting—while her hands moved down his chest, all the way to his loins. He came alive under her caresses. He strained toward her. The girl laughed and moved her lips down his chest, nuzzling the wiry hair on his rock-solid chest, and moving on down almost to his crotch. Fire enveloped him as her tongue explored his pelvis, then moved up his back. Her hands touched him boldly, measuring his potency with an eagerness that caused him to sweep her under him.

She cried out softly, her head flung back, at the force with which he entered. She turned her head, her eyes wide, her teeth clenched. "Oh," she gasped, "there's so *much* of you!" It was not a complaint. Her legs rose behind him to lock fiercely around his thrusting buttocks.

Their first climax came quickly, more quickly than Longarm wanted. He stayed up and kept himself in her. Taking his time now, he grabbed both of her buttocks in his big hands and hauled her in closer under him. Each stroke brought a feverish, shuddering response from the girl. Alice dug her nails into his back and crossed her heels tightly behind him. Longarm was reaching bottom with almost every thrust. When he tried to pull back a little to make it easier on her, her face became a naked mask of fury as she lifted her pelvis and jammed upward to get the full impact of each stroke.

"Damn you, Mr. Long!" she cried. "Deep! Go deep! I want *all* of you!" Then she began to gasp, her face and neck growing scarlet. "Now! *Now!*" she cried exultantly. "Yes! Oh, Jesus!"

Her fingernails were like bear's claws now, as they raked down his back. She shuddered once, twice, and then Longarm climaxed himself, joining her with one last, deep thrust, expending himself with involuntary ejaculations that left him—finally—soft and warm and exhausted.

She had gone limp under him. He rolled off, satisfied. She turned to face him and rested her cheek on the palm of her hand. "Mmmm," she murmured contentedly. "That *was* nice. I feel warm—all the way down to my toes."

Longarm said nothing, just watched her.

"You are all I thought you would be, Mr. Long."

"Call me Longarm," he said quietly.

"Oh, that's much better. Yes. Longarm," she said, leaning close and kissing him on the lips, softly. He could smell the sweetness of her perspiring body. There were tiny beads of sweat on her upthrust breasts. "Take a nap," she told him softly. "Maybe afterwards . . ."

"Just what *I* was thinking."

She got up and pulled down the sheets. Bouncing lightly back down beside him, she pulled the blankets up around both of them. She snuggled against him, fitting herself into his back. He felt her warm body relax, and closed his eyes.

She dropped off to sleep, or appeared to. Her breathing became regular. For a while he was certain she was asleep. Still he waited, allowing his own breathing to grow heavy. It was difficult not to fall asleep. Once or twice he almost drifted off, the warmth of her body lulling him.

She sat up slowly, waiting for some sign that her movement had disturbed him. He lay still. She lifted back the covers and was on her feet, moving swiftly around the bed, as silently as falling snow. Longarm was facing toward the dresser. He opened his eyes just enough to see what she was doing. He saw her reach into his inside coat pocket and remove his wallet and papers. She took the papers over to the lamp—the warrant for Shortslef, the notes on his physical description, a copy of the telegram Tanner had sent Washington—and read them swiftly by the lamp's light.

Satisfied, she folded the papers, replaced them in his wallet, and tucked it back into his inside pocket. As she started back around the bed, he sat up, withdrawing his Colt from under the pillow. She froze in her tracks as he leveled the gun at her pale, almost luminous breasts.

"My God," she breathed.

"Who put you up to this?" he asked, without a trace of emotion.

"Ruby. She told me I had to do it," she answered quickly.

He smiled. "And I thought it was all because you couldn't wait to pleasure a real man."

"That was part of it, honest. Ruby asked which one of us new girls wanted to do it. I volunteered because I liked you."

"What were you looking for just now?"

"They want to know what you're really doing here."

"Who are 'they'?"

"Constable Seegar and Slade Desmond, his boss. Seegar works for Slade. He's suspicious of you. He told Ruby she had to do it or he would tell Desmond she had refused to help."

Longarm believed her. He had been suspicious the moment he found her in his bed. No madam would allow herself to be this careless concerning the whereabouts of one of her girls, and certainly not for this length of time.

Still standing before him, Alice ran a nervous hand through her long hair. "You never believed anything I told you," she said softly. "Did you?"

"No, Alice, I didn't."

"Can I leave now?"

"Of course."

Longarm put the Colt down and watched her as she swept up her nightgown and let herself out. He listened to her bare feet running from his door and down the hall. When he heard a door open and close at the other end of the hall, he threw back the covers and dressed rapidly.

A thin, freckled-faced man in steel-rimmed glasses was behind the front desk as Longarm strode through the lobby and started for Sheriff Tanner's office. The uproar in the Silver City Saloon was still in progress. As Longarm walked along the boardwalk, he saw an occasional logger stagger drunkenly from the place and reel off into the night, like a wagon with its wheels coming off.

Entering the sheriff's office, Longarm found it empty. A kerosene lamp on the sheriff's desk was lit. The desk had obviously gone unused for some time. A smaller desk in the corner—most likely Constable Seegar's—was littered with old dodgers, official correspondence, dirty cups, and an old coffeepot with a broken spout. A cot along the far wall sat next to an open door that led to the lockup. Glancing into it, Longarm saw four empty cells. He returned to Seegar's desk and eased himself into the constable's swivel chair. Propping his boots up on the desk, he listened to the drone of the horsefly convention being held on the ceiling and prepared himself for a long wait.

That silly constable was most likely questioning Ruby or Alice at that very moment—and might even be staying for a while.

The sound of horseshoes striking stone alerted Longarm. He pulled his feet down and stood up. Someone was riding into town. Blinking the weariness out of his eyes, he stepped outside and peered into the darkness. A horse and rider were angling onto the town's main street. The rider, slumped well over the saddle horn, seemed dangerously close to falling off.

Longarm left the frame shack and hurried out to meet the rider. Once he got close enough, he reached up and grabbed the horse's bridle, pulling the animal to a halt. Longarm reached up and steadied him. Peering carefully up at him through the darkness, Longarm saw that his eyes were closed. His tan shirt front contained two large, irregular dark patches—and a sheriff's badge.

Sheriff Tanner had returned.

Both of Tanner's hands were clasped tightly about the horn. The man did not seem aware of Longarm's presence. Longarm led the horse down the street to the sheriff's office. Dropping the reins over the hitch rail, he reached up to pull Tanner out of his saddle. For a moment, the sheriff clung obstinately to the horn. When he did let go, Longarm found himself hefting a surprisingly light burden across the walk and into the office.

Longarm carried Tanner to the single cot against the wall and eased the sheriff's bird-frail body gently down upon it. Tanner could not have been more than five and a half feet tall. Soaking wet, he must have weighed a hundred and fifty pounds. His face was small. The boy that used to be Tanner stared up at Longarm—an old, wrinkled boy. The skin on his face was as weathered as old boot leather and drawn tightly about the skull, causing his cheekbones to stick out prominently. His closed eyes rested in dark hollows. The thin line of his mouth was drawn straight and grimly down. The man was obviously close to death. Only a fierce instinct had kept him on that horse.

Longarm leaned close. "Tanner! What happened? Who did this to you?" he asked.

Tanner's eyes opened and the expression on his face grew terrible. The sound of Longarm's voice had aroused him, but he had not understood the words. He reached up, grabbed Longarm's vest, and pulled him closer.

"That you, Seegar?" he gasped

"Never mind Seegar," Longarm said. "Was it Shortslef? Did he do this to you?"

"Illegal!" The man raved, wide-eyed. "Wrong place! Settlers—right. Stop him! Stop. . . !"

"Tanner!" Longarm said, leaning still closer. "Where's Shortslef? Is he the one who shot you?"

The man's eyes focused on Longarm for the first time. "Shortslef? You want Ned Shortslef?"

"Yes," Longarm replied. "Is he the one who bushwhacked you? Where is he?"

"Who are you? Where's Seegar? That idiot, Seegar!"

"Never mind him. I'm here to get Shortslef—Ned Shortslef. I've got a copy of your telegram to Washington."

Tanner laughed, and his skull-face turned hideous. As he laughed, his eyes closed and his boy's fist relaxed, releasing Longarm's vest. Martin Tanner's hand dropped to the cot. His shrunken head sank deeper into the pillow. His eyes remained open only because there was no force still left in the man capable of closing them.

Longarm pulled a blanket over the dead man's face and stood up. He looked down at the quiet form for a moment, then turned and walked out of the office. A couple of loggers stumbled out of the saloon. Longarm took out his Colt, stepped into the middle of the street, and pumped two slugs into the night sky. The detonations reverberated thunderously throughout the sleeping town. The tumult inside the saloon quieted instantly.

The two loggers halted in confusion and looked down the street at Longarm. A second later, those still in the saloon charged from the place. Some of Bat Lawson's men had their guns drawn.

As they came to a halt in the middle of the street, Longarm called out to them, "Sheriff Tanner's dead! Someone find Constable Seegar—and get an undertaker!"

Longarm holstered his weapon and went back into the late Sheriff Tanner's office.

As the coach carrying Whipsaw's fresh supply of girls and the wagonload of loggers left Silver City the next morning, Longarm climbed to the crest of the hill that was the town's graveyard and saw to the burial of Sheriff Tanner. Town Constable Pete Seegar, the owner of the livery, and the bespectacled hotel nightclerk were the only ones besides the gravediggers who joined Longarm at the grave site. Longarm had selected what he felt were appropriate verses from a hastily procured Gideon Bible and read them over the body of his fellow lawman, then stood back as the cheap, hastily constructed pine coffin was lowered into the ground.

The rest left hastily after that. Seegar looked furtively back at Longarm, while the tall deputy remained behind at the grave, hat in hand, contemplating the small rectangle of ground it had taken to cover a man's life forever. It was true that there were never many tears shed at a boot-hill burying, but that didn't make it any easier for Longarm to accept.

Like Longarm, this lawman had known the loneliness of long days in the saddle, of dry camps and dark nights with the yapping of the coyotes as his only lullaby, his only comfort. Tanner had exhibited a rare tenacity of purpose shown not only in his determination to bring in a man he had once called a friend, but also in the way he had ridden for a day, at least, with two bullet holes in his back. When Longarm thought finally of the size of the man in contrast to the fierce spirit that must have driven him, he felt peculiarly close to him. He wished he could have met the sheriff while he had still lived and shared a glass of rye with him, perhaps, or a game of poker.

Longarm took out the man's badge, buffed it on his trouser leg, then drove its pin into the top of the rude wooden grave marker. In the bright early morning sunlight, the badge gleamed brilliantly. Longarm stepped back. The badge would soon be dusty. The wind and the rain would tear it loose. Perhaps then it would become buried in the shifting sands of the gravesite, resting at last with the man who had worn it with such dedication.

Longarm put his hat back on and pulled it down snugly. The dry wind whipped and bellied the tails of his Prince Albert coat as he turned and started down the hill. He had a score to settle with that weasel, Seegar. He was anxious to see to it and ride north to Whipsaw, for he rode now with a renewed purpose—to find Ned Shortslef and bring him in. Not only for desertion, but for the backshooting of Sheriff Martin Tanner.

Longarm found the constable waiting for him behind his desk. The man was sitting bolt upright. His desk top had been cleared off somewhat—as if he wanted a better view of Longarm as the man approached him. For the first time since Longarm had known him, Seegar was wearing a huge old Remington sixgun that tugged heavily on the man's gunbelt and was worn ludicrously low on Seegar's hip. If Seegar got up suddenly and started running, he would most likely trip over it and break a leg.

Longarm pulled out Tanner's chair and sat down beside Seegar's desk astride the seat, his arms folded on the back. He chucked his hat back off his forehead and smiled at the town constable.

"Why in blazes did you send that girl to my room last night, Seegar?"

"I don't know what the hell you're talking about."

Longarm didn't say anything for a moment or two, then repeated his question a second time, a bit more softly. "Why did you send her, Seegar? What were you expecting to find? I told you what I was doing here."

"Hell! I didn't send no girl to your room. Why in Hades would I do anything like that?" He smirked. "You're just popular with whores, Longarm."

Longarm stood up, kicking his chair halfway across the room, reached over and grabbed Seegar by his checked vest. He snapped a few buttons as he hauled Seegar out of his chair and dragged him across the top of his desk. Black ink spilled over the desk top, smearing a dark stain over the front of Seegar's checked trousers. Longarm lifted Seegar until both of his heels were off the floor, then flung him after the chair. Seegar came to rest against the overturned chair, spraddled as loose as a rag doll. He seemed not entirely conscious but as Longarm approached, he clawed for his Remington. Longarm waited until the hog leg was clear of its holster, then kicked it out of Seegar's hand.

"All right!" Seegar cried raggedly. "I sent her! I just didn't believe you was only after that army deserter is all."

"What else *would* I be after? Why didn't you believe me, Seegar?"

"I . . . I just didn't, that's all. Who the hell cares about something that happened so long ago? Them Indian Wars is over now. Why should Washington send a guy all the way up here for a turd like that?"

Longarm considered the trembling man sprawled at his feet. His naked fear was like a stench in Longarm's nostrils. The constable got his picture of the west out of

40

them books he was always reading, only this wasn't no book—and if it was, it sure didn't read like all the others. Longarm realized then that there was really no way he could make this poor excuse for a lawman tell the truth—even if the man knew what it was.

He took out a cheroot, lit it to clear out his nostrils, and left the office. Longarm had already checked out of his hotel. Soon he would put the dust of this town behind him. And he would make damn sure he didn't return to it the way Sheriff Tanner had.

Chapter 3

The rough wagon road Longarm followed north to Whipsaw took him through a bleak, rocky, alkali wilderness. So deceptive were distances in the clear, high air that rock formations on far distant ridges appeared to leap into view as he rode toward them. At times Longarm felt he could reach out and pluck a giant cottonwood from the bluff it was sitting on, even though it was maybe five miles away.

The mountain barriers hemming in this bleak hinterland were hazy escarpments lost in the distance. Longarm was continually surprised by the sudden green valleys he came upon. They had the impact of mirages. Riding through them, he found them to be cool, meandering belts of green vegetation following the banks of streams, most of which fed the Humboldt, many miles to the south. Cottonwoods, quaking aspen, and fragile willows grew in abundance in these valleys. Longarm was always sorry to ride out of the cool, whispering fragrance of these valleys into the denuded passes that led from them.

Well past midday Longarm found himself riding through deep draws and canyons, putting him almost constantly in the shadow of towering ridges spiked with pinyon and juniper. The sharp, medicinal tang of pine resin filled the air. Soon he was climbing past gaunt, wind-blasted bristlecone pine, their indomitable roots

42

clutching at the rocky cliffsides, their branches reaching out like the gnarled fingers of an arthritic.

The road kept to a ridge for a long while, then dropped gently to the floor of a canyon. Longarm rode for close to a mile along the canyon floor, until the wall to his left dropped away, and he glimpsed the heavy, shouldering peaks of the Santa Rosa Range, its flanks clothed in pine. Below its foothills Longarm saw the beginnings of another broad, fertile valley with a river snaking through it. It was, as usual, a beautiful sight. Longarm pulled up to drink it in.

A rifle shot shattered the silence.

The bullet ricocheted off the trail just in front of Longarm's horse. It had come from the top of the ridge to his right. Even as Longarm yanked his Winchester from its boot and rolled off the Morgan, a second slug —this one much closer—sent rock splinters into the air just beside him.

A fusillade of rifle fire followed him as he dashed to the foot of the ridge and flattened himself against the rock face. He looked around for a trail that would lead to the top of the ridge. He spotted what he hoped was a way to the ridge and looked back at the Morgan. The animal was in among some rocks, casually cropping the sparse grass. Longarm crouched low and raced up the broad slope of a boulder into a cover of juniper. As he reached the timber, three more shots poured down upon him, each round shearing through the branches, sending pine cones flying. He left the shelter of the junipers and raced about ten feet along a steep-sided gully that led up among the rocks. Once inside, he found the draw widening and followed it for a couple of hundred yards until he caught sight of a game trail that led up a steep incline.

The loose gravel made the footing treacherous as he raced up the slope. More than once he had to slam the butt of his rifle into the ground to keep himself from sliding back down on his belly. Close to the top of the ridge, he found himself clinging first to one pine and then to another as he hauled himself up hand over hand, the toes of his boots finding precarious purchase on the thin limestone ridges that poked out of the almost sheer wall. He almost lost his rifle at one juncture and thought seriously of abandoning it. Instead, he carefully kept it ahead of him, sometimes wedged into crevices and at other times snugged under the exposed roots of the scrub pine that clung to the side of the mountain.

At last he pulled himself after his rifle over the lip of the ridge and found himself on a large, flat caprock that was as gouged and weathered as an old man's face. About thirty paces from where he lay grew a thick stand of pine. About a hundred yards down the ridge, partially hidden by the timber, three men lay flat on a rock as they peered over its edge at the canyon floor below. Scrambling to his feet, Longarm raced swiftly across the caprock. He was almost to the pines when one of the men turned and caught sight of him. The fellow's shout of alarm echoed along the ridge.

Longarm kept on into the pines. Once under their cover, he headed toward the spot where he had seen the men. After twenty paces or so, he ducked back toward the open ledge and flung himself down behind a pine at the edge of the stand. One of the bushwhackers had mounted and was just galloping past where Longarm lay. The two others were racing through the pines behind Longarm, their spurs clinking heedlessly.

Longarm waited until they were past his position before he opened fire on the rider. He tried to bring down the horse, aiming at the base of its tail, hoping for a spine shot. The round carried high, however, and caught the rider in the shoulder. The man reacted as if a two-by-four had slammed into him. He was flung sideways off the horse, landing on the rock face and skidding a good distance on his belly. His nose made a poor rudder. For a moment he lay still; then—moaning in pain—he began to crawl toward the pines.

The downed rider's cries brought the others to the edge of the pines. They were well past Longarm. As they left their cover to aid their fallen comrade, Longarm got to his feet and stepped out of the pines, pointing his rifle at the sky. He fired. The two men halted in their tracks and whirled. As Longarm lowered his rifle, training it on them, both men quickly—almost eagerly —dropped their sixguns.

They were *too* eager, and something in their faces warned Longarm. He flinched to his right. A slight *thunk*, followed by an agonized gasp, came from behind him. He spun and saw a thin shadow of a cowboy slumping forward onto his knees. There was a small arrow lodged in his back above one shoulder blade. The gun in his hand clattered to the ledge. He sagged over onto his side, careful not to fall back on the arrow, looking up at Longarm, his eyes filled with surprise and pain.

Longarm swung quickly back around to face the others. They were crouching, their hands only inches from their sixguns. Longarm fired. The Winchester's round sent one of the sixguns spinning across the rock. Both men sprang erect without their guns, their hands jerking upward as though pulled by strings, as Longarm reflexively levered another round into the rifle's chamber.

"All right, Tigbee!" one of them cried. "All right, goddamnit! You got the drop on us! Now call off your damn Diggers!"

Without a word, Longarm moved back behind the downed cowboy, his rifle still leveled at the two bushwhackers, and kicked the man's sixgun off the ledge. "You two better split up," Longarm suggested, "and see to these men."

As the two uninjured men hurried to the aid of their

stricken partners, Longarm kicked their dropped weapons over the edge of the rock into oblivion, then scouted about the ledge and into the pines for any sign left by the Indian who had sent that arrow. He saw nothing and heard nothing. He was not surprised. When an Indian puts his mind to it, he can be as quiet as a cheating woman—and just as cold-blooded. But why had a Digger Indian saved *him?* Why were they *his* Diggers?

And who the hell was this fellow Tigbee, for whom these bushwhackers had evidently mistaken him?

Longarm returned to the ledge and found the four in a miserable, huddled group. He almost felt sorry for them. The fellow with the arrow in his back had had it pulled out. It had left a large, ragged hole. The wound had been plugged with a sweaty bandanna, but was still leaking badly. The fellow with the gunshot wound in his shoulder was just hunkered down and trying to stay quiet, his mouth a straight line, his eyes closed. The man's shoulder appeared to be broken.

The two healthy ones stood up to face Longarm. The fellow who had called him Tigbee looked to be about forty-five. He had a long, narrow face and a lantern jaw covered with white stubble. His eyes were gray, frank, and, at the moment, alight with indignation. The other man, considerably younger, had light blue eyes, a wide face, and round cheeks, reminding Longarm of a squirrel with its cheek-pouches full. Both men wore the dress of working cowpokes; their hats and boots were as weathered and as dry as the country.

"Who are you?" Longarm asked the older one.

"Lyle Butts," answered the man, "if it's any of your damned business."

"Mighty perky for a bushwhacker on the wrong end of a rifle barrel, ain't you?"

"I ain't crawling for no damn gunslick." The anger in the man's eyes kindled to a brighter glow. He appeared

46

ready to leap at Longarm—despite the obvious foolhardiness of such a move.

"Mind telling me who this fellow Tigbee is?"

Butts frowned angrily. "You trying to deny who you are, Tigbee?"

"Let me tell you something, Butts. You better thank that Digger Indian, if you ever find him; he saved your friend from killing me. I'm a deputy U.S. marshal; my name is Custis Long. If I'd been just a mite unluckier, you would pretty damn soon have found this place crawling with federal marshals.''

"Hell, you ain't no federal marshal," the younger one said. "You're Clyde Tigbee, the gunslick Slade sent for!"

"Now, just how the hell do you know that?"

The two men exchanged quick, apprehensive glances. It was Butts who swore softly, his narrow face darkening. "Jesus, Billy. Tim Caulder! *That son of a bitch!* He was lying!"

"Hey, mister," Billy said, grown suddenly sheepish, "You got any identification?"

Longarm reached into his breast pocket, withdrew his wallet with its badge, and flipped it to the cowpoke. Billy looked it over and passed it to Butts without comment. Butts sighed deeply and handed the wallet back to Longarm.

"Tim Caulder's one of Slade's men," Butts explained. "We thought he was on our side. He sure wanted us to think so, anyway. He reached Whipsaw a few hours ago, riding a lathered horse, and ran into us at the Paradise Valley. He told us Tigbee was riding in. That's the gunslick we've been waiting for—the one Slade's bringing up here to keep us cattlemen in line. You've heard of Tigbee, ain't you?"

"No, I ain't heard of Tigbee," Longarm replied wearily. "There's a new gunslick popping up every week. Looks like they just want to get into Buffalo

47

Bill's Wild West Show before it closes. This one's probably some flannelmouth wearing a load of hay on his skull and packing enough artillery to make his horse swaybacked. Hell, you men ought to know the type. Usually those characters are as yellow as mustard, only without the bite. But what's Slade bringing in a hired gun for? What are you cattlemen up to, anyway?"

"It ain't us!" Butts exclaimed. "It's him—and that company of his. They're ruining the valley—cutting and slashing the pines off the ridges and the mountainsides, chewing up everything till there ain't no place left to graze a single cow. The water's either running off or standing in ditches, instead of going into the ground. Some of us cattlemen are already losing water in our wells. Hell, even the sage on the desert floor is drying out. If they don't stop cutting the way they're doing, there won't be nothing left but tree stumps and mudholes. And then that damned company will move on to tear some other valley up, leaving us with homesteads not worth a plugged nickel."

"This *is* federal land, Butts," Longarm said. "This lumber company must have rights to the timber on it. You can't go against that."

"You watch us."

"That's right," Longarm snapped, glancing down at the two wounded men. "That's just what I'm doing right now—watching. What I see is four damn fools who just threw down on a stranger—and lost. Maybe you better go talk to Slade. You couldn't do any worse than this. And he just might listen to you."

Billy shook his head. "You don't know Slade Desmond, Mister Long."

Longarm shrugged. Satisfied that the two men were no longer a threat to his life, he put down his rifle and helped them gather their horses, after which he did what he could to make it easier for the two wounded men as they mounted up. Once they were in the saddle,

Longarm felt only pity for them. Both were as white as new-spilt milk and were hanging on with guts alone, bowed over their saddle horns—coffin-fodder on their way to hell. If they didn't get to that home spread of theirs pretty damned soon, they would likely never get to choke on the alkali dust of another roundup.

Longarm looked up at Butts as soon as the older man had mounted. "Just one thing, Butts. Did this Tim Caulder give you a description of the hired gun?"

Butts smiled bitterly. "The son of a bitch did, all right. It was a good one, too. He did a fine job of describing you and what you was wearing—in detail."

Longarm stepped back. The four men rode back down the long slope of the ledge, heading west, away from Whipsaw.

Bat Lawson had known Longarm was riding to Whipsaw. Pete Seegar had told him that much, at least. So it could simply have been Bat Lawson's idea, his way of squaring accounts with Longarm. On the other hand, if Slade Desmond was having trouble with the local cattlemen, what better way to put them on the defensive—to discredit them entirely—than to trick them into killing a deputy U.S. marshal?

Neat. Very neat indeed, he thought, as he thumbed three fresh rounds into the Winchester's magazine.

Longarm reached Whipsaw close to four o'clock that same afternoon. It was Longarm's first glimpse of a logging town. He didn't much like what he saw—here or in the countryside surrounding it. From a mile back, the valley floor and the mountain slopes had resembled a torn, muddy wound extending as far as the eye could see; and now, in the midst of that desolate, stump-filled landscape, sat this raw, unpainted logging town, both sides of its main drag lined with wooden shacks and tents of varying sizes, selling whiskey, gambling, or women. The larger tents provided all three.

Railroad tracks snaking alongside a sluggish, silted river led directly to the sawmill and lost themselves behind a mountain of sawdust. Sitting on a side spur were several triple-decker bunkhouses-on-wheels. These rolling bunkhouses had probably been used once in the construction of this railroad, and now served as living quarters for the loggers.

In sharp contrast to the ramshackle impermanence of almost everything else were three large, substantial frame buildings at the end of the town farthest from the sawdust and whining screech of the mill. They were the first buildings Longarm approached on his way into Whipsaw. One was the Paradise Valley Saloon, the building next to it was the Western Lumber and Land Combine General Store, and the third building was a three-story hotel set back on a slight rise.

Riding past the hotel, Longarm glimpsed a girl sitting in a window. She waved to him. Longarm knew at once that this was where Ruby's girls held court. Longarm rode on into town past the mill, until he found the livery stable. It was a sprawling collection of tents, corrals, and wooden barns constructed crudely of unpeeled logs. Longarm dismounted in front of the largest barn and was giving the Morgan a drink at the trough when a shout, followed by a string of magnificent oaths, pulled him up short. A wagonload of recently cut logs was on its way past to the sawmill. It was the driver—a powerful, raw-faced logger—who had warned Longarm. As the man's whip cracked over the backs of his horses, Longarm pulled the Morgan out of the way and entered the livery.

He emerged a moment later, having learned from the liveryman that Ruby's place was indeed a hotel—for those who had the money to patronize what the man told him—with some pride—was probably the most famous establishment of its kind in northern Nevada. It was also owned, lock, stock, and roulette wheel, by the

Western Lumber and Land Combine, like everything else in Whipsaw.

There were no sidewalks. Longarm slogged through the muck, doing his best to avoid the constant stream of huge logging wagons and their massive workhorses. His tall, lanky, obviously well-muscled figure did not go unnoticed. He recognized some of Bat Lawson's men; he could tell they remembered him as well. Those of Bat's men whom he did not recognize from Silver City he knew by their flashy dress and their willingness to freight themselves down with artillery. Many fancied double rigs and ivory-handled sixguns, with cartridge belts worn lower than good sense would dictate. They swaggered.

As Longarm neared the Paradise Valley, an obviously disgruntled Bat Lawson stepped through the batwings with one of his lieutenants to watch Longarm walk past. He was not dismayed, it seemed, only resigned to the necessity of having to cook up another scheme to rid himself of Longarm. Longarm nodded solemnly to the man. Lawson turned and disappeared back into the saloon.

The lobby of Ruby's hotel was expansive and, considering its clientele, not at all what Longarm had expected. Its decor was subdued, even prim. Well to the right of the front desk, however, a short flight of red-carpeted stairs led up to an ample archway. Beyond this, Longarm glimpsed a wall hung with gilt-edged mirrors, fleshy portraits, and over it all, the soft glow of pink lamps. The tinkle of women's laughter and the occasional bellow of some early celebrant having a good time came clearly to Longarm. Yet the laughter, the click of poker chips, and the rattle of dice all were kept to a soft, barely audible level. It was most civilized, indeed. Ruby—and the Western Lumber and Land Combine—ran a disciplined house.

"A room for the night," Longarm told the desk clerk.

Abruptly, Longarm felt someone plucking gently at his sleeve. He turned to see a brilliantly liveried bellhop pointing at Longarm's boots.

"Please, mister," the boy said, "you got to take them off in Ruby's place." The bellhop indicated a wall alongside the entrance where at least ten pairs of boots were already lined up.

"Okay," Longarm said. "But I'm taking them up to my room with me."

The boy offered no objection, and while Longarm signed the register, he lifted first one foot and then the other as the bellhop tugged off his boots. Longarm carried his boots up to his room while the bellhop carried the rest of his gear. Longarm tipped the boy, and as soon as he had closed the door behind him, went to the window and looked down at Whipsaw.

The logging town was obviously a gut-it-and-get-out operation. From the look of things, the logging company was doing a lot of gutting, not only of the land but of the loggers as well. The company probably charged the loggers outrageously for their miserable accomodations in those railroad bunkhouses, and then saw to it that wherever in Whipsaw they spent their wages, most of the money found its way back into the company's coffers.

But the loggers probably didn't mind as long as the booze hit hard enough and the girls were plentiful. It was the settlers, the cattlemen mostly, who would find it impossible to live with this operation. At the rate the Western Lumber and Land Combine was going, the valley and the ridges and mountainsides flanking it would soon be a wasteland. Longarm knew with some certainty how long it took high desert land like this to regain its cover and survive the ravages of a one-purpose company town like this one. The west was pockmarked with abandoned mining towns and rail-heads, and the ruined landscapes that surrounded them.

It was still light. Bands of loggers just quitting work were gathering to begin their night's carousal. The loggers crowded first into the company's general store, where they were probably paid their day's wages, then left to drift up and down the line. A few headed directly for the hotel. Longarm could hear their heavy boots mounting the low porch, then their booming voices—almost immediately silenced—as they entered the lobby. He could imagine the bellhop hurrying among them, removing their brogans with swift dexterity.

His attention was suddenly drawn to a brawl in front of one of the tents. A floozy had been on a logger's arm and been about to entice him into her place of business when another logger with a thick mane of silvery hair rushed up and pulled the floozy away. At once the two men started clobbering each other. The first fellow, smaller by a foot at least, had enormous shoulders and the biggest head Longarm had ever seen. Big Head seemed to know precisely what to do with it. Tucking in his chin, he rammed Silver Hair repeatedly, at last catching him amidships and sending him sprawling backwards into the mud.

As the crowd that gathered cheered him on, Big Head took a running jump and came down with both of his calked boots on the man's chest and face. Treating the downed man as if he were a log running downstream, Big Head began to birl him, driving Silver Hair's head and shoulders down into the muck and then up again and around—faster and faster, to the delighted shouts of the onlookers—until Silver Hair was little more than a mud-caked, bloody torso. Only then did Big Head cease his logrolling and jump off.

The crowd broke up. A large contingent led Big Head into the Paradise Valley. Only the floozy remained. She sat back on her haunches in the mud beside her fallen champion. But not for long. Soon she left the still figure on the ground, caught hold of a little fellow in a red stocking cap, and drew him into her tent.

Longarm turned from the window. He was weary and needed a bath, but he knew he would have to wait until the next day. Not until the loggers drifted off to their bunkhouses for the night would there be a place in town safe enough for a quiet bath; booze would be the only liquid allowed to flow until then.

Longarm saw to his gear, then went downstairs to the lobby. It was crowded with bootless loggers, all of whom seemed strangely subdued without their boots as they filed up the low stairs past Ruby, who was greeting her favorites at the arch. Her ample figure was poured into a long red dress agleam with sequins. Her thick curls crowded her pale shoulders and broad bosom. She was being welcomed by everyone and seemed genuinely pleased to be back in harness. The day's exhausting journey seemed to have left no mark on her.

The dining room was at the end of a long hall that led off the lobby. There were chandeliers and liveried waiters. The silverware gleamed brilliantly on white, freshly ironed linen. Despite himself, Longarm found himself comparing its quiet elegance with one of the many fine restaurants in the Windsor hotel back in Denver.

Just as Longarm finished ordering, Bat Lawson walked into the dining room with a companion. From the deference Bat showed the man, Longarm surmised that he was Slade Desmond. The two men approached Longarm's table, Bat Lawson hanging back a bit. The dining room grew silent. Knives and forks froze in mid-air or were put down carefully as all eyes followed Slade Desmond's progress to Longarm's table.

"I'm Slade Desmond," Bat's companion introduced himself. "I'd like a word with you, Mr. Long. May I join you?"

Slade Desmond was almost a foot shorter than Bat. He was barrel-chested and stubby-limbed. He held a chocolate-brown derby in one hand, revealing a domed, hairless cueball of a head. His jaw was forward-thrust, his nose was small, and his eyes—set wide in his round face—were cold and humorless and deadly, reminding Longarm of spent buckshot.

Assuming that Longarm would have no objection to his request, Slade started to pull out a chair for himself at Longarm's table. Longarm smiled coldly at the man and shook his head. "I like to eat alone," he said, "or at least choose my own company, and that lackey behind you is sure as hell not welcome at any table of mine."

Slade Desmond pulled back and glanced with surprise at Bat. When he looked back at Longarm, his buckshot eyes had narrowed dangerously. "You and I *should* talk, Long."

"At your office, Desmond."

Slade nodded curtly. "It's in the company store, in back. I'll be waiting for you." The man turned and strode out of the dining room with Bat Lawson on his heels.

The dining room was small enough for everyone in it to have heard the exchange. From the glances that came Longarm's way, Longarm realized he had created a sensation by treating Slade Desmond that curtly. The tone of their meeting would be common knowledge throughout the town before morning. But what bothered Longarm was that someone like Slade Desmond should have this much power. Desmond had entered the dining room and strode out of it again like an absolute monarch.

The frown on Longarm's face left the moment his steak arrived.

Slade Desmond rose to his feet as Longarm entered his office. Bat Lawson stood up also. The deputy ignored Lawson as Slade walked around his desk and shook Longarm's hand. The handshake was firm, even hearty. There was a slight, approving smile on the company manager's face.

"I like a man who says what he thinks, Long. Bat,

here, has been filling me in on a few details. It seems you and he had a little misunderstanding in Silver City."

"I don't think 'misunderstanding' really catches the gist of it, Desmond."

"Call me Slade, please. And do sit down. No need for us to stand on ceremony. I am sure we can all work together nicely."

"I don't mind standing," Longarm replied. "Been using my bottom most of the day. My feet could stand the straightening." That was not the reason and Slade knew it, but it preserved some civility.

Slade nodded curtly. "I am afraid Bat is somewhat overzealous at times. He's sorry for any trouble he might have caused you. Isn't that right, Bat?"

"Sure. I'm sorry, Long. I just got carried away," Lawson said.

"And later? When you sicked those four cowboys on me?"

"That was Tim Caulder's doing. I never could hold him down. He has all kinds of crazy ideas sometimes."

"This one almost worked." Longarm had no intention of telling Bat that two of the men had been wounded in the encounter.

"Yeah." Bat glanced nervously at Slade. "Well, that's the way it is. You win some, you lose some."

Longarm pointed a callused finger in Slade's direction. "I'll tell you this once, Slade. Then I'll just figure you've got it straight so I won't need to repeat it. Leave the Indians alone. They are wards of the federal government. You are working on federal land. I am an officer of the federal government and I will enforce its laws. And if anything happens to me, there will be other federal marshals along right soon to take up where I left off."

"Them Diggers are causing us real trouble," Lawson protested. "We sent a wagonload of supplies to Cedar

56

Ridge two weeks ago for the few loggers we got working up there. The little bastards killed the driver and made off with most of the supplies. Are we supposed to just stand by and take that? Like I told you once, I wanted to set an example with them four Indians."

"Don't set any examples," Longarm said. "Report what's happening and let the proper authorities take care of it."

Lawson snorted. "By proper authorities, you mean Digger-lovin' federal marshals."

"Bat!" Slade said sharply. "That's enough!" Slade turned back to Longarm. "There's no calculating the mischief those little devils can accomplish, Marshal." Slade's voice was filled with sweet reason. "I'm logging this land under a tight schedule. I can't afford to pussyfoot around when armed heathens attack my men and carry off my supplies."

Longarm nodded. "I'll check around and file a report. If action is to be taken, the army will see to it. I repeat, Slade, this is federal land—not yours or your company's private little kingdom."

"I appreciate that, Marshal, I can assure you."

"Good."

"Now, what brings you to Whipsaw? Since we've cleared the air, Marshal, I am sure Bat will be more than willing to cooperate in your—investigations. It would be surprising if there weren't one or two renegades among those loggers out there. They're a hard bunch. They work hard and they play hard. Whatever they call themselves, whatever deeds their past may be filled with, I don't pry into—not as long as they pull their weight."

"I'm looking for an army deserter—name of Ned Shortslef. A big guy with bushy hair and a beard. He's a squaw man—or was. An ex-Mountain Man. He may not be using his own name, of course. Sheriff Tanner spotted him working up here."

"Yes, so I understand. I was sorry to hear of that man's death. He was a good lawman, Marshal. We all respected him. Do you think this Shortslef is the one who killed him?"

"Seems likely, if Tanner was getting too close to him. Did you give Tanner any help in locating Shortslef when he came to bring him in a couple of weeks ago?"

"We gave him the run of Whipsaw, let him ask all the questions he wanted. It seems he spent considerable time at one of the cattle ranches, too." Slade turned to look at Lawson. "Isn't that right, Bat?"

Lawson nodded. "Yeah. When he wasn't nosing around here, he was out there."

"Which cattle ranch?"

Slade glanced at Bat.

"The Flying T," Bat replied. "You should know them fellows pretty well by now." He could not keep the smirk off his face.

"Did Tanner have any contacts among the loggers?" Longarm asked, ignoring the smirk.

"Gus Dodds," Bat said. "He went straight to Gus when he got here."

Longarm nodded, remembering the one-eyed logger from Silver City. "What's Gus's job in this camp?" he asked.

"A chopper. And he's one of the best. Averages close to sixty a day. You could see Fitz about him."

"Fitz is the chief foreman," Slade put in. "His full name is Arnold Fitzpatrick."

Longarm nodded. "Thanks. I'll talk to him."

The two men, obviously relieved by this time at Longarm's reasonable manner, expected him to take his leave now and go about his business. Longarm could feel them waiting for this, and said, "I understand you're sending for a gunslick to keep the ranchers in line, Slade."

The man's buckshot eyes grew cold, and his bulldog

chin became more set. "Who I bring in is my business. If you are referring to Clyde Tigbee, he's a fine, experienced lawman who has worked for me in the past as a sort of town marshal. He may have killed a few men, but only in the line of duty. He's not a gunslick." Slade smiled then, somewhat sardonically. "If you'll walk around Whipsaw tonight, you'll see we could use a town marshal capable of banging a few heads."

"What's wrong with Bat, here?"

"Bat has other, more important business to attend to. He's in charge of the security of this entire operation. Him and his men."

Longarm could see Bat swelling up as Slade sang his tune. Slade, of course, was lying, but he was doing a fine job of it.

"You don't expect any trouble with the cattlemen, then."

"Didn't say that, Deputy. But any trouble they and their vigilantes can stir up, Bat and his men can handle."

"Vigilantes?"

"Yes, Marshal, vigilantes. These ranchers have been doing some night riding. They threatened one of my crews at Elk Springs. They were pretty rough on my men. Said they were logging on their homesteads. It was a lie, of course."

"I guess that means you got a federal land survey to prove that."

Slade smiled. "The men from the Bureau of Land Management were here from the Department of the Interior less than three months ago to extend the area allotted to us. We're waiting now for their map to get here from Washington. If you have had any dealings with that city, you know how long it will most likely take for it to get here."

"Those men saw the way your loggers are tearing up the land around here?"

"I must confess, they were not happy about it. But we're cutting timber, not digging gold or silver out of a few holes in the ground. In either case, Marshal, there has to be some damage to the land. As it is, we are turning what amounts to scrub pine into wealth. Furthermore, we have many friends—and I might add, powerful friends—in Washington, who have a stake in our operation here. I repeat, Marshal—we are creating wealth where there were only alkali sinks, rock, and desert. This is progress, Marshal, and I do not need to apologize for our role here."

Longarm had no urge to dispute with the man. Slade had puffed himself up like a bullfrog in a hog wallow as he had delivered that spiel. Longarm had heard potbellied bankers in barber chairs in Denver spouting the same bilge. He had no doubt that the fat cats in Washington felt the same way. They were perfectly capable of aiding and abetting this plundering of the West, now that robbing the Indian on his reservation was no longer as profitable as it had once been. A list of the stockholders of this lumber company would prove most interesting, but it would be worthless. Everything would most probably be set up legally, with no loopholes. Longarm shrugged slightly. It was not his concern. He was after that deserter and murderer, and he thought he'd best keep his mind on that.

Longarm nodded curtly to the two men. "Guess I'll be thanking you for your time, Slade."

"I hope we've been of some help, Marshal," Slade said, leaning back in his chair, his tiny black eyes gleaming. He was obviously pleased that Longarm was proving so easy to get along with, and he had apparently defused a potentially explosive situation between his lieutenant and Longarm.

"You have helped," Longarm assured him. He turned and walked back to the door. Pulling it open, he glanced back at Bat.

"I'm going to find Tim Caulder now, Bat," Longarm said. He smiled slightly. "If that bit of tomfoolery was his own idea, I'll take it out of his hide. If it was your business to begin with, I'll be back to see you."

He stepped through the doorway and closed the door firmly behind him.

A moment later, leaning back casually in the shadow of the building, Longarm watched Lawson leave the general store and plunge headlong into the traffic of the main drag. Longarm followed. In the night, dodging among the crowds of loggers in and around the tents and shacks, Longarm almost lost sight of Bat. He stayed close to him however, and saw him duck into the rear of a larger-than-usual shack at the far end of town.

As he reached the door, he paused. From within, he heard Bat's rough voice: "I'm saying it was your idea, Tim—and I'm telling you to get on your horse and vamoose, if you know—"

Longarm pushed open the door and strode into the room.

The small, smoke-filled place went silent—except for the continued clicking of the roulette wheel along the far wall. Three poker games were in progress; the games were being played on surprisingly bright green felt-topped tables. At the table closest to Longarm, the man Bat had been talking to when Longarm had entered was sitting with his cards down, his face turned upward as he looked at Bat.

He was a slightly built fellow with a weasel face— long nose, receding chin, and gray, furtive eyes that now shifted in sudden panic from Bat to Longarm.

"Are you Tim Caulder?" Longarm asked.

"Yeah." Caulder glanced at Bat, his tongue flicking out to moisten his upper lip. "That's me. So what?"

"So your boss just told me it was your idea to sic those cowpunchers on me this afternoon."

Slowly, and as silently as possible, the loggers at the other tables began sliding their chairs back. The men at Caulder's table seemed prepared to dive under it. Tim Caulder's face had gone gray with Longarm's words.

"Hell," Caulder managed, "it was all Bat's idea. He sent me on ahead because I knew the punchers. I been keeping on the right side of them."

Longarm believed Caulder. Bat's story had sounded phony from the start, but he wanted Caulder—and as many others as possible—to know who had tried to put the finger on him. Longarm turned his attention to Bat. The man took a step back. Longarm faced him squarely.

"Sure is nice, Bat, to see a man who'll stand up for his own riders. I guess these men would follow you straight into hell, now, wouldn't they?" Longarm smiled. He was deliberately goading the man and knew he should feel ashamed—but he didn't.

"Damn you, Long!" Bat hissed. "I ain't afraid of you!"

" 'Course you ain't," Longarm said softly. "I never thought you were yellow. And now you're going to prove that, ain't you?"

The men at Caulder's table—including Caulder himself—dove under it as the others in the room broke for the walls, out of the line of fire. Bat slapped leather. Longarm strode quickly toward him, his Colt appearing in his hand as if by magic, its muzzle trained on Bat's startled face. Bat's right hand froze on his gun, halfway out of its holster. Before he could take another step back, Longarm moved closer, and with one brutal swipe, he brought his gunbarrel down on the crown of Bat's head. The man's hat was driven from its perch. Bat, his eyes closed, dropped to the floor with all the grace of an empty grain sack.

With the toe of his right boot, Longarm nudged Bat's shoulder. The man groaned and opened his eyes. Longarm kicked Bat's gun the rest of the way out of its holster. It skittered across the floor and came to rest against the wall with a solid clunk. It was the only sound in the place. Longarm returned his own gun to its holster.

"Now, you listen to me, Lawson," Longarm said. "Two damn fools are hurt pretty bad because you had some idea you could get them to bushwhack me. They weren't very bright or they wouldn't have listened to Tim, here, and I suppose they deserved what they got. The thing is, I just figured it wouldn't be fitting if I let you walk away scot-free."

"My head," Bat muttered, reaching up to feel the bump rising on the top of his skull. "It's bleeding. It must be bleeding. I can feel it!"

There was muted laughter at this. No blood was showing at all. Bat, in a kind of panic, kept feeling about his head.

"You'll be all right," Longarm told Lawson, "as long as you keep your nose clean. I don't hold grudges."

He turned and left the shack. His anger at the attempted ambush had been building steadily since that afternoon. He felt much better now. Despite the late hour and the fact that the loggers would have to be busy with their axes come morning, the town was still jumping. Kerosene lamps had been hung on posts almost everywhere along the line of shacks and tents. The lamps glowing from inside the tents cast a pale, feeble glow over the men roaming past in the street. Horsemen were still riding and carts were still being driven through, as small gangs of drunken men roamed back and forth across the single wide street. The place was noisier than a Mexican revolution, Longarm reflected as he sidestepped a drunken logger who had just reeled out of a small shack. The man disappeared past him into the night, zigzagging dangerously.

Longarm had about decided to go back to his hotel

room when he caught sight of the logger Gus Dodds. Remembering what Lawson had told him, Longarm halted and changed direction, following Gus into the Paradise Valley. The saloon—obviously a company run operation—showed considerably more class than any of the other watering holes in Whipsaw. The dark mahogany bar ran the length of the saloon and was easily forty feet long. The rear of the saloon was given over to roulette and poker. As Longarm stood for a moment in front of the flapping batwings, the place quieted noticeably. He could hear clearly the ticking of the roulette wheel, the croupier's droning voice, and the clicking of celluloid chips between the fingers of the dealers at the tables.

The bar was crowded and most of the tables were taken. The brass rail seemed to bend under the weight of so many calked boots. The floor was at least an inch deep in clean, recently spread sawdust. Over it all hung stratified layers of tobacco smoke, the clouds changing and swirling with each movement of the men.

Gus was at the bar, his big shoulders hunched as he leaned on it, giving his order to the barkeep. The bartender said something to Gus, then ducked to get a glass. Gus turned and looked directly at Longarm with his one good eye. The place was a lot quieter now. The clicking of the roulette wheel in back had ceased. Longarm walked across the slippery sawdust and pushed up to the bar beside Gus.

"Join me in a drink, Gus?" Longarm invited him.

Beneath a bushy eyebrow, Gus's eye focused unwaveringly on the lawman. "I'd let the devil himself buy my booze, if he's of a mind to," said Gus.

The marshal chuckled. "He's of a mind to."

Longarm glanced over his shoulder and spotted an empty table against the far wall. He turned back around, paid for Gus's whiskey, and ordered his own.

"Since you're paying," Gus said, "we'll just take this

here bottle with us." As he spoke, he took the whiskey from the barkeep's hand.

Longarm shrugged and dropped three silver dollars onto the polished mahogany. The barkeep said, "Four dollars."

Longarm was a little taken aback. He saw the broad smile on Gus's face, shrugged, and paid the ransom. "Let's go over to that table," Longarm suggested.

Gus voiced no objection and followed Longarm across the saloon floor, clutching the bottle of whiskey in his hand tightly about its neck. Longarm took the chair against the wall. Gus sat beside him, facing the door. The level of noise and activity in the saloon gradually returned to its former level. Gus finished his glass and poured himself another. Longarm sipped at his whiskey.

"I remember you from Silver City," Gus said. "You freed them Diggers, and I was glad you did. What do you want with me?"

"You knew Tanner."

"So?"

"He was bushwhacked."

"I knew that too, mister."

"Call me Longarm."

Gus downed another shot of whiskey. His eye reddened slightly as tears crowded into it. He coughed, then cleared his throat. "I don't know where the company gets this tonsil varnish, Longarm. It sure enough tastes like it was brewed in one of them circles in hell I hear tell about."

"I'd like to get the man who did that to Tanner," Longarm said quietly.

Gus pondered this for a moment, then looked squarely at Longarm. "I suppose I would, too. I liked Tanner. For a lawman, he was pretty square with us when we got in a jam."

"Maybe you can help, then," the deputy suggested.

"Sure."

"I'm looking for the same man Tanner was after."

"The deserter?"

Longarm nodded.

"Well, I helped Tanner all I could on that. I got to know a logger pretty good who fit that deserter's description. He lit out of here just after Tanner rode through on his way to collar a horse thief." Gus paused to pour himself another jolt. "A week or so later, Tanner came back asking about him, then took after him. Now Tanner is dead. I guess all I can do is give you the same information I gave Tanner."

Longarm sipped the low-grade rotgut. "I want a better description of Ned Shortslef than I got from that constable in Silver City."

Gus frowned thoughtfully, pushing his glass in small circles over the damp tabletop. "You sure he's Ned Shortslef? He called himself Tom something-or-other. I never got the last name and I never asked."

"Why don't we call him Ned? Nothing like thinking positive. That's the name of the deserter, and if Tanner went after him, he's Ned Shortslef. But like I said, I need a better description than the one I've got now that Tanner's dead."

The logger shrugged massively.

"How do you describe a guy? I don't remember nothing special about the way he looked. He was big, is all."

"Lots of hair? The color of his eyes?" Longarm prodded.

Gus shrugged again. "He wasn't bald and he had a full beard. I don't guess I ever really looked at his eyes to tell what color they was. He wasn't no girl I was romancing."

"Any limp or scars? He was supposed to be a Mountain Man at one time. Maybe he got into a rasslin' match with a bear or something. I understand he lived with an Indian woman for a time. Is that right?"

"Yeah. But that didn't leave no scars that I could see." Gus grew thoughtful. "Ned loved her quite a bit, as a matter of fact; her and the boy. He used to talk about them a lot."

"What happened to them? The squaw and the breed?"

Gus looked at Longarm sharply. "He never liked anybody to call her a squaw, or the boy a breed. That used to get him real mad."

"What else, Gus?"

"How's this going to help you? You said you wanted a description of Ned."

"Just answer my questions. You'd be surprised. It'll all fit in somewhere when the time comes; it usually does."

Gus went back to his whiskey glass, again pushing it about before him, tracing the wet circles, the patterns of which seemed to fascinate him. "She was a Cheyenne woman. Tall, and as graceful, he would say, as a flower in the wind. Fact is, that's what her Indian handle was. Black Flower Woman."

"What did Ned call her?"

Gus smiled. "Ned called her Muddy Face."

"Muddy Face?" Longarm echoed, a mite surprised.

The logger nodded.

"She worked so hard on the hides and stuff during their first months together, trying to impress him, that all he seemed able to remember of her was her dirty face at night when she poked her head in through the door of their lodge."

"And the boy?"

"Ned Flower Shortslef, he was called." Gus spoke somberly now.

"What happened to them?"

"Dead. Both of them. They died on the way to the reservation after the Rosebud Campaign. Probably froze to death. Ned wasn't sure what really happened —not that it makes all that much difference."

"Where was he during all this?"

"Running, I guess. The Cheyenne had made him a brother of the Dog Soldier Lodge, and he had taken an oath to defend the camp alongside the Dog Soldiers while the other warriors were away doing battle. When Custer's men stumbled on the camp, he sided with his wife's people. That was when he was spotted by one of Custer's lieutenants. So after the campaign, he lit out. He knew that if he hung around he'd only cause more trouble for his wife and her people. And his son."

"And Tanner was at the Rosebud, too."

Gus nodded.

"So now Tanner's dead. Do you think Ned killed him?"

Gus stopped fiddling with his glass. "How the hell should I know?" he muttered, as he tossed the glass of whiskey down in one gulp and reached for the bottle.

"It's just that you seem to know so much about this jasper," Longarm persisted. "Maybe you could tell me if he was the sort of man who could shoot Sheriff Tanner in the back—twice."

Gus kept his eye averted from Longarm. His shrug was elaborately casual. "I only knew him for a few months while we bunked together. He was good with an axe, so after a while we teamed up. He was a quiet one and kept pretty much to himself. When he saw Tanner, he knew he'd have to make tracks. So he did."

"Where did he go?"

"He didn't want to leave this area. His people are still up north, cooped up inside a reservation near the Snake. He went north, to work on one of the ranches."

"Which one?"

"Biggest one around—the Flying T."

Longarm considered this. He was going to have to pay that outfit a visit, it seemed. There wasn't any way around it and he wasn't looking forward to it—but everything so far pointed in that direction.

"I wish you could have given me a better picture of Shortslef, Gus."

"Just look for a big man—a *very* big man. Moves like a cat." Gus looked appraisingly at Longarm. "The way you do. And he's a man who don't smile often and likes a goodly distance between himself and the next guy."

"And I can find him at the Flying T?"

"I didn't say that. I said he went to them looking for work. I didn't say he found it. He might just have gone on north into Snake River country. Could be he's back with his people."

Longarm nodded a bit wearily. If this logger was giving him help, he was also making it seem as though the apprehension of Ned Shortslef was going to be a damned sight more complicated than he had anticipated.

A loud crash startled Longarm and caused him and Gus to turn in the direction of the noise. A logger had just gotten to his feet in a hurry and overturned a poker table in the process. The chips were rolling over the floor, the cards scattering in every direction. The two other loggers at the table were backing away. Everyone else, including those men at the bar, was cautiously moving away from the overturned table. The outraged logger was standing over the wreckage of the game, his chair lying on its back behind him. The house dealer was facing him from the other side of the overturned table, a Smith & Wesson pocket .38 in his right hand.

The dealer—in white shirtsleeves, a black vest, and a black, wide-brimmed, flat-crowned hat—smiled a reptilian smile. His mouth moved, while his eyes remained coldly amused. He had a pale, almost greenish face with a pencil-thin mustache on his upper lip, giving him the look of a stage villain. But there was nothing stagey about that Smith & Wesson in his hand.

"Put that gun down!" the logger said. "I ain't armed.

And you been cheatin'! I saw you dealing from the middle of the pack!"

"You ain't armed, mister. But you're a couple of feet taller than I am. I figure this here revolver makes us even." The dealer smiled and straightened.

"I saw you cheat!" the logger shouted. "I want my money back!"

"That's a libel, mister, and you know it. I don't have to cheat to outplay you. And if I did cheat, you'd never see a thing."

"Abruptly, one of Slade's men broke away from two of his companions at the bar and, coming up from behind the logger, brought the barrel of his sixgun down hard on the top of the logger's head. With a barely audible sigh, the logger sagged to the floor, his face sliding through the muddy sawdust.

At once, the place exploded. Every logger in the place—including Gus—swarmed toward Slade's men and the house dealer. There were five dealers in all, along with two bartenders and three of Slade's men against about nine loggers. Calculating swiftly, Longarm joined the loggers. Under the circumstances, the tall lawman would have avoided a donnybrook like this, but he decided that he might need the loggers' help someday against Bat's men. Shouts and threats rent the air. Someone leaped onto the bar, a chair in his hand, and hurled it at one of the barkeeps. Longarm saw one of the leaders industriously hammering with the barrel of his sixgun on the skull of a logger. Longarm waded toward the dealer, ducked a chair that whistled just over head, then brought his own Colt down across the dealer's wrist, sending his gun flying into the milling crowd.

The logger whose head was being pounded so diligently blinked once, straightened, and swung a roundhouse right, catching the dealer on the side of the head. The dealer went spinning backward into the melee. The logger, a broad crimson slash running down the side of his head, grinned widely and waved at Longarm, then turned and set off after another dealer. Almost knocked off his feet by a tumbling body, Longarm turned and was able to regain his balance just in time to duck under a wide, sweeping blow from one of the barkeeps. He was using a sawed-off peavey that just caught the crown of Longarm's hat, knocking it off. This upset Longarm. He kicked the fellow in the groin, and when he doubled over, brought his knee up into the barkeep's face, permanently altering the shape of the man's nose. His eyes snapped shut, and with a solid left jab to the chin, Longarm sent him flying backward over one of the few tables still upright.

Before Longarm could look around for his hat, a chair crashed down on his head and shoulders. He blinked, and staggering under the impact, he went down on one knee, shaking his head in an effort to clear it. It cleared just in time for him to dodge a fellow lunging at him with eyes as wild as a spooked steer. It was one of Bat Lawson's men, thinking only of getting out of the saloon. Longarm stuck out his boot. The fellow left his feet and went sailing into a wall, head first. Longarm straightened up then to ward off a clumsy attack from a dealer. Longarm reached out, grabbed the fellow's vest and yanking him toward himself ducked aside, flinging the fellow across the bar. The man, his arms and legs flailing willy, crashed into the shelves of bottles.

Surprisingly, this living projectile was the first missile to hit the bar's stock of firewater. The crash of breaking bottles seemed to alert the surging mass of bodies to the damage they were doing to their favorite watering hole and at once, it seemed, the mayhem quieted remarkably. Longarm looked quickly around and saw that the loggers had matters well in hand. Gus was in a corner with a dealer, the joyous look on his face in sharp contrast to the bloodied, glazed look on the face of the fellow he was holding up by the vest. Gus let go of the dealer, who sagged unconscious to the floor. A logger on top of the bar hurled one of the barkeeps in the general direction of the door.

The other loggers scrambled out of the way. The barkeep landed on his knees and then lunged frantically for the batwings. He was assisted by several well-aimed boots in his wide rear, and was airborne by the time he got to the door.

"Let 'em go, boys!" said one logger standing on the bar. "We don't need them anymore tonight."

With that he dropped down behind the bar and started placing fresh bottles and glasses upon the bar.

"Drinks are on the company!" he yelled.

With a roar, the loggers bellied up to the bar while someone stepped outside to announce the news to the rest of Whipsaw. Longarm spied his hat and hurried over to it. It was scuffed a little, but it would do. He clapped it on and caught Gus's eye.

The logger smiled at him and saluted. Longarm nodded back and left the saloon along with those dealers and company men who were still conscious. Once outside, he had to sidestep quickly to avoid the stampeding mob of loggers hurrying toward the Paradise Valley to share in the sudden wealth. Glancing across the street, Longarm saw a sullen crowd of battered men reporting to a now fully conscious Bat Lawson.

Bat was evidently trying to decide whether or not to try and take back the saloon. He evidently thought better of it and stalked off into the night with his unhappy band of enforcers. Longarm chuckled. The man would have a difficult time explaining this to his boss. This had not been Bat Lawson's night.

Chapter 4

Longarm spoke softly to the Morgan and pulled up. It was early in the morning. He was on his way to Wolf Creek to interview the foreman, Arnold Fitzpatrick, and found himself on a ridge overlooking Whipsaw. He dismounted, walked to the edge, and looked down.

From this height, he saw how the river lost its gleam as it neared Whipsaw and became only a dirty, sluggish moat looping halfway around the town. Great, misshapen clods of earth, composed of tree stumps and roots with ridges of mud and sand piled up behind them, dotted the mountain slopes on both sides. Those that were nearest the ridge were large enough to block Longarm's view of much of Whipsaw. Long, raw scars —skid marks from logs that had been snaked down the slopes—ran down both mountainsides, some leading into the river, others disappearing into the town. Whipsaw, the source of this spreading blight, festered just below—the bright, clean yellow of the mill's growing pile of sawdust reminding Longarm of the pustulous core of a boil that needed lancing.

He turned away from the sight and mounted up again.

On the rest of his ride to Wolf Creek, he found the same desolation. Slope after slope was denuded of all but the stumps of trees, littered with branches and other discarded portions of trees, all of it ground into the soil, obliterating what little vegetation had managed to grow in the rocky, inhospitable soil before the logging. When he reached what had been described to him as Wolf Creek, he found the waters muddy, but a significant number of pinyon and juniper still crowded the surrounding slopes, and there was considerable grama grass growing on the flats alongside the stream. The smell of pine resin hung heavy in the high, clean, bracing air.

As he rode up the stream, he could not help comparing this sudden explosion of green and standing pine with the country he had just ridden through. It was with a keen sense of disappointment that he watched the waters of Wolf Creek grow muddier, and saw the traces of broken branches and bark caught in the shallows along the shore. Crossing a low flat, he topped a rise and looked down on sudden desolation. Closest to him was a small camp made up mostly of tents for the men, and barns and corrals for the wagons and the horses. Beyond the camp, both slopes leading down to Wolf Creek were swarming with loggers. The crests had already been shorn. Now the loggers were busily chopping down the pine on the slopes. Tiny figures straddled the downed trees, swiftly hacking off the branches. Here and there on lower portions of the slopes, he saw loggers building neat skidways of gleaming, freshly peeled pine logs. Wagons piled high with logs were moving off along a heavily rutted road that followed the creek and then cut south toward Whipsaw, following a longer but less arduous route than the one Longarm had taken.

Longarm rode into the town and asked the cook, scouring out a pot in front of the huge eating tent, where he could find Fitzpatrick. The cook pointed with his scrub brush to a slope on the other side of the creek. "Halfway up," he said, then went back to his scrubbing.

Longarm nodded and rode down to the creek, searching for a place to ford it. As he started across, the cook poked his head out of the large pot and yelled something to him about Fitzpatrick wearing a green jacket. Longarm waved his thanks and a moment later gained the far shore.

The cook's directions had been clear enough, but Longarm had difficulty finding the foreman. Finally, he came across a crew chief in a red-checked shirt standing apart from a crew of loggers. His arms were akimbo as he angrily supervised the building of a fresh skidway. As Longarm rode up the slope toward him, the foreman turned to look at him.

Longarm nodded. "Howdy. Maybe you might be able to help me." Out of courtesy, the lawman dismounted to face the man on foot.

"Do I know you?" the crew chief asked.

"You will. Call me Longarm. I'm a deputy U.S. marshal. Right now I'm looking for your foreman, Arnold Fitzpatrick."

"You are, are you? Well, you'll just have to wait, Marshal. These so-called loggers are messing up this here skidway something awful."

The crew chief turned away from Longarm then, shouting, "Keep that log even! You'll never have a smooth deck less'n you keep them logs moving even!" he cried.

There were six men in all. Using a kind of four-foot-long pointed stick with an iron hook swinging from a socket near one end, the men were jacking logs up onto the skidway, which was a neat pile of recently cut logs kept in place with chains. The slopes were dotted with these skidways of fresh logs waiting for the wagon that would eventually transport them to the sawmill in Whipsaw.

The loggers appeared to be quite skillful with those hooked sticks, called peaveys, and Longarm found it difficult to understand why the crew chief was so critical of the loggers' performance. He watched as the crew chief snatched one of the peaveys from a logger and showed the fellow how to use it in jacking the log up the pole ramp onto the skidway. Longarm had to admit, the crew chief indeed knew how to handle a peavey. There seemed to be some kind of dispute raging in the camp as to which was more effective: the small, mean-looking peavey—the tool preferred by the younger loggers—or a much longer pole called a pike pole, which a few of the old-timers carried about with them much as shepherds carried their staffs. From the manner in which this crew chief in front of Longarm used the peavey, Longarm found it difficult to imagine a more efficient tool.

The crew chief returned the peavey to the chastened logger, then stepped back to join Longarm. The loggers worked even harder than before as they jacked the logs up the ramp onto the deck of the skidway, and now Longarm saw what the crew chief was after. The logs were falling into place neatly, seeming to slide up onto the skidway in a steady, effortless flow.

Satisfied, the crew chief turned to Longarm. "All right, Marshal. You say you're looking for Fitz."

Longarm nodded. He realized abruptly that the foreman was nervous—perhaps trying to stall.

"I just want some information," Longarm said.

"Just information, eh?"

"About a logger who used to work for him."

Obviously relieved, the fellow grinned slyly. "Nothing at all to do with last night, eh?" He broke into a broad grin. "Thought maybe Slade might have sent you. But then, you was pitching in along with the rest of us."

Longarm smiled. The crew chief must have been one of the loggers he had battled beside the night before. "That's right. Nothing to do with last night. I just want to talk to Fitzpatrick."

"Fitz is through that pass somewheres, checking out the log scale on what pine we got left on that slope."

"Thank you."

"That's all right, Marshal. Glad to help. If you see Fitz, tell him Jock's almost through here."

"I'll do that," Longarm said, swinging into his saddle.

He headed for the low, wooded pass Jock had indicated and was beyond it about a half hour later, approaching a small clearing, when he caught sight of Fitzpatrick on the far side of it. The green jacket stood out clearly as the foreman, standing on what appeared to be a small stump, spoke to some ten or twelve loggers gathered around him. He appeared to be excited about something, waving his arms as he talked.

But Longarm was too far away to hear the words spoken by the foreman, and before he could get close enough, a shot echoed from the hillside to Longarm's right. He pulled up at once and looked in that direction. When he glanced back at the group in the clearing, he saw the loggers moving off into the pines, their axes over their shoulders. The foreman was walking across the clearing to meet Longarm.

Longarm rode closer, then dismounted. That shot, he realized, was a signal.

"Are you Arnold Fitzpatrick?" Longarm asked.

The fellow nodded. "That I am. And you'd be that federal marshal."

"I'm Deputy U.S. Marshal Long. You can call me Longarm; it's easier to remember."

"Call me Fitz, then. What can I do for you, Longarm?"

"Slade said you might be able to help me. I'm looking for an army deserter who used to work for you."

"If Slade says I got to talk to you, then I'll talk." Fitzpatrick's white teeth gleamed in a sudden smile.

Like the crew chief back at the skidway, he seemed to be relieved to learn what Longarm wanted.

The foreman looked to be in his late thirties. He was of medium height, thick about the chest and arms, with a gut only just beginning to strain against his belt. He wore a red cotton shirt under his open jacket, and heavy pants of a coarse woolen material tucked into his laced boots. A narrow, flat-crowned hat covered most of his thick, dark hair. His face was full and his dark, handsome eyes peered alertly out at Longarm from under jet-black, bushy eyebrows.

"This fellow I'm looking for, Fitz, worked for you until a few weeks ago. His name is Ned Shortslef, but I don't expect he'll be using that name. Like I said before, he's gone now—but I thought you might have some idea where he went. Anything you could give me would be a help."

"You got more than his name? A description, maybe?"

Longarm described Shortslef as best he could, relying on Seegar's and Gus's descriptions. By the time he had finished, he realized how inadequate his description was. The foreman's dark eyes reflected Longarm's misgivings.

"Well, now," the foreman began, "I suppose you might think that to be a fine description, but it don't tell me much. You say this bucko is tall. We got plenty of tall loggers, Longarm. He has a beard, has he? Look around you. My men don't have time to shave—not out here, they don't. Moves like a big cat, you said. Well, these loggers better move like a cat or they'll get flattened in no time at all by some falling tree or by a load of logs breaking from a skidway. Longarm, you just about described most of my loggers."

"This one was a good friend of Gus Dodds."

The foreman arched an eyebrow. "Gus Dodds, you say?"

Longarm nodded.

"Gus Dodds is a loner," Fitz told him. "A fast man with an axe, make no mistake about that. One of my best. He can drop a tree on a stake already set in the ground and bury it every time. But he keeps to himself, he does. And that's a fact, Longarm."

"How about two weeks ago?" the lawman asked.

"He's a loner, I said. And he has been ever since I've worked here. All the men like him, though. They just don't mess with him. They let him be."

"You're saying he's been lying to me?"

"I wouldn't say that. No, sir! Not to his face. Like I said, Longarm, he's a fast man with an axe."

"Is Gus working out here with this crew?"

Fitz shook his head. "Nope. He's on the other side of that ridge behind me."

"Maybe I'd better go have another talk with him."

"Just don't slow him down any. We need his production."

Longarm thanked the foreman, remounted, and picked his way along a steep slope beyond the clearing. Reaching the ridge, he found it alive with loggers cutting through a thick stand of juniper. Unlike the gnarled pinyon being cut downslope to be used for railroad ties and firewood, these junipers were tall and straight enough to be used for telegraph poles. As he rode past, Longarm saw the trees being barked and trimmed with almost startling rapidity in preparation for their trip downslope to the waiting skidways.

Longarm kept going, crested the ridge, then slanted down the far slope toward a small army of loggers busily cutting through a thin but valuable stand of red fir. Watching the loggers chopping at the trees—white chips flying, each axe blade sounding as steadily and surely as a pendulum—Longarm no longer questioned these loggers' gargantuan excesses at nightfall. Men who worked this hard should be allowed to play the same way.

Nearing the stand of fir, Longarm watched as one of the tall firs came crashing down among its fellows. It was so skillfully placed, he noted, that it completely missed the surrounding trees as it crashed to earth. Into the timber by this time, Longarm caught sight of Gus. The big logger was about to resume his chopping of one of the tallest of the remaining firs.

"Gus!" Longarm called out, pulling up.

Gus turned, saw him, and put down his axe. He said something to another logger stripping a fallen log nearby. This other logger took up Gus's axe and began chopping at the tree as Gus strode through the slash to Longarm. Dismounting, Longarm waited for the one-eyed logger to reach him.

"Gus," Longarm said, "I need a little more information about Ned Shortslef. You say you worked with him for a while?"

"Look, Marshal, I told you all I know. He's up north somewhere if he ain't at the Flying T."

"Gus, the foreman says you never worked with anyone. He says you're a loner—that you didn't have any such buddy as Ned Shortslef."

"He's calling me a liar."

"You look like a loner to me. I haven't seen you with anyone yet, except that time in the hotel in Silver City when you got to be spokesman for those other two bashful loggers."

"I pick my own friends. I keep to myself if I want. I told you the truth about Ned Shortslef, no matter what you or Fitz says."

The big logger was getting angry. Before Longarm could say anything to soothe the man, a shot rang out from the slope above. Longarm never found out who fired the shot, and it didn't seem to matter at that moment as a crowd of hooded horsemen swept down off the slope, encircling the stand of fir. At sight of the riders, the loggers at once dropped their axes and reached for their weapons. Longarm heard the sound of shooting coming from the ridge above and the slope beyond.

A twig from a branch over his head was snipped off by an errant bullet as a volley of shots rang out from the enclosing vigilantes. Longarm went for his gun and darted with Gus behind a tree. By this time it became apparent to Longarm that the loggers had not been completely surprised as the withering fire cut from the trees. The hooded riders pulled up somewhat indecisively. It was obvious that their appetite for bloodshed did not match their desire to intimidate the loggers.

One of the riders pulled up swiftly, turned his horse, and waved the others back. Before they could follow his lead, slugs tore into two of the riders. Longarm saw them slump forward over their pommels as other riders came alongside them to help the wounded men stay in their saddles. The firing from the trees let up a bit after that.

But the vigilante who had waved his men back away from the timber now turned his horse around and charged recklessly back toward the timber. Longarm swore softly at the rider's gallant but foolhardy gesture, then ducked as the fire from the fellow's Winchester began slashing through the branches above his head.

"Jesus!" Gus muttered. "Why's he picking on us?"

By this time the loggers in the timber had opened up once again, sending out a fierce fire at the rider. But the vigilante did not falter. He was angry. Abruptly, he ran out of ammunition. Pulling up, he began to reload his Winchester.

Longarm stepped out from his cover. "Hold it right there, mister!" he called.

The firing from the timber behind Longarm ceased, and an eerie silence fell on the scene as the gunfire on the ridge above and the slope beyond ceased also. The hooded rider looked up in surprise as Longarm strode swiftly out of the timber toward him. Then he continued in his insanely determined effort to reload his Winchester.

When Longarm had approached to within five feet or so of the vigilante, he unholstered his Colt. "This is a fool's errand, mister. What are you up to? You think those flour sacks are going to scare anyone?"

At last the vigilante looked up from his rifle and stared down at Longarm through two ragged slits in the sack. There were none for his mouth and nose. With the fellow's every inhalation the flour sack was sucked in, then blown out. It had to be as hot as a chicken's ass inside that mask, Longarm mused.

"This is a warning!" the vigilante cried, his voice muffled grotesquely by the hood. "You loggers are ruining this slope. Ruining this entire valley! If we can't stop you one way, we'll stop you another. Tell that to Slade!"

"Why, hell, man! Don't you think he knows that already? He's not logging on your homesteads. He's cutting on government territory. You can't scare him off this land. You try that and you'll be going against the law. The fact is, you ain't much better than outlaws right now!"

With a furious oath, the hooded rider swung up his reloaded Winchester and levered quickly. Longarm ducked low and crabbed sideways as he fired almost without conscious volition up at the rider. The man grabbed his left shoulder and peeled back off his horse, his Winchester discharging harmlessly into the air.

At that, the rest of the vigilantes, who had been waiting not more than a hundred yards away from the timber, immediately spurred back toward Longarm. Longarm did not think he could make it safely back to the trees. Darting forward, he grabbed the bridle of the vigilante's horse and yanked powerfully, pulling the mount down on its side. As he did this, he kicked the Winchester out of the downed vigilante's right hand, then stomped on the rifle's stock, snapping it. The man groaned and swore bitterly at Longarm. Longarm ducked low behind the horse and began to track the lead rider bearing down on him.

He fired; the shot went high. Then he no longer had time to aim. He fired rapidly, riding the recoil up with each shot. The nearest rider lost his hat. The one just behind him spun his horse when a slug whined too close. At that moment, the sudden rattle of rifle fire came from the ridge. Glancing up, Longarm saw about ten horsemen charging down the slope with their guns blazing, and two mounted vigilantes running before them. The foreman, Fitz, was leading the chase.

From the dress of the pursuing riders, Longarm knew they were Bat Lawson's men. They must have been waiting somewhere for just this kind of foolishness on the part of the ranchers. As Lawson's men swept down the slope, the rest of the vigilantes broke off their attack on Longarm and galloped away, abandoning their wounded comrade. Lawson's men, letting out whoops like cowboys on a Saturday night hurrah, galloped after the vigilantes to the delighted cheers of the loggers behind Longarm in the timber.

Fitz and one other rider pulled up. Longarm waved; Fitz waved back. Then the two riders rode over to him. The loggers had already left the cover of the timber and were forming a grim circle around Longarm and the wounded vigilante. Fitz and the other rider rode through the circle of loggers. Longarm bent down and yanked the flour sack off the vigilante's head.

He was a very young man, not yet in his twenties. His face was pale and drawn from loss of blood, but his dark eyes were alive with anger as he glanced about him. He had a lean face, deeply tanned, the jaw slightly outthrust and square. At the moment he was intent on trying to stanch the flow from his wound with his bandanna.

"What's your name, mister?" Longarm asked, holstering his Colt.

The wounded man glared up at him for a moment, but refused to reply. Then he turned his attention back to his shoulder wound.

"That's Wally Troy," Fitz said, looking down from his saddle. "Terry Troy's brother. The Troys own the Flying T. You got yourself a nice catch there, Marshal."

The rider with Fitz grinned wolfishly. He was wearing a black vest over a bright red cotton shirt. The butt of his pearl-handled Colt gleamed against the shining flap of his black leather holster. "We know just what to do with him, don't we, Fitz?"

Longarm looked up at the man. "What's your name, mister?"

"Jack Wilson."

"And just what in tarnation do you plan on doing with this man, Wilson?"

"What we do with vigilantes—string him up. That's the word from Bat. And you ain't going to stop us this time, Marshal. This man and his band of lawless vigilantes killed one of our loggers."

"Prove it."

"We don't have to."

The rest of Slade's private army was galloping back toward them now. Wilson glanced at the oncoming horsemen, then smiled back at Longarm. "Here comes all the evidence we need, Marshal."

"Wilson, if you—or any men here—take part in a lynching, I'll come after you. If I can't bring you in, there'll be other deputies, and still more after that. On this government land, I'm the law. Not Slade, or Bat Lawson, or any of you gun-happy flannelmouths."

84

"Guess that means you, Wilson," Fitz said, his teeth flashing in his tanned face.

"Shut up, you dirty mick!" Wilson cried.

Fitz's smile vanished in an instant and in one powerful move he brought his huge left fist around in a backhand swipe, catching Wilson on the tip of his jaw. Longarm thought he heard a bone go as Wilson went flying backward over his cantle. He landed close beside Wally Troy and sat up holding his jaw. Tears of pain and rage flowed suddenly from his eyes.

Wally Troy laughed.

Longarm pulled Troy's horse to its feet. Then he reached down to help the young man. As Wally stood up and steadied himself, he told Longarm, "We never tried to hurt anyone. We was all aimin' high, deliberate. We couldn't've hurt no loggers. He's lying."

"I was wondering how come you were all such lousy shots," Longarm drawled. "Let me give you a hand up."

With his teeth firmly clenched and his eyes closed from the pain, Wally Troy swung himself up into his saddle just as Bat's riders closed in around the circle of loggers. A rider, whom Longarm recognized as the same man who had stood in the entrance to the Paradise Valley with Bat the night before, guided his mount through the loggers toward Longarm.

"Who told you to butt in here, Longarm?" the rider demanded.

"Just who the hell wants to know?" Longarm replied testily, eyeing the man with a swift and sudden dislike.

"I'm Ruel Tyson. I'm in charge here. You ain't going to interfere in this, Longarm. I got the word from Bat. We catch any of these here vigilantes, we string 'em up."

A roar of approval came from the loggers as they pressed closer. Many of them were still carrying those ancient but formidable weapons they had grabbed when the vigilantes' attack had first begun. Longarm could not blame the loggers. They were the ones who had been the target of all that lead. It didn't much matter to them that the damn fools in those flour sacks were aiming high. And there was little chance they would believe such a thing, anyway.

"You're not stringing anyone up, Tyson," Longarm said. "Young Troy here says the vigilantes were all aiming high, just trying to scare the loggers. It was a damn fool thing to do, I admit. But scaring hell out of loggers isn't a hanging offense that I know of. So back off. I'm taking this fellow back to his spread."

"No, you ain't," Ruel said, his eyes suddenly going cold. His hand flashed down to his holster.

Longarm's Colt appeared in his hand with such speed that it seemed to have been hanging in the air between the two men all the time. In the act of drawing his own weapon, Ruel's right hand froze. His face was suddenly pale, his eyes wide and focused on the muzzle of Longarm's steady sixgun.

"Ease your gun back into its holster, Tyson," Longarm instructed him quietly. "Then tell these loggers to stand back or you'll be wearing a hole where your heart ought to be."

"Stand back, you men!" Ruel shouted, letting his Colt drop back into its holster.

Longarm heard a scuffle to his right. Glancing swiftly over, he saw a logger go down heavily. Gus, standing beside the downed man with a large chunk of wood in his hand, nodded solemnly at Longarm. The downed logger had evidently tried to save Ruel's ass. Ruel glanced in that direction, furious.

"I told you knuckleheads! Get back! Don't try nothing!"

"Gus!" Longarm called. "Get my horse! It's still back there in the timber."

Gus ran for Longarm's mount and brought it back through the ranks of grim loggers. Longarm thanked the man and swung up into his saddle, his gun still trained on Tyson. He spoke to Troy: "Start to ride, Wally. I'll catch up to you."

Slumped painfully forward over his saddle horn, Wally Troy dug steel into his mount's flanks and started up. Longarm waited until the man was beyond Lawson's riders, then told Tyson, "Now, you follow Troy. And remember, there's a Colt looking at your back!"

With a muttered curse, Ruel followed Troy, Longarm riding close behind. Once through the loggers, Longarm glanced back at Gus. "You going to be all right?" he asked.

"Never mind me, Longarm. You got enough to handle right in front of you!"

Longarm nodded and waved to him, then turned back around. Ruel glanced at him. "Keep going, Ruel. I'll tell you when you can go back to your gunslicks. Just keep riding."

Ruel did as he was told. Glancing ahead of Ruel at young Troy, he saw that the kid was doing all right. He had more guts than brains, it appeared. Longarm decided he would keep Ruel with him for a couple of miles at least before letting the man return to the logging site.

Then all he would have to worry about would be Wally Troy's friends, and after that, his reception at the Flying T.

Chapter 5

The Flying T was a good distance away. Longarm found himself riding through high, surprisingly fertile country. The floors of the valleys they crossed were covered with thick grama, the few dry stretches dotted with waist-high sagebrush. Jackrabbits leaped away through the scrub pine, and once Longarm thought he caught sight of a pronghorn antelope high-kicking his way around a clump of sagebrush.

They were crossing a narrow creek when Wally slumped suddenly forward over the pommel. Longarm had been riding just behind him. He dismounted quickly and was in time to ease the man out of his saddle and onto the ground. He took off the young man's hat and went back to the stream for some water. Wally drank it greedily. Longarm felt his forehead. It was burning up. Wally had evidently lost a lot of blood.

Easing him over to a boulder, Longarm propped him up against it and inspected the wound. It was suppurating by this time, and partly scabbed over. Ugly, raw streaks of red radiated up over the shoulder and down into the armpit. Wally Troy watched him through cold, heavy-lidded eyes, making no effort to hide his contempt for Longarm. When Longarm probed the wound with the barrel of his Colt, the young man's eyes didn't waver.

Longarm stood up and gazed down at the man for a moment, considering. Often it wasn't the bullet that killed a man; it was the infection that usually followed. And this inflammation was advancing rapidly. Longarm had seen a wound similar to this take a man in less than two days. There was nothing for it then, but to cauterize the wound as best he could.

Going to his horse, he untied his bedroll and secured his coffeepot. Filling it with water from the stream, he built a small fire and heated the water to a boil. Then he ripped a portion of Wally's shirtsleeve off and dropped it into the boiling water. While it boiled, Longarm took out his knife and held the blade over the open flame until it began to glow.

Wally watched him, his eyes narrowing ever so slightly. Longarm approached him with the glowing knife in his hand, hunkered down beside him, and before the fellow could pull back, plunged the blade into the wound, cutting deep and scouring the edges. The stench of burning tissue assailed Longarm's nostrils. Only when he felt Wally's body slump sideways did he glance up and see that the man had passed out.

It was what Longarm had hoped would happen. He took the piece of shirt out of the boiling water and thoroughly cleaned the wound. The blood was beginning to flow again, but it was cleaner blood. Longarm was encouraged. He tore off another piece of the unconscious man's shirt. Stuffing the bloody shirt fragment into the wound to stanch the flow, he used the other piece of shirt to bind it tightly in place.

He stood up then, and surveyed the still unconscious man for a moment longer. Satisfied that he had done all he could, given the circumstances and the tools he had, Longarm cleaned off the knife's blade, emptied the water on the fire, and repacked his bedroll. He was in the act of knotting the rawhide thong around it when he heard a movement behind him.

Ducking low and turning in one swift motion, he was astounded to see the wounded cowboy coming up behind him, a sixgun in his raised right hand. Wally brought his weapon down. Just in time, Longarm managed to thrust his arm up to ward off the blow. Nevertheless, the impact of the gun barrel on his forearm was such that for a moment Longarm thought the fellow might have broken it. But only for a moment. Longarm grabbed the sixgun's barrel and twisted the weapon out of Wally's hand. At the same time, he smashed the cowboy in the midsection.

Wally Troy went down suddenly, as if someone had cut the strings holding him upright. Longarm stuck the fellow's sixgun into one of his saddlebags. Massaging his throbbing forearm, he turned back to the cowboy, whose head was sagging forward, his hair falling over his face. Slowly and painfully, he lifted his head to look at Longarm.

He spoke then in a voice so soft Longarm had to lean forward to catch his words: "You skunk! Damn your eyes to hell! I'll get you yet!"

Longarm smiled at the fellow. He liked his courage. "As soon as you're ready, I'll help you back up onto your horse."

"I'm ready," the fellow croaked weakly, and held up his right hand. Longarm pulled him to his feet.

The sun was sitting just above the mountains when Longarm followed Wally Troy into a narrow pass that led onto a vivid green flat. As he rode closer to the flat, Longarm could make out the cattle feeding on the grama. Emerging from the pass, he saw the ranch buildings, blue in the distance. They were a slightly darker smudge set against the lighter blue of the low hills beyond. The jingle of harness and the sound of shoes striking stone behind Longarm alerted him—but too late.

He swung around in his saddle and saw the semicircle of riders falling in behind him. Longarm recognized the lead rider. It was Lyle Butts. As Longarm caught the man's eye, Butts touched his hat brim and smiled coldly.

"We meet again, Marshal," he said, his stubbly, narrow face grimly serious.

Longarm glanced around at the other riders. There were six of them, all told, including Butts. Longarm had little doubt that all of them had been riding not too long before with flour sacks over their heads. But obviously others had joined this bunch, since there had been considerably more vigilantes in that gang at Wolf Creek. The ranchers were getting together then, acting in concert against a common enemy.

"Don't make a play for your sixgun, Marshal," Butts said, as he rode past Longarm to reach the side of Wally Troy.

"How you doin', Wally?" Butts asked.

The young man looked at Butts through a curtain of pain. "Hell, Butts, I'm doing just fine. All I got's a slug through my shoulder."

"You look peaked."

"I wonder why?" the young cowboy said sarcastically. "Shit, Butts, don't ask so many questions. Just get that sonofabitch riding behind me off my back."

"Sure, Wally. Sure," Butts said. He pulled up slightly and fell in beside Longarm, then guided his mount closer. He reached out his right hand. "Let me have that weapon of yours, Marshal."

"You can take it if you want, Butts, but it'll cost you."

"Hell! I got five men backing me—each one with a hogleg pointing at you. Do as you're told, mister."

"Call me Longarm—and keep your distance, Butts. If you lay a hand on that Colt, you'll just get my balls in an uproar and all hell will break loose. They'll be sending both of us to hell on a shingle, but you'll be going in just a little bit ahead of me." He smiled. "You got a hankering to make that trip, have you?"

Butts shrugged. "I can wait. We'll be at the ranch soon enough. Just follow Wally."

"What the hell do you think I've been doing, Butts?"

The older man's narrow face darkened, but he offered no further comment and pulled his horse out and away from Longarm, then drifted back with the rest of the Flying T crew. Glancing back, Longarm saw blued steel glinting darkly in six hands. Turning around, Longarm felt a coldness creep up his spine. He felt as if he had bedded down in a nice, cool, shaded nest of rattlers—he would be all right if he didn't move too suddenly . . . maybe.

About a half hour later, with the riders still close behind him and Wally Troy keeping himself erect in the saddle just ahead of him, Longarm rode onto the Flying T spread. The low, long bunkhouse and the cook-shack adjoining it were of adobe and formed two sides of a rough, sandy plaza. The opposite sides were taken up by the blacksmith shop and several wagon sheds. All of this, the working heart of the ranch, lay sprawled under giant cottonwoods. The house was separated from the work building by a high stone wall, and stood some distance away.

As Longarm rode in, a powerful, stocky fellow stepped out of the small ranch office near the north end of the bunkhouse. He was wearing a black, flat-crowned hat with its brim turned down in back, a dark blue shirt, and gray pants tucked into well-cared-for boots. The man's face was handsome in a casually brutal way, with sensual lips, lidded eyes, and an habitual insolent downturn at the corners of his mouth. He looked like a man who was happy only when he was riding someone hard. When he saw the drawn guns all pointed at Longarm, he licked his lips and stepped eagerly toward the group of riders.

Longarm pulled up. Butts dismounted and hurried to help Wally off his mount. As he was doing this, the other riders pulled up in a circle around Longarm.

"What happened to Wally?" the fellow in the dark blue shirt asked Butts.

It was Wally who answered. Hurrying toward the ranchhouse, he glanced back at the man who was evidently the foreman and snapped angrily, "That lawman shot me. He's working with Slade and Lawson!"

"Hey, Russ!" a rider behind Longarm called out. "That's the marshal that messed up Teeter and Slick."

Longarm glanced back and recognized Billy, one of the four who had attempted to bushwhack him the day before. As Longarm glanced back at the foreman, the fellow took a step toward him.

"You're the one, huh? I was hoping you'd turn up. I hear your name's Long."

"That's right. Custis Long, deputy U.S. marshal out of Denver."

The foreman glanced quickly around at the grim faces of his riders, most of whom still had their sixguns trained on Longarm. He smiled back at Longarm. "Slick Hansen and Jim Teeter are two pretty sick boys, no thanks to you."

"I see. I was supposed to let them bushwhack me, is that it? A funny kind of law you've got here." The Morgan shied. Longarm reached forward and patted its neck, and settled it down. "You the foreman here?"

"That's right. Russ Blodgett's the name. You can call me Mister Blodgett."

"Russ, I reckon you better tell your men to put their guns away. There's a law against vigilantes—even damn fool vigilantes like this bunch. Wally Troy drew on me; that's attempted assault. Two of your men are already flat on their backs for attempting to murder me, and a man sitting his horse right now behind me was part of that same conspiracy. Looks to me like you've got yourself a passel of trigger-happy cowpokes who've been making a mess of things so far. You tell them to quit while they're ahead."

"And if they don't?"

"I just might have to take them back with me," Longarm answered evenly.

"All five, Marshal?"

"As many as I have to."

Blodgett laughed, and a set of crooked teeth flashed in his otherwise handsome face. "You ain't bringing anybody back with you, Marshal." The man looked quickly around. "Ain't that right, boys?"

"He's just going to have an accident," Billy drawled from behind Longarm, cocking his sixgun. The sound of the other four sixguns being cocked filled the tense silence. Again Longarm had to quiet his skittish mount. He patted the Morgan's neck gently and talked to it. Then he looked down at the foreman.

"I tell you what, Russ. Looks like I'm a dead man anyway, what with all this firepower pointed at me. The only thing a man can do in a case like this is pick one fellow and make sure he takes that jasper with him. I pick you."

"I ain't armed!" Blodgett protested.

"That doesn't make any difference, the way I look at it. Your friends have got enough artillery for both of us. I've got a Colt in a cross-draw rig under my coat. Some say I'm fast, and I guess I do practice some—for situations like this."

"Just a minute there." The foreman held up a hand and took a step back.

"Hang in there, Blodgett. I ain't started counting yet."

"It's a bluff, Russ!" a cowhand called.

"Sure! That's all it is!" another cried. "Give us the go-ahead!"

Longarm smiled at Russ. "Maybe I don't have time for counting. . . ."

"What in hell's going on out here, Russ?"

A woman had strode into view behind the foreman. She had come from the house, it appeared. Russ spun to face her. He was obviously more than a little relieved to see her. She strode angrily toward him, her fierce eyes raking the ring of horsemen.

"What in tarnation are all you men doing, pointing your guns at this one man? Put those irons away!"

She swept past Russ Blodgett and came to a halt in front of Longarm. "You're Marshal Long. Wally just told me what happened. Thank you for not killing the damned fool, Marshal. Light and stay awhile. You're welcome at the Flying T anytime. My name is Terry Troy. I own this spread."

Longarm took a deep breath, touched the brim of his hat to the woman, and smiled down at her. "Much obliged, Miss Troy."

She spun around then to face the foreman. "You heard me, Russ. Get these men back to some kind of honest work. And from now on, I don't want them playing cowboys and Indians on Flying T time. Do you understand that, Russ? They are cowpokes, not vigilantes!"

"Sure, Terry, but it was Wally's idea! he said you—"

"Never mind what that *kid* told you, Russ. I thought you had better sense than that! *That's* why I made you foreman."

With a sudden, dangerous sullenness, Russ waved the riders back away from Longarm. Looking suddenly sheepish, the riders turned their mounts toward the barn. The tension lifted immediately.

The woman turned back to Longarm and smiled. "I

95

asked you to dismount and stay awhile, Marshal. Or do you intend to spend the night on that Morgan?"

"Not when I've got a better offer," Longarm said, swinging off the horse.

Standing before the owner of the Flying T, Longarm realized that she had appeared taller than she actually was. She wore Levi's that had shrunk to fit and looked as if they might have to be peeled off, judging from the way they clung to her full hips and lushly rounded thighs. A faded-blue man's shirt was pulled almost as tightly across her bosom, giving the shirt a shape it sure as hell never had on any man. The gaps between the two top buttons threatened to grow larger any second. High-heeled boots and a thick crown of chestnut hair were what had imparted the illusion of height. Her stance, proud and not a little arrogant, completed the picture of a woman used to giving orders and seeing them obeyed.

"What's a woman doing," she asked him mockingly, "running a ranch? Is that it, Marshal? I think that's what I am reading in your eyes. I am not usually wrong."

"And you weren't far wrong this time, either. I reckon if you can read minds, you won't have any trouble buffaloing a few foolish cowhands and a thousand head."

"There are more than a thousand head running the Flying T brand, Marshal. But the cattle aren't what's giving me the trouble." She turned, called one of her hands over, and told him to see to Longarm's horse. Then she looked back at Longarm. "There's hot coffee at the house, Marshal, and a place to sit that's not moving all the time."

She turned and started for the ranchhouse. Longarm left his horse with the hand she had called over and followed after her.

The ranchhouse was massive, one story high with a

fluted tile roof. A porch extended around three sides. Deep within its cool adobe fastness was an inner court paved with black cobblestones, the surfaces of which shone like glass. They crossed the court to reach a bedroom where Terry's brother, naked from the waist up, was being tended by a young Mexican girl. Longarm remained behind in the doorway and watched as Terry consulted the girl on Wally's condition. Wally's eyes were closed, but he did not seem to be sleeping.

Terry thanked the girl and started from the room. Her brother opened his eyes and looked at her. "Carla says that son of a bitch did a good job when he cleaned out my wound."

"You're luckier than you deserve," Terry said, carefully keeping her concern out of her voice. "The bullet went on through."

Terry left the room and Longarm followed her back across the court to a huge parlor with pine rafters. It was comfortably furnished with leather sofas and easy chairs. A huge stone fireplace dominated the long outer wall. There were hunting trophies above the long mantelpiece—the heads of a pronghorn with an impressive pair of prongs, an elk, and a bighorn. Longarm settled into a leather chair.

This was a man's parlor, he thought, in spite of the curtains over the bank of windows facing the porch. Terry Troy didn't seem to go in much for frills and lace any more than she did for petticoats.

She sat down on the corner of the sofa facing him, and noted the way he surveyed the room. "Yes," she said, "this is still the way my father left it a couple of years ago. I saw no reason to change a thing. It is a big, comfortable room without any foolish clutter of knicknacks. It's like my father—a big man without much fuss or show."

The housekeeper—an enormous and absolutely

silent Mexican woman—entered the room with a tray containing a battered coffeepot, cups, milk, and sugar. She set the tray down on a solid oak table between them, and poured the coffee. Watching her, Longarm realized that this woman was the mother of the girl in the room with Wally. The milk came out of a can and the housekeeper was quite generous with it. She handed Longarm his cup first, then served her mistress.

"Thank you, Juanita," Terry said. "Leave the pot."

The big woman padded silently out of the room. Longarm drank the coffee. Despite the generous portion of canned milk, it had the strength of a mule's kick. He savored it.

Putting down her cup, Terry smiled at Longarm. "Juanita uses aged coffee grinds, I believe. But I do like its bite."

Longarm met her smiling gaze with his own serious one.

"I am sorry about your brother, Miss Troy," he said.

"Call me Terry," she suggested with a smile.

"My friends call me Longarm."

"All right, Longarm. I understand, I think, about Wally. He's a terrible hothead, and right now—along with the rest of us—he is desperate about this logging. If my father were still alive, his action would have been a lot more drastic than Wally's was this afternoon, I am afraid. But tell me about it. Wally said he tried to shoot you."

Longarm told her everything. When he got to his account of Wally galloping back to the timber alone through the gunfire, she closed her eyes, shuddering at the picture in her mind. When Longarm was finished, she took a deep breath.

"Then you saved Wally's life. Bat Lawson's men would have hung him."

"That was their intention."

She shook her head. "Thank you, Longarm. I'm sure that when Wally comes to his senses, he'll thank you as well."

"Two other men were wounded, I noticed."

"Yes. They were Bar B hands. The Bar B is a small ranch to the south of us. The two men will be all right, I understand." She smiled wryly at him then. "And there are two other hurt cowboys in our bunkhouse, one with an arrow hole in his back. They'll be all right, too, if I can keep them quiet."

"They mistook me for a gunslinger Slade was bringing in. What can you tell me about him?"

"Nothing much. But he's a threat to all of us. This gunslick can call any of my hands out and cut them down easily, one at a time. Wally would be the first to answer such a challenge. But, Longarm, I didn't know those four men were going after you. If I had, I would have stopped them. Butts said he tried to talk them out of it, then went along to keep them out of trouble— if he could."

"He wasn't very successful."

"That arrow—from the wound, I could tell it was a Digger arrow. Were Diggers with you at the time?"

"I've been doing some thinking about that, Terry," Longarm said, scratching the back of his neck. "In Silver City I made Bat and his men release four Diggers they were about to hang. I figured those four Diggers—or one of them, at least—was up there, sort of looking out for me, when your boys opened up."

Terry frowned in thought, then nodded. "It's likely," she said. "What's that about casting your bread on the waters—"

"Or, one good turn deserves another."

"And these Indians are like that. They never forget a kindness—or an offense."

"That's about it, Terry," he said.

She took a deep breath and leaned back. He held

his own breath at the sight, wondering if the buttons down the front of her shirt would hold. Her face was darkly tanned causing her white teeth and light blue eyes to gleam like precious stones. She wore her hair down to her shoulders, loosely curled, utterly without concern as to how this might be regarded by others. The lines of her face were clean, her nose uptilted slightly. There was a faint dimple in the center of her bold chin. She was a handsome woman—and strong. The wildness of her father was apparent in Wally. It was in her, too, but she had her father's strength as well.

"You're staying for the night," she said. "You must allow my hospitality to make amends for whatever indignities you suffered at the hands of my men—and the Flying T. Really, Longarm. I insist."

"That's right kind of you. But are you sure your hands will be able to understand that? They seemed pretty anxious to have me for dinner—after I'd been drawn and quartered, that is. Your foreman especially."

"This is *my* ranch, Longarm. I run it and every man on it." She smiled to take the sting out of her words. "Except, that is, for my guests."

"Even guests who shoot your hands?"

"You saved Wally's life, Longarm. That makes you more than a guest. That makes you a friend."

She stood up. As if some kind of silent command had been given, Juanita appeared in the doorway.

"Juanita, Marshal Long will be our guest tonight," Terry informed the woman. "Show him to the main guest room, see to his gear, and draw him a bath. We'll sit down for dinner at six."

Juanita looked with large, liquid eyes at Longarm— there was just a trace of a smile in them—and waited for Longarm to follow her from the room.

As Longarm rose to his feet, Terry smiled at him.

100

"Enjoy your bath, Longarm. Nap for a while afterwards, if you wish. I'll have Juanita wake you in time for dinner. I have some business. That is, I think I should see to Wally and talk to him—and then to the rest of my hands."

Longarm nodded to her, then moved off down the long, cool hall after the massive, silent housekeeper.

Juanita spent almost a half hour lugging steaming kettles of hot water to Longarm's tub. She said nothing to him during all this time, but her eyes watched him closely, noting his long torso and its equipment with some approval. The harsh yellow soap she gave Longarm peeled the dirt off with a vengeance.

When the water was at its hottest, and filling the bedroom with clouds of steam, Juanita came back in without a kettle and fell upon Longarm, scrubbing his back with such enthusiasm that he could hear her panting in his ear from her exertions. But it was just what he had wanted. He let her have her way with him, hoping only that she would see her way clear to leave some of his skin.

Scrubbing his chest, she dropped the soap and fished in the water for it. Her hand brushed him. She uttered a tiny cry when she discovered what her attentions had been doing to him. As she pulled her hand quickly away, Longarm reached up casually and pulled her down, kissing her on the lips. For a moment the woman tried to pull back. Then, with a deep, almost convulsive sigh, she answered his kiss, her hand plunging back down into the steaming water. . . .

When she pulled away at last, her dark face was no longer impassive; the large eyes were warm.

Longarm smiled at her. "Thank you, Juanita. Nothing a man likes better after a long ride than a hot, steaming bath."

She nodded, reached back for the huge bath towel,

and held it out for him. He stood up. She wrapped the towel around him as he stepped out of the tub, then patted him all over, leading him to the bed. As he sat down upon it, he looked at her questioningly.

She smiled very slightly, her miraculously white teeth showing for the first time. Then she shook her head, declining his invitation in such a way as to inform Longarm that she was not offended and did indeed appreciate the offer.

In a few moments the housekeeper and a tiny, much older woman—she looked part-Indian—carried the tub from the bedroom. Longarm removed his Colt from his rig and tucked it under his pillow. Lying back on the cool bedspread, bare-assed and content, he slept.

It was Carla who awakened Longarm. His nakedness did not appear to bother her. The warmth in her eyes indicated approval more than anything else. As he sat up, she presented him with fresh longjohns, stockings, Levi's, and a gleaming white broadcloth shirt that fit perfectly. His own clothing, Carla told him in excellent English, was being laundered.

As he entered the dining room a moment later, Terry, already seated, glanced up at him approvingly. "Those were my father's," she told him. "I knew you were big enough to fill them."

"Thank you," Longarm said, sitting down. "I was wondering whose they were. I'm usually a hard man to cover."

"Yes," she said. "I imagine you would be."

Sitting across the table from Longarm was the foreman, Russ Blodgett. He was startled to see Longarm enter and appeared slightly outraged at the lawman's presence at the dinner table. Longarm got the distinct impression that it had something to do with the nature of his relationship with his boss—the foreman was unwilling to share Terry with him. Longarm nodded curtly at the man.

"Wally's too worn out to join us," Terry told Longarm, "but he's resting comfortably, and Carla takes good care of him. He admitted, by the way, that most likely he would be dancing from a tree limb now if it weren't for you. I am sure, Longarm, that he will thank you himself when he's stronger."

"No need," Longarm said. "I'm a law officer. I get paid by the federal government to stop such nonsense when I can."

The meal was brought in then by Juanita and Carla, great plates piled high with thick slabs of steak, fried potatoes and steaming hot biscuits. The coffee was plentiful and even stronger than that potion Longarm had sampled earlier.

The three of them ate with quiet gusto, in a silence that grew more ominous as the meal progressed. Russ was evidently not going to dignify Longarm's presence at the table by noting it. Terry, aware of his sullenness, became increasingly irritated. Longarm could sense her growing impatience as her remarks, directed at Russ and intended to lighten the tension, seemed only to increase Russ's black, disapproving silence. In reply to her he did little more than grunt. He refused to look at Longarm.

At last, her blue eyes flashing angrily, Terry put down her knife and fork and spoke directly to the problem: "Longarm is a guest at my table, Russ. You are not being very friendly. I had hoped you would be man enough to use this opportunity to apologize for your behavior earlier this afternoon."

"Apologize!" In his amazement and fury at such a suggestion, Russ slammed his knife down upon his plate with such force that Terry visibly winced.

Her tanned features growing suddenly pale, she

103

said quietly, "Yes, Russ. Apologize. And if that temper display cracked that plate, it'll come out of your salary."

"But—but, Terry! This man—"

"This man," she cut in, "saved Wally from a mob of rope-happy loggers. He shot Wally in self-defense. If he had killed him—God forbid—he would have been justified, since Wally turned his rifle on him. If he had left him to the loggers, he would have been justified. But he didn't do that. He took Wally from them at the point of a gun and brought him home through our own guns—"

"But, Terry, how the hell did I know all that? And what about Teeter and Slick?"

"Those two deserved what they got," she replied with some venom. "And if you didn't know all I just told you, you should have. That's the point, Russ. You had no idea; so why didn't you take this opportunity to find out from Longarm what happened? And while all this business with the flour sacks was going on, by the way, where the hell were you? If you were part of it and didn't tell me, I want to know why. If you didn't know about it, I'd like to know what the hell you've been doing masquerading as my foreman all this time."

"Why, sure, I knew what the boys was up to, but Wally wouldn't have it no other way, and I didn't want to bother you with it. You'd only worry."

"You mean I'd only stop it. If Wally had lost his life on account of this foolishness, I'd have blamed you, Russ. And I'd have wanted satisfaction!"

Russ jumped to his feet. "Now, Terry, you can't talk to me like that. Not after all we been to each other!"

"Russ," Terry said, "I pay your salary and that means I talk to you any way I want to. Right now I'm treating you like a damned fool because that's just what you've been. You can leave this table now.

You've been excused. And say good night to Mr. Long before you go."

"Terry!" the man fairly wailed. "You can't *mean* that."

"Yes, I can, Russ. Now get out."

"But—but what about—" He looked with enormous embarrassment at Longarm, his handsome features suddenly turning crimson.

"You can sleep in the bunkhouse tonight, Russ," she said coldly.

"Terry! I warn you! I won't forget this!"

"Get out, Russ."

He stood there for a moment, too stubborn to be dismissed like this by a woman and too terrified to disobey.

"Git!" Longarm thundered. "You heard the woman! She means *now*, mister!"

The force of Longarm's verbal blast seemed to buffet Russ physically. He turned on his heel and lunged from the room. A moment later the outer door was heard to slam.

Terry looked down at her plate, her face pale with fury and embarrassment. At last she glanced up at Longarm. "Forgive his manners, Longarm. And forgive me for allowing the likes of him to share my bed. It is not good for discipline, I know. But this is a lonely, barren land in some ways—and for too many things you have to make do with what you have."

"Say no more," Longarm said quietly. "I've traveled over some pretty sorry land in my time, where the pickings were just as lean."

"Some wine, then, to finish our meal?" she suggested, calm once more.

Longarm smiled. "Sounds fine."

"We'll have it served in the parlor. Nights are chilly here; I'll have the fireplace lit."

The wine warmed Longarm almost as much as the fire. As Terry talked about her father and his struggle to survive in this high desert country, the lawman developed a liking for the girl and an appreciation of her love for her dead father—as well as a strong admiration for the man himself. Everything this man had built depended on the wells that fed the ranch's water holes, and the almost miraculous cheat grasses that sprang up after even the most insignificant rain. Fortunately, as Terry explained, there was always some snow in the winter and just enough melt-off in the spring to feed the rivers and streams, which, together with the wells, gave them the water without which they would perish during the hot, almost bone-dry summers.

But now the stripped mountainsides and ridges no longer trapped the occasional rainfall. The water table throughout the valley was beginning to drop alarmingly. The wells were drying up and even the sagebrush on the valley floors was burning off. This meant that the pronghorn would soon be gone as well, leaving the land to the coyotes and the jackrabbits—and the Digger Indians.

"They can live anywhere," she said, almost in wonder.

"Well, maybe," Longarm said. "They depend on water too, don't they?"

"Yes, of course," she said, correcting herself. "And on the nuts of the pinyon. Their women go about with these enormous baskets they weave themselves, filling them with these nuts." She grimaced. "They also eat ground-up grasshoppers mixed into a kind of cake, I hear. For them, it's a delicacy."

The lawman tugged thoughtfully at a corner of his mustache. "So you're losing your water and the Indians are losing their pine groves, it looks like."

Terry nodded. Then, seeing that his glass was empty, she got up with the bottle, crossed to his armchair, and refilled his glass. As she bent close to him, intent on her task, he could feel the animal warmth of her—the sweet, clean, almost intoxicating perfume of her body. She also had bathed this afternoon, it seemed. She returned to her corner of the sofa and sat down, tucking her legs under her and smiling back at him.

He sipped the wine, knowing that she was perfectly well aware of the hell she had just raised with that brief visit.

"Tomorrow," she said, "I'll take you over our land, so you can see for yourself why Wally acted the way he did today. It was foolish, of course, and it will only bring Slade and his men down on us harder—but at least you'll be able to understand the depth of our concern. These lumber companies will be gone someday; they will have taken every tree, stripped every ridge, every hillside, leaving us with a silted-up river, gullied-out slopes, and barren valleys. It will be a dead land, Longarm."

"I wish I could tell you that telegraph poles, railroad ties, and firewood were worth all this, Terry. But I can't. The thing is, you ranchers are using government land mostly for grazing—and this government has some high and important officials who stand to line their pockets with silver and gold if they only let this company operate. The law is on their side."

"The law!" She spat out the word contemptuously.

"They *make* the laws, Terry. I never heard tell yet of a law passed *against* progress. And progress means mining the wealth out of the West, wherever you find that wealth and whatever it is—gold, silver, or lumber."

"This *land* is a kind of wealth, Longarm. Perhaps you could make a report to your superiors—someone in the federal government, anyone who might care what's happening here to this land."

Longarm sipped his wine. He knew such a course of action would do no good at all. The Western Lumber and Land Combine could not be stopped now, not legally. Their claim to cut this timber could not be withdrawn at this late date. It would be like trying to stop a boulder in mid-course down a hill. "I'll try," he said. "Raise a little hell in Denver, maybe. Speak to my chief, find out who I should contact in Washington. But I sure don't want to get your hopes up. I never saw the like of those clerks and middlemen. Seems like someone should blast away all that red tape, but if that *did* happen, the whole government would collapse." He smiled ruefully. " 'Course, maybe that wouldn't be such a bad idea."

"All of us ranchers would appreciate anything you could do. I know it seems like that company is un-stoppable—that they can do anything they want in order to bring out that lumber—but there's something about Slade and that henchman of his . . . I can't put my finger on it. It's just that they seem so anxious to get this lumber out *fast*. It's almost as if they were afraid of someone coming and taking it away from them. Of course, it's just a feeling. When you're desperate, you clutch at straws, I guess."

Longarm nodded. "Desmond did mention to me that he was on a tight schedule. I just figured that was normal. The faster they can cut the lumber and ship it out, the lower their expenses'll be, and the more profit for them."

"I suppose," she sighed. "That's what Tanner said, too."

Longarm looked at her levelly, and said in a quiet voice, "Tanner's dead, you know."

"Yes," Terry said. "One of my hands was in Whip-saw picking up supplies, and he heard one of Bat

Lawson's men mention it. I was sorry to hear it. Tanner loved this country and had promised me that he would see what he could do."

Longarm decided then not to press any further with inquiries about the deserter. That could wait until tomorrow. He suddenly realized how tired he was. The wine and the heat from the crackling fire had lulled him. He put his glass down and stood up.

"This has been real nice, Terry—the fire, the good wine. Sorry what we talked about couldn't have been a little more pleasant. I'll be looking forward to that ride you mentioned."

She stood up also. "Yes, it's been very nice, Longarm." Her blue eyes gleamed in the firelight. "You do fill a room, you know. That's something I've missed." Juanita appeared in the doorway. "Marshal Long will be retiring now, Juanita," Terry told her. "See to his bedroom. I'll pick up in here."

Juanita nodded.

Longarm said good night and followed the housekeeper from the room.

Chapter 6

An eagle with angry blue eyes was screaming as it plunged at Longarm out of a moonlit sky. Longarm flung up his arm to ward off the raking talons. He felt himself tumbling backward off his horse. Whinnying in fright, the animal plunged away as Longarm twisted slowly in space and began to fall. . . .

He awoke to find himself sitting bolt upright in the large bed, cold sweat standing out over his naked body; he had automatically reached under his pillow for his gun and held it now in front of him, its muzzle probing the darkness of the room. There was an open window beside his bed. No moon hung in the black night sky; the sense of nightmare persisted.

He became aware of angry voices coming from down the hall. Terry Troy and her foreman were arguing heatedly. Terry seemed quite angry. The foreman's heavy voice was alternately wheedling, then demanding. The man did not sound stable. It was an ugly, dangerous confrontation. It must have been this, Longarm realized, that had awakened him.

He left his bed, slipped into a robe Juanita had left for him, and padded on bare feet down the hall. The door to Terry's bedroom was open. He stopped just outside the doorway. In front of an ample fireplace the two of them faced each other. They had already clashed physically. Terry's long nightgown had been ripped completely off and now lay in a shimmering,

110

silken pool at her feet. A livid tracery left by Terry's fingernails extended down the side of the foreman's face. Even as Longarm stood there, the welts appeared to swell and brighten as the blood began to flow. But it was Terry who riveted Longarm's attention. She stood boldly naked before Blodgett, a quirt in one hand, her naked body gleaming from head to toe with perspiration. Hers was a powerful figure, every inch of it as darkly and thoroughly tanned as her face. A lit kerosene lamp stood on a table behind them, shedding a pale light over the scene. So intent were they on each other that they did not appear to be aware of Longarm's presence in the hallway.

"You want *him* too, don't you!" Blodgett cried, his voice thick with rage and jealousy. "You were going to go in to him! I saw you at the dinner table—the way you looked at him!"

"So I looked at him! Why not? You fool! Do you think you own me? Because I let you sleep with me, does that make me your property?"

"It should, damn it! It should!"

"Ugh! You make me sick."

"But I—but I *love* you, Terry."

"Is that your excuse, then, for stealing in here like a thief, for attacking me in my bed? You call that love? And besides, Russ, I never told you I loved you. Never! That was all your idea!"

"But why, then? You must have felt *something*!"

"Yes, damn you! Need! I felt need for a man. And that—as best you could—you satisfied, and for that I suppose I should thank you. But that's all I wanted from you. That's all I needed."

"You *used* me!" the man cried, choking now with baffled rage.

"Of course! And you used me. We used each other!"

"A whore!" Blodgett spat, aghast at her words.

"That's what you are! That's *all* you are! A whoring slut!"

She stepped toward him and brought the quirt around. It whistled in the small room a split-second before it caught him about the shoulders. He yelped and reached out to grab it from her, but she was too quick for him. Again and again she brought the quirt around, driving him back relentlessly, her eyes shining pleasure, her head thrown back, her breasts upthrust, her nipples erect. Soon she was panting from the exertion as the foreman—his back to the wall now—covered his face with his arms and sank slowly to the floor while the slashing strips of plaited rawhide ripped at him, cutting his arms, his neck, his head.

Only when she was physically exhausted, her fury finally appeased, did she pull back to gaze down at the whimpering man at her feet. In a voice icy with contempt, she said, "You should always speak with respect when addressing your betters, Blodgett. I recommend it as an excellent course to follow in the future. Pack your gear and get off this ranch. Tonight. You may take two horses of your choosing from the remuda. Now get out!"

He pulled himself upright and, leaning on the wall, glared at her like some captive animal still fearful of the lash of his new master. "You . . . owe me a month's wages . . . and that bonus . . . " His voice trailed off hopelessly.

She turned and strode to the strongbox on top of her dresser. Using a key she had secreted in a small jar of what appeared to be face cream, she unlocked the box and lifted the lid. A small Smith & Wesson revolver gleamed on the black velvet cloth that covered the box's contents. She lifted out the gun, reached into one of the compartments, and pulled out a small, heavy leather pouch. Pulling its drawstrings open, she swiftly counted out several gold coins, then turned and flung them on the floor before Blodgett.

It was a regal, cruel gesture. As Russ scrambled about the floor on his hands and knees snatching up the coins, she watched him with amused, flashing eyes, her naked contempt for him filling the room. Once he had retrieved all the coins, Russ scrambled to his feet, looked about for his hat, found it on the floor by her bed, then—head down, like something wild fleeing a fire—he bolted from the room.

He was too anxious to get out to be startled at Longarm's presence in the hallway. As he disappeared down the dark passage, Longarm stepped through the doorway.

"I suppose you saw it all?" Terry asked, standing in the middle of the room, facing him, completely unconscious, it seemed, of her dark, lustrous nakedness or its possible effect on him.

"A couple of wildcats in a potato sack would have been quieter, Terry."

"I caught him in your room, Longarm, with a lantern. He was a little upset to find you in that bed, I am afraid. And back in my bedroom he was not much of a gentleman about it."

"I was able to figure that out."

"I'm tired, Longarm. Very tired. Of course, Russ was right. I would have visited your room this evening. But perhaps you have seen too much of me already. Sleep now. We have a long ride ahead of us tomorrow."

He nodded. "Good night, Terry."

As he turned to leave, she said, "It would be best if you didn't sleep until you hear Russ ride out."

"And if I were you, I'd keep that Smith & Wesson handy," he suggested.

Longarm returned to his bed and waited. It wasn't too long before the sound of racing hoofs drummed past his window and faded rapidly as the ex-foreman fled through the gate. Longarm tucked the Colt under his pillow and closed his eyes again. The last image be-

113

fore sleep came was of Terry's nakedness. She stood boldly and provocatively before him, her quirt in her hand, a challenge in her blue eyes. . . .

They had been riding since the cool hours just before dawn. Now, close to midday, they rode through a steep-sided canyon and out onto a broad benchland that appeared to have been the scene of some titanic struggle between contending giants. The flat as well as the hillsides looming above it bore the familiar scars of the Western Lumber and Land Combine. Debris covered the ground everywhere. The sawed-off trunks remaining after the cutting looked like the humped, misshapen heads of defeated legions. Skid marks— slick, snaking gashes—wound down the hillsides onto the bench to a deeply rutted road that led back— Longarm had no doubt—to the lumber mill in Whipsaw. The only trees still standing were the few stunted pinyons that had been judged not worth the effort of cutting. Yet even they were not unscathed. The fever-ish cutting and skidding around them had left the trees with maimed branches and deep slashes in their trunks.

As Terry rode across this ruined landscape beside Longarm, she said nothing to him, content to let its appearance speak for her. Longarm was hesitant to say anything, since all that he had seen here he had seen elsewhere. He was not surprised. It was ugly. It was disturbing. But if this timber was to be cut to pro-vide the country with the railroad ties, fuel, and telegraph poles it needed, this sad devastation had to be the result. There was simply no comfort he could offer Terry.

"You've seen all this before around Whipsaw," Terry said, glancing at Longarm. "I know that. But there's something else you probably haven't seen yet."

They rode until they reached the edge of the bench

where they found themselves looking out over a semi-arid valley dotted with sagebrush and grama. As Terry pulled up, she pointed without a word down the slope at a tangled mess of debris and mud lodged in a narrow stream bed. A great muddy pool was backed up behind the obstruction. On the other side of what must have been a mud slide, the stream's channel was completely dry. Gaping cracks in the ground radiated out from it to lose themselves in the dry, sage-covered valley floor.

"Look closely at that mud slide in the stream bed," Terry told him.

Longarm looked back down at the great pile of debris and thought he saw, sticking up out of the top of it, pieces of framing, a shingled portion of a roof, and the stones of a chimney. Looking still closer, he saw what remained of posts and poles that had once formed a corral sticking up out of the mass like the quills of a giant porcupine.

"Guess that slide took a house with it," Longarm said. "I see some roof shingles and parts of a corral."

"That was one of our line shacks," Terry replied. "It used to stand ten feet back from where we are now. You see what's happening to this land? A mud slide after a short rain two weeks ago and we lose a line shack and a valuable stream." She pointed to a broad slash cutting the slope behind them. "The slide came down from there, as near as I can figure, then hit this bench and rolled across it with enough force to dump the line shack. Longarm, that was a solid, two-room cabin, a corral, and a small stable. Now add to that the loss of that stream for none of us knows how long, and you'll get some picture of what we're up against."

Longarm noded soberly.

"Can you see now why we've got to stop them? Do you understand why my cowhands go around shooting up logging camps with flour sacks over their heads?"

"Yes, Terry," Longarm replied. "I understand. I'll do what I can. I told you last night that I would, and I meant it."

She smiled suddenly, her teeth flashing in her dark face. "Forgive me, Longarm. I know you meant it. But we are desperate, and I want you to know why."

Longarm swung around in his saddle and gazed up at the hills reaching up from the bench. "Are there any timberlands on the other side of this range, where cutting wouldn't do this kind of thing to the valley?"

"Yes, there are. That's where we thought they would be cutting. It wasn't until they began their operation that we realized they were logging this side of the range."

"Well, like I said, I'll see what I can do, as long as you realize I'm not about to promise what I can't be sure I'll be able to deliver."

"That's enough for me, Longarm."

Terry pulled her horse around, apparently satisfied, and led the way back across the bench. As they rode from it into the canyon, Longarm took one last look back at the ravaged landscape and shook his head. Once they were well inside the canyon's cool shadows, Longarm turned to Terry.

"I'm up here, Terry, to find the same man Sheriff Tanner was after—the army scout who deserted. Tanner spotted him in Whipsaw, and I think the deserter was the one who killed Tanner. I want him. I won't be able to do much for you ranchers concerning this logging until I bring that man in. Gus Dodds— one of the loggers—said this jasper left Whipsaw when Tanner spotted him, and might have ridden out to your spread looking for a job. He was a big man, and most of the descriptions I've heard say he has a heavy beard and blue eyes." He smiled at her. "Like yours, I reckon."

"I know the man," she replied. "Tanner was at the Flying T to pick up a horse thief we caught. He told us he'd spotted the deserter and was going to send a wire to Washington when he got back to Silver City. He didn't have much confidence in Washington, though. I remember his saying he'd probably end up going after the man himself. Anyway, as soon as Tanner left with the horse thief, a logger fitting that description you gave showed up looking for work. I didn't connect him with what Tanner told me until you mentioned it just now."

"Did you give him a job?"·

"We didn't have anything for him. He drifted north into Digger country then. None of us has seen hide or hair of him since, but then, we haven't been looking. Like you say, though, he's a big man, all right. A bear. And he rode a horse well."

"What was he riding?"

"A grullo.

"That means he could be a long, long ways from these parts by now. Did you tell all this to Tanner?"

"He never returned to the Flying T after he left with that horse thief."

Longarm frowned at that. "So I go north, then— into Digger country, and maybe all the way to Snake River. I want him, Terry."

"I'm sure you'll get him, Longarm."

They were halfway back to the Flying T when Longarm felt the sudden chill of an impending storm. He glanced to the west. A great, dark cloud, looking like the wing of some enormous bird, was sweeping toward them from the mountains. The smell of rain was in the air. Dust devils whipped sand into his eyes and he lifted his bandanna to cover his mouth and nostrils.

Lightning flickered in the bowels of the cloud. The dim muttering of thunder rolled toward them, echoing ominously in the high, rocky land through which they were riding.

Terry looked at Longarm and smiled. It was not a nervous smile. She seemed genuinely pleased—and excited—at the prospect of a storm. "We still have time before it reaches us, Longarm. I know a place where we can hole up until it's past."

"Is it near here? We don't have as much time as you might think."

"I know this country, Longarm. Besides, we were going there anyway. The view is lovely. I wanted you to see it." A sudden gust of wind made her reach up and grab the brim of her hat to keep it from flying off. "It's my favorite spot. I'm sure you'll be very impressed."

"Lead the way," Longarm told her, aware that her excitement had caught him up as well.

Terry followed a winding trail, quite steep in spots, that took them presently up onto a high bluff overlooking a vast desert valley that stretched all the way to distant peaks, dim ramparts shrouded now by the building storm. Keeping just ahead of him, she rode the full length of the bluff until she came to a boulder larger than that fancy hotel in Whipsaw, and kept on until she was in under the great rock. It seemed to be balanced precariously in the center of a large, smooth dish worn out of the cap rock.

There was a narrow trail that took them under the boulder and out the other side. Terry followed it as it wound still higher. The horses were somewhat skittish on the steep trail. At last they emerged onto a smooth rock shelf only slightly bigger than her parlor. A surprisingly large pinyon grew out of a fissure at the rear of the ledge, its gnarled, misshapen branches offering the only available shelter.

Dismounting under the tree, they tied their horses securely to it. She led Longarm to the edge of the ledge, where they stood together silently and gazed out over the desert valley, watching the approaching storm. The thunder was louder and more powerful here, and seemed to strike at the foundations of the bluff itself. The lightning lit the underside of the clouds almost continuously now, as if a series of powder kegs were being set off deep within them. Longarm could not help noticing Terry's reaction. She was watching the storm eagerly, with an excitement so intense that she seemed almost to be a part of it.

She saw the look in his eyes and laughed. "Yes, I love it," she said. "It's like we're the only ones left in the world, watching God put on one of his displays for us. To warn us, perhaps. Do you wonder, now, why this is my favorite spot?" Her eyes grew suddenly fierce. "You are the only one I have ever brought to this ledge. The only one. Do you understand that, Longarm?"

"Reckon I do. This is some spot. I can see why you'd like to keep it just for yourself."

"It's where I come to sort things out," she said. "Where I come to lie in the sun and drink in that warmth, that fabulous warmth that pours out of the sun—that pours over all of me, every bit. I can feel it drugging me, loving me, Longarm, caressing me. Do you understand what I mean?"

"You don't have to keep asking that. You speak plain enough."

"But have you ever let the sun caress you, as I have?"

Longarm shook his head. "No, I guess I ain't, Terry. I've been too busy lately to lie down in the sun."

She smiled and shook her head. "You don't understand," she said, stepping back. "You don't understand at all—but you're going to."

To his astonishment and growing wonder, she unbuckled her gunbelt, then peeled down her Levi's.

"You, too, Longarm," she said. "I want you to feel that warmth with me."

Longarm felt slightly ridiculous. There was a storm coming, even though at that moment the afternoon sun was still blazing down. Terry unbuttoned her shirt and flung it aside. She was wearing longjohns underneath her outer clothes, and promptly proceeded to unbutton them, her fingers moving swiftly all the way down the front. Kicking off her riding boots, she stepped out of the longjohns and stood before him naked.

He was having trouble with his shirt. His fingers were all thumbs, it seemed. There was a strangely tight feeling in his throat. Terry moved swiftly against him, her fingers rapidly unbuttoning his shirt. She peeled it back off his shoulders. Thunder, much nearer by this time, cracked like a giant bullwhip overhead. The ledge seemed to shudder beneath his boots. Terry paid no heed to it as she deftly unbuckled Longarm's gunbelt, then peeled his Levi's down his thighs.

"Your boots," she said softly. "Step out of them."

He complied quickly, astonished at how easily he was able to kick them off. It was the incentive, he realized, smiling to himself.

She stayed close until her help was no longer needed. Then she stepped back to survey Longarm. Like Adam and Eve before the serpent's blandishments, they faced each other's nakedness without blushing.

"Men don't often see a woman naked, do they, Longarm?" she asked. "Women are supposed to keep themselves wrapped in armor, it seems. That must be why men know so little about a woman's body. It's such a bore, Longarm, to be constantly pawed over by men who know so little about how to please a woman." She frowned angrily. "We are only supposed to be compliant receptacles into which you men pour your seed, then roll over and sleep with your mouths open."

"I reckon when you put it that way, Terry, it doesn't hardly sound very pleasureful."

A shattering crash of thunder shook the ledge soundly this time. Terry's eyes grew wide with sudden exultation. She lifted her arms up to the darkening sky and flung her head back. A bolt of lightning seared the sky over their heads and turned her figure momentarily blue. Longarm felt the hair on the back of his neck stand up a fraction of a second before another thunderclap almost flung him to the ground.

Terry was laughing wildly now as a sudden fierce wind tugged at them. The wind brought with it a damp, musty smell that reminded Longarm of a root cellar. Another bolt of lightning flashed above them. Through the deafening crash of thunder that followed, she called out to him: "Save me, Longarm! Protect me!"

"Get dressed!" he told her. "We've got to get off this damned ledge!"

"No!"

"You heard me!" he cried, reaching for his discarded clothes.

"I said no!" Terry shouted. Removing her sixgun from its holster on the ground, she cocked it and fired at Longarm—point-blank. The hammer came down on an empty chamber. She cocked it a second time. "There's only one round in this Colt," she cried as the wind wildly tugged at her hair. "It wasn't in that last chamber. Do you want me to try again?"

"Never mind!" Longarm laughed, the madness in her suddenly overtaking him as well.

"Then *cover* me, Longarm! Shield me! Keep your body between me and the storm."

The wind gusted wildly and the first faint drops of rain began to sting his naked shoulders. He stepped toward her, took the revolver from her, then dropped to one knee, pulling her down beside him. She stretched out on her back like a large cat. Longarm bent close to kiss her. She reached up, flinging an arm around his neck, and drew his mouth down hard upon her lips. Lightning played about them. A chill wind, laden with stinging drops of rain, swept over his naked body. He moved to cover her. Her tongue probed deeply into his mouth and then she fastened her teeth firmly but gently about his upper lip and began to tease it.

Another series of lightning bolts crackled in the sky above them. An almost continuous roar of shattering thunderclaps split the air. But Longarm no longer cared. There was another storm building beneath him —and within him.

Terry pulled her lips away and with surprising ease rolled him onto his side, her hand thrusting boldly, insistently, between his thighs. She found that he was ready for her, and grasped him with a strength that almost made him cry out, then buried her face in the thick hair on his chest, and began nibbling on one of his nipples. He was astonished at the effect this two-pronged attack had on him. With a deep, guttural mutter of delight, he grabbed her firm buttocks and pulled her hard against him. As lightning turned her tanned body an unearthly blue, he rolled over onto her, his knees slamming down hard on the wet rock surface.

For a moment he thought he would need something to place under her, but she thrust her thighs up with an angry urgency, and he felt the tip of his erection probing the entrance to her womb. She cried out and thrust up still higher, then wrapped both legs about his waist. He plunged deeply into her and gasped in pleasure. The rain was pounding down on them both now, and rivulets of water were pouring off his shoulders onto her. The sound of their entangled bodies slapping together filled Longarm's universe. The mindless rhythm of his thrusting caused him to lose all sense of time, while the difficulty of gaining a secure purchase with his knees kept him hovering, with a kind of maddened frustration, on the edge of his orgasm. She began turning her head rapidly from side to side, her eyes shut tight, swearing in a steady stream with a fluency that astonished him. And this was what did it for him. With a grim, wild plunge he drove into her, driving her buttocks down hard on the rock, grinding her into it. The lightning flashed, the thunder muttered and crashed over them, and the rain poured down with sudden intensity.

He felt her shudder convulsively under him. She let out a piercing scream that was more like a wail of terror. It sent shock waves of desire through him and he began to come, pulsing completely out of control. Constantly buffeted now by the wind and the rain, they clung together on the wet, slippery rock, entwined, as progressively more violent climaxes convulsed them. They grew fiercely into each other, and became one flesh, one twisting, moaning entity. . . .

Lying on his side, his head propped on his palm, he looked at her. Her long hair, soaking wet and stringy, hung over her face, partially obscuring her left eye. She smiled. The rain continued to pelt down with increasing force, and the almost continuous thunder made speech nearly impossible. She reached over and down as she moved closer. To his surprise, he found that he was ready again. She flung her hair back off her face and crawled over onto him.

"Now I'll cover you," she said into his ear, nibbling it for a moment.

She lay full length upon him, her legs closed tightly about his erection. An awesome peal of thunder deafened Longarm. She pressed her mouth hard down against his, while her tongue began probing with an insistent, delicious wantonness that caused him to twist involuntarily under her. With a sudden, delighted laugh, she leaned swiftly back, sat up, and with a violence that he was afraid would hurt her, drove herself down onto his erection. Gasping with pleasure, she began to pound on his chest—as almost continuous strokes of lightning played about them with a crackling intensity that seemed to singe the very air.

She was like some wanton female warrior, some Amazon or Valkyrie, and she rode him as if he were a beast, twisting and plunging, first forward, then sideways, gyrating around and around. She began to come repeatedly. Each time she did, she let out a cry that was like a sob. At last he found he could not keep himself from climaxing any longer. She felt his pulsating, thrusting orgasm and clung to him then, tightening her muscles about his shaft in a fierce, sobbing effort to keep him erect.

It worked. Laughing exultantly, she began to move once more—steadily, slowly this time. His shaft probed so deeply at times that its tip seemed to him to be on fire. Still thrusting gently, she leaned away suddenly, and flung her head back, drinking in the still pounding rain, allowing the thunder and the lightning to become a part of her frenzy. Longarm began to wonder if it would ever end—if, perhaps, they had stumbled into some hellish world where desire was never satisfied, where coupling became an end in itself, the only reality. . . .

He found himself coming alive again, lifting to meet her every thrust. Suddenly he reached up to grab her thighs. He wanted her under him, to drive upon her, to plunge deeply into her as, within him, a door opened that had never opened before.

"Down!" he cried above the howling storm. "Down! I want you under me!"

"Of course!" she cried, laughing, reaching down toward him.

A surging, shattering peal of thunder rent the air. Multiple forks of lightning turned the rain-filled gloom unnaturally bright. Still riding him, Terry's nakedness gleamed in the cold, flickering light. Thunder pounded again and again—as if some maddened smith were using the ledge for his anvil. She screamed. He paid no attention as he rolled her over, his hand firmly in the small of her back, his erection still deep within her.

On top of her again, he buried his face in the wet fullness of her breast. A warm, thick wetness smeared his cheek even as the rain washed it away. But its flow persisted, its salty, metallic sweetness invading his probing lips. He pulled back with a cry. Continuous lightning flickered like a serpent's tongue about them. He caught sight of a gaping hole between her breasts. He flung himself away from her and looked down to see her blue eyes wide, unblinking in the rain, the full, ripe slash of her mouth slack now, empty of desire at last.

A movement near the tree caught his eye. He dove to the hard surface of the ledge, scrambling for his holster where he had placed it under his coat. A shot, this time not covered by the roar of thunder, rang out from the tree. Longarm felt the slug whine off the surface of the ledge just in front of him. Tiny, cutting shards of stone flew up into his face. He drew the Colt and rolled swiftly to one side. Lightning gave him another glimpse, through the sheets of rain, of the man crouched beside the two plunging horses.

Blodgett! Russ Blodgett! Longarm squeezed off a shot and saw the man stumble back. Then darkness and a sweeping, obliterating curtain of rain swept across the ledge. Longarm waited for the next lightning flash. When it came he saw no sign of Blodgett, but only the wide-eyed, plunging horses, maddened now by the storm and the shooting so close by. As Longarm started to get up, he saw one of the horses break sud-

125

denly loose. A shattering peal of thunder exploded just above his head. He heard the plunging hooves of the crazed animal as it charged blindly across the ledge toward him. When a lightning stroke revealed the animal almost on him, its eyes bulging, Longarm flung himself out of the way.

But he was unable to clear the horse. One driving hoof slammed into his chest, smashing him down on the rock ledge as the great, wet beast passed over him. Barely conscious from the force with which his head had struck the ledge, he heard the horse's sudden whinnying terror as it plunged off the ledge into the rain-filled void.

He shook his head and tried to get up. It was no use. The storm's fury made it impossible for him to concentrate. He thought of Terry, beside him on the ledge, and Blodgett, gone by this time, and groaned in frustration. He managed to roll over onto his face. The rain pounded down on him. The lightning and thunder rocked him, then lulled him. The beat of the lashing rain faded and he lost consciousness.

He awoke with the warmth of the sun on his naked body. Rolling slowly over, he opened his eyes. The sun was low on the western horizon, gleaming out of a clear, pale sky. The dark stormcloud was sweeping away over the land, smoky tendrils of rain beating the ground before it. Thunder muttered softly. Lightning still winked. But for Longarm and Terry, the storm had passed.

Slowly Longarm got to his feet, his eyes avoiding Terry's dark, sadly shrunken body. He felt his chest where the horse's hoof had struck him, and took a deep breath. There was an ache, but no stabbing pain, and he was satisfied that the horse had not stove in one of his ribs. But his head pounded. Fingering the back of it, he withstood a sharp needle of pain and felt a sticky smear of coagulating blood where his scalp had been lacerated. From the way the pain rocked behind his eyes, he realized he probably had a slight concussion.

With great care, much like a man suffering through the granddaddy of all hangovers, he dressed himself in his still-wet clothes, finding it a difficult, time-consuming task to pull on first his sodden longjohns, and over them, the skintight Levi's. Fully dressed at last, he turned to the grisly business of dressing the dead woman. The sun was setting when he stood up at last, finished. It was her horse that had bolted, leaving him the Morgan. From his bedroll tucked behind the cantle, he took out his slicker and wrapped her in it, then flung her over the pommel. The trip back down the narrow trail was an unpleasant, dangerous business that was made even more so by his unsteady vision, the gathering darkness, and the constantly shifting weight of Terry's body.

Once he reached the bluff beyond the huge boulder, he relaxed a bit, feeling grimly pleased not only to have negotiated the narrow trail safely, but also at the growing evidence that he had winged Blodgett severely. From the pink glow still remaining in the sky, he could clearly see dried puddles of blood. They grew larger with each yard or two. He was able to follow the bloody spoor all the way down to the desert floor.

Then he turned his horse back toward the Flying T. He would be back for Blodgett soon enough. He would not need a warrant, and he wanted the man to resist.

It was a good deal later when he rode into the Flying T spread. Butts, holding a lantern high, stepped out of the bunkhouse and peered up at him through the darkness.

"Hello, the bunkhouse!" Longarm called.

"It's the marshal!" Butts called to those behind him in the bunkhouse.

Dismounting, Longarm led the Morgan toward Butts. "Take my horse," he told the man.

He lifted the burden off his pommel, turned with it in his arms, and started toward the house. Behind him, he heard Butts gasp. Turning his head, Longarm spoke coldly to him. "Yes, this is Miss Troy. Russ Blodgett shot her. She's dead. Now do as I told you, Butts. Take care of that horse of mine. I'll be needing it tomorrow, early."

The housekeeper was waiting in the parlor for him when he entered. She must have seen him from one of the windows as he approached the house. Her reaction did not surprise Longarm. She simply turned her head away for a moment as he put his burden down on the sofa, then bent to fold the yellow slicker back gently. Carla entered the room with Wally and began to cry softly. Wally controlled his feelings admirably while Longarm gave him a tactfully expurgated account of Terry's death. Only when Longarm had finished and the weeping Carla was leading him back to his room did Longarm hear—dimly—the grief that wrenched itself from the young man's heart.

The voices of angry men came to him then. He walked out onto the porch to speak to the unhappy crowd of Flying T hands. Longarm quieted them and told them what he had told Wally. None of the hands, it seemed, had any difficulty at all in believing the ex-foreman capable of such a deed.

"We'll go after him with you, Longarm," someone cried, his voice hoarse with rage.

"A rope'd be too good for him," another infuriated hand called out.

A sullen roar of agreement greeted that sentiment. Longarm held up his hand. "I'll handle it. I'm the law here. He won't get away, I promise you that. You've got a spread to run for Wally Troy. He's still hurt bad, and he'll need you. I'll handle Russ Blodgett."

With vague, futile threats and unhappy mutterings, the men filed away into the darkness, back to their quarters. Longarm went back inside. The housekeeper saw the gaunt, drained look on his face, stepped quickly closer, and kept him from collapsing to the floor. As her big arms held him, she inspected the back of his head and made a soft, sympathetic sound. In his bedroom she gently washed the wound clean, using warm water and that harsh soap he'd used in his bath, then bound a bandage around it after soothing it with a greasy, evil-smelling dressing.

He had been lying face down on the bed while she worked. Before she finished her task completely, Longarm began to drift off to sleep. Dimly, he felt her undress him and pull the sheets up gently over his long, thoroughly exhausted frame.

As Longarm rode back to the bluff the next morning, he found it difficult to shake the sense of nightmare that still clung to him. The storm and the surging, elemental passion that had grown along with it, the sight of Terry's suddenly stilled body and the crazed horse plunging through the rain toward him, all combined to fill him with an uneasy sense that none of it had really happened.

Then he saw the splayed, broken body of the horse among the rocks at the foot of the bluff. Humped, waddling buzzards were already tearing at the fly-covered carcass. He rode on past it and came finally to Blodgett's sign. The blood was barely visible now—a faint, rust-colored stain on the surfaces of a few rocks. Blodgett had taken two horses, as Terry had suggested. It soon became obvious that he was keeping the second horse with him. This would make it much easier for Longarm to track him. It would not make it easier, Longarm mused, for him to overtake Blodgett. The Morgan still had reserves of speed and endurance, but she had been ridden hard the day before. Aware of this, Longarm had nursed her along since he had left the Flying T.

Still, Russ Blodgett was wounded. Longarm hoped grimly that his slug was still lodged in the man's carcass.

Along about midday, Longarm found Blodgett's trail leading into higher, wilder country. As Longarm rode into a canyon, he realized Blodgett was no longer intent on making distance. He wanted only a place to go to ground, and, more than likely, a vantage point from which he could command the trail with his rifle. The man was probably holed up at that moment, waiting for Longarm.

Longarm forded the muddy stream that cut through the canyon, found a shaded overhang of rock face, and dismounted. Hobbling the Morgan in a lush growth of grama, he took his Winchester from its saddle scabbard and began to climb. Better than halfway up the side of the canyon, he found a man-sized cleft in the canyon wall. Straddling it, he looked through it and spotted a trail that could take him around, well behind the rim of the canyon. It was treacherous going, but when he reached a grassy bench well above the canyon floor, he found Blodgett's two horses quietly cropping the grass. Beyond them, a game trail led to what appeared to be the highest point on the canyon wall.

Longarm did not use the trail. He kept to the rocks until he found his progress barred by a steep, bald, rounded upthrust of sandstone. The incline was less than forty-five degrees; he could make it if he ran full-tilt. He removed his spurs and his boots. Levering a fresh cartridge into the Winchester's chamber, he raced up the steep rock-face and burst onto a sandy

130

ledge. Russ Blodgett was lying facedown on the far side of it, less than twenty feet away. He was turning swiftly to face Longarm, but his back was still to him, his rifle barrel still hanging out over the ledge, waiting for a target on the canyon floor below. Before Blodgett could haul the rifle around, Longarm fired.

Nothing happened. The rifle had misfired. As Longarm levered swiftly a second time, he realized that the magazine was jammed solidly. So eager was Blodgett, however, that as he swung his rifle around, the barrel struck a rocky projection. The force of it ripped the stock out of his hand. He grabbed frantically for it, but the rifle dropped out of sight.

By then, Longarm's momentum had carried him close enough to Blodgett to enable him to reach down and haul the man to his feet before he could grab for his sixgun. Blodgett cried out in pain. Longarm saw the sodden, bloody pants leg. His round had caught the man in the thigh above the knee. Eyes wild, panting with fear and pain, Blodgett clawed at Longarm's coat to gain his balance.

"Please!" he cried. "For God's sake, Longarm! Take me back for a trial! Please! I need a doctor!"

Longarm took the man's revolver from its holster and tossed it off the ledge. Then he released Blodgett and let the man crumple to the ground.

"A trial," Longarm said, coldly and implacably. "You'd love that, wouldn't you? Your lips would be smacking as you told the jury what you saw on that ledge. Hell! You'd probably get off, the way you'd tell it!"

"No! No! I wouldn't say a word about that! You have my promise, Longarm. My solemn oath!"

Longarm took a deep breath. The man before him was helpless and disarmed. Longarm would have to take him in. There would be a trial. The lawman considered what that would mean and grew cold at the prospect. Then he shrugged and turned away to retrieve his Winchester. He had dropped it as soon as he had realized it was useless to him.

As he bent to pick it up, he heard Blodgett's heavy, labored breathing as the man bore down on him from behind. Dropping to one knee and picking up the rifle—barrel first—Longarm swung it around in a complete arch as if he were swinging a bat. The rifle's heavy stock caught Blodgett flush in the ribs and sent him reeling back.

The man stumbled, found himself on the rim of the ledge, and tried to catch himself. His good foot stepped into space. Uttering a cry of dismay, he pitched forward off the ledge. For a moment he managed to catch hold of a small pine sapling growing on the edge, but as soon as his full weight tugged on it, the sapling pulled free of the sandy soil. Blodgett tried to grab for a narrow crack in the ledge, but missed. His hands still clawing frantically, he disappeared from sight, screaming.

The scream ended too abruptly. Longarm walked to the edge and looked over. Blodgett's fall had been broken by a bristlecone pine growing out of the side of the canyon wall. He lay on his back on a narrow sandstone ledge not more than twenty feet below. The man was still conscious, though he seemed unable to move. His mouth opened, but all that came out was a hoarse, barely audible whisper. Longarm looked around until he saw a way down to the ledge. He would have given a lot at that moment for a pair of Apache moccasins. His unshod feet were painfully sore by this time. With a weary shrug, he dropped his rifle and worked his way down the steep face of the canyon wall until he was crouched beside Blodgett, peering into the man's slack face.

"I'm hurt bad," Blodgett whimpered softly. "Real

bad. I hurt my back when I hit that tree! I can't move a muscle! You got to help me!"

"No, I ain't. There ain't any way I can get you off this ledge."

A shadow passed over them both. And then another shadow. Longarm glanced up. Buzzards, two of them, were circling over them, already dropping lower with each pass.

"I'm going to have to leave you here," Longarm said.

"You can't!"

"Yes, Blodgett, I can."

"Then *shoot* me, damn you! For God's sake, Longarm! Don't leave me for them buzzards!"

Longarm knew what Blodgett was thinking. The fellow couldn't move a muscle. Vultures do not smell a carcass rotting in the sun. They do not have any sixth sense concerning death. What they watch for while coasting high in the desert sky is a body lying perfectly still—unnaturally still. When they spot such a body, they drop closer. After a few passes, during which there is still no movement, they land beside the still body and waddle close.

At such a moment Blodgett would try to scream in an effort to frighten them away. For a while, perhaps, he would be able to drive the foul birds back. But only for a while. Paralyzed, there would be nothing he could do, no movement he could make to stop them as the two buzzards roosted on him. Black wings would shut out the sun and pairs of cold eyes would peer into his. Abruptly, the crooked yellow beaks and red necks crawling with lice would snap forward. They would begin to rip and tear. . . .

Longarm straightened up, then stepped off the ledge and began to climb back. Behind him, Blodgett's frantic, barely audible pleas faded. As Longarm reached the ledge, he glanced skyward. Another buzzard had joined the first two.

Chapter 7

Two days later Longarm found himself at midday taking refuge in the shadows of a narrow canyon. As he had learned from Wally before setting out, they were supposed to be coming to the end of the dry season, but this one was hanging on. That morning the air had been so dry that Longarm could barely shave. The water and soap had dried on his face even as he had reached for his straight razor. The day before, he had seen a cloud releasing rain high above the basin. Halfway between cloud and earth, the falling water had evaporated. Longarm saw curtains of blue rain dangling out of reach in the sky while the parched land beneath panted for the needed moisture. At that moment Longarm had recalled Vail's scathing description of this high desert land: *a godforsaken patch of alkali basins and black rock populated by bush Indians and a few damn fool settlers.*

Longarm pulled up. He had come at last to what he had been searching for. Water. He dismounted and took both of his canteens to the canyon wall. Water was seeping out between two horizontal formations, through a crack that looked no wider than a newspaper. Longarm had spotted it by the dark stain beneath it and by the hanging garden of orchids, monkeyflower, and maidenhair fern that fed on the steady trickle of moisture. Fortunately, even after these thirsty plants drank their fill, there was still enough water left to form a small water hole at the base of the canyon wall.

He filled his canteens while the local gnat population fought him for every drop. To keep them out of the canteens, he had to place his bandanna over the openings as he filled them. Infuriated, the miserable little bastards attacked his eyes, drawn irresistibly by the liquid shine of his eyeballs.

Longarm drank his fill, emptying one of the canteens, then filled it again. Returning to the Morgan with his hat filled with water, he gave the horse what it needed, then mounted up, the damp hat a welcome relief as he pulled it down snugly.

Once out of the canyon, he turned north again and began climbing into the same range that enclosed Whipsaw twenty miles or so south. Once into the foothills, he caught sight of a few cottonwood following the banks of a cracked, dry river bed. The shade of the trees was soothing. Longarm kept going, climbing steadily. He crossed a ridge and found himself suddenly entering a broad valley, both sides of which were clothed in juniper and pinyon. The air was heavy with the smell of pine resin, a smell Longarm had come to associate with these high, wooded hillsides.

Shots. Distant. But shots, he had no doubt. He pulled up. The Morgan blew through her nostrils and jingled her bit. Longarm patted the side of her neck softly. Then he listened intently. Nothing. A few gray desert sparrows flew from one tree to another, then seemed to wait with Longarm. A wood dove called mournfully in the distance.

The shots had come from off to his left. Longarm guided the Morgan in that direction, and after a quarter of an hour, he came to a small mountain stream. He pulled up and let the horse drink her fill, then pushed on, following the stream.

Coming around a bend, he found himself confronted

135

by two loggers with rifles. Beyond them, Longarm saw a small campsite consisting of two large tents, three fire pits, and a rope corral with good horseflesh inside. He recognized Fitz standing in the entrance to the largest tent. Longarm pulled up and waited. Fitz called out something to the two loggers. They lowered their rifles.

Longarm rode into the campsite and dismounted. Fitz walked over. "Well, now," he said. "Fancy meetin' the likes of you up here!"

"Hello, Fitz. How are you?"

"Just fine, me bucko, just fine."

"I thought I heard shots."

"You did that."

"Game?"

The logger winked meaningfully. "You might say that, in a manner of speaking."

"Fitz, let's have it plain."

"Relax, Marshal. No need for you to worry about a thing. We handled it perfect. We kept our asses down and waited for the damned heathen to pull out. We were outnumbered, you see."

"Heathen?" Longarm echoed.

"Diggers. They don't want us here, you know. Something about the pine seeds they harvest from the valley. It's too bad, I guess, but I have a job to do. Anyway, the only casualty is one of my men. When he tried to bring up his rifle to fire on the leader, an arrow pinned the poor fellow's arm to a pine. That sort of took the heart out of my boys."

"They just cleared out? No threats? No palaver?"

"That's the way it was, Marshal."

"You'd better get back to Whipsaw—now. That was probably just a warning. The next time your men might not be so lucky."

"You call getting an Indian's arrow through your forearm lucky?"

"Have you got any idea, old son, where else that

136

damned arrow could have gone? Like up the man's ass?"

Fitz frowned. "I see your point."

"What are you doing up here? You're a long way from Whipsaw."

"Whipsaw is where the railroad and the sawmill are. This is where the lumber is. We'll be getting to it soon. I been scouting the area, and I figure we could put a pretty big camp right here and use the river on the other side of that pass to carry the logs into Whipsaw."

"You're going to log this entire range—use all that river?"

"That's how we're supposed to do it, Marshal." He smiled. He was an honest Irishman whom Longarm found he could not dislike.

Longarm shook his head and looked about him. This entire valley was like a miracle after his day and a half in the desert. A high, clean miracle. The pinyon and juniper stands appeared taller and more lush here. Cottonwood and aspen were mixed in with the pine. On the ridges, crowding the rimrock, he saw giant cottonwood.

He looked back at Fitz. "I still think you ought to get on back to Whipsaw, Fitz. And let me find the Indians and warn them."

"Well now, Marshal, that sounds like a fine idea. And I'm bettin' that Mr. Desmond and Mr. Lawson would be happy to know you was sticking your neck out for them."

"I just don't want to see the army in here herding the Diggers back onto their reservation," Longarm explained. "And if they keep harassing this operation, I imagine that's what'll happen. I guess I'm thinking of the Indians as much as I'm thinking of the Western Lumber and Land Combine."

"All right, then," Fitz said. "We'll move out this afternoon. I seen enough here. It's good quality timber, better than that scrub we been logging on the ridges around Whipsaw. You tell them Indians—if they *let* you—that we'll be back in less than a month and we'll stand for no deviltry."

Longarm swung up into his saddle and looked down at the foreman. "You got any idea which way the Diggers went?"

"They came out of nowhere like bloody little pixies and disappeared the same way," Fitz told him. "Maybe your coming scared them off. They're pesky, silent little savages, and that's a fact. I'm thinking of my own folk fighting the British and can't help but sympathize—but I've a job to do. You understand that, Longarm."

The lawman nodded. "I understand, Fitz. I've got a job to do as well."

Longarm pulled his mount around and prodded it toward the stream. Following the stream out of the camp, he kept with it until he had passed through a small canyon at the other end of the valley. The stream became faster and shallower, the ground rockier. Great boulders and sharp pinnacles of rock barred his way at times. He worked the horse carefully around these obstructions and kept climbing, reaching at last a long bench dotted with sagebrush and with thin stands of grama holding the sandy soil in place. Beyond the benchland rose abrupt slopes clothed with pine and juniper, but not as thickly as the valley through which he had just passed.

From what Wally had told him, he was deep in Digger country. This jasper, Shortslef, was supposed to have married an Indian. He would have no difficulty, then, in communicating and perhaps living for a while with the Diggers. If he was not with them, they would know which way he had gone after leaving them—not that they would tell him anything, he realized somewhat ruefully. And if the son of a bitch was not here with these Indians, he was more than likely well north of here in Snake River country on the Cheyenne reservation, safely hidden out with his wife's people.

Snake River country. That was high, lush land—considerably more hospitable than this basin country. Longarm found himself hoping he did not find Shortslef with the Diggers. He would not mind shaking this troubled land, and he was in no hurry to return to Denver and its smells. . . .

His thoughts were broken off by something he saw out of the corner of his eye. A small, dark figure had gone from one large sage bush to another. Dangling from its skinny, gleaming arm was a long black bow. Longarm took a deep breath, talked softly to his horse, and kept riding. He was almost to the end of the bench and could see the slope ahead of him leading into a narrow, winding valley thick with juniper.

By this time he could feel the eyes at his back. The small of his back began to crawl. Another swift movement, on his left this time, as silent as thought. They were keeping up with him on foot, making not a sound and moving only when they could be sure of cover. He kept his back straight. *Hell, might as well give them a good target,* he thought. The horse dipped down the slope. Longarm angled the horse carefully, looking neither to the right nor the left, intent on guiding his horse down the slope.

He reached a narrow trail and was soon well into the valley, with the trees crowding close upon him. A meadow spread out ahead. By this time he was sure the timber was teeming with small, nearly naked Indians, all of them keeping pace with him. Still, they had not yet loosed any arrows at him. That was a good sign.

The horse was almost to the meadow. As if that were the signal, the Indians left their cover along the trail and appeared from the deep grass just before him. He pulled up quickly as their naked bodies pressed close upon the horse, their impassive faces turned up to his, their eyes bright in their dark, wrinkled faces. There were no smiles, only the incredible silence broken occasionally by the clack of their bows. So close together were they that as they held their bows up, they knocked against their neighbor's.

One of them took the bridle and led Longarm and his horse onto the meadow. The Indians kept pace, still as silent as before. The only sounds were those of the horse's passage across the thick grama and the rustling of their bare legs brushing through it. They were—taken as a whole—the most wretched-looking creatures Longarm had ever seen. They looked even worse than those four Indians he had helped in Silver City. Many of them wore capes made of strips of rabbit skin, twisted and dried, and then tied together with strings and drawn around the neck by a cord. The capes extended to just below their hips and didn't appear to give much protection to the body, since they wore no leggings or moccasins. The men all cut their hair square in front, but for the most part it hung down in greasy streamers at the temples.

The meadow dipped, revealing a campground ahead, situated in the bend of a shallow stream. There were about ten wickiups, some conical, others domed, with a hole in the top of each for a smoke vent. They had no look of permanence about them, no sense at all that they could offer any real protection from the elements. As he rode closer, he saw that the pole frames were covered with bark and dried brush. In a few cases, mangy, matted army blankets served. Longarm had seen collapsed and abandoned sod houses that looked more habitable. The women standing in front of their wickiups, some with children clinging to their breasts, wore nothing above the waist. Their hair was filthily matted and unkempt and seemed to be growing in all directions.

Diggers. Yes, the name was apt.

When he reached the outskirts of the encampment, the Indian who had hold of Longarm's horse released the bridle and, with astonishing suddenness, trotted through the camp and plunged across the creek. Longarm watched him and was surprised to see—on a slight rise overlooking the stream on the other side, partially obscured by a stand of pinyon—what appeared to be an army tent. The Indian hurried up the slope and came to a halt in front of it.

A tall woman stepped out of the tent. The two appeared to have no difficulty conversing with each other. At last the Indian left the woman and hurried back across the stream. When he stopped in front of Longarm, he spoke in good English.

"Miss Tate say you are not to worry and she will speak to you at her tent when she has made herself ready." He peered intently at Longarm, the ghost of a smile in his black eyes. "And I say you not to worry, Marshal. Do you know my face?"

Longarm looked more closely at the Indian. The features were only vaguely familiar, but they *were* familiar.

"In Silver City," the Indian said. "You come in and sit down at the table. We have ropes on our necks and you take out your gun and free us. Yes! You remember now?"

Longarm still didn't recognize the face, but when he recalled the smoky interior of that saloon and the ring of drink-sodden faces lusting after blood, he did not wonder that the faces of those four Indians standing on the tables had failed to stay in his mind.

"Yes," Longarm said, "I remember. Where are the others?"

Immediately three Indians, grinning from ear to ear, stepped forward. Looking about him now, Longarm saw, if not outright pleasure, certainly an absence of ferocity. He was, it seemed, quite welcome.

Longarm dismounted. Admiring hands played over the Morgan's coat. A sharp command came from the Indian who had addressed Longarm, and a woman came forward and led the horse away to a pasture.

"I need the saddle and the rest of my gear," Longarm told the Indian.

The Indian nodded and said something to the squaw. She answered him without looking back, and continued to lead the Morgan away. She was heading toward the stream. Longarm relaxed, and looking up, saw the woman emerge from her tent. He started toward her. The Indians stepped aside for him and he negotiated the stream with a couple of quick strides.

Mounting the bank on the other side, he found himself as fascinated by the woman's tent and accessories as by the woman herself. Her wall tent was at least twelve feet high at the center peak, enclosing a living area the size of a good-sized living room. What looked like a rubber bathtub propped on telescoping legs peeked out from the rear of the tent, and farther back, tucked for modesty's sake behind a canvas screen, he saw what he recognized as a toilet commode. Just in front of the tent—on the front lawn, as it were—there was a scattering of folding camp chairs. Among them was a collapsible table of considerable size, upon which were piled writing materials, notebooks, and several bulky volumes.

The woman who stood regally amidst all this was at least as tall as Longarm. She was wearing a pith helmet, a tan hunting jacket—open casually to reveal a high-necked silk blouse—jodhpurs, and high English riding boots. She was blonde, her hair worn in a tight bun at the nape of her neck. Her forehead was high, her eyes hazel under clean-lined brows. Her light eyebrows had been bleached almost into invisibility. Her chin was cleft and angular, her nose patrician, and nothing in her gaze at that moment gave Longarm any encouragement. She appeared more than ready, in fact, to do battle with him.

"You're the marshal from Whipsaw, I understand. I can't understand why Wanowi was so pleased at your arrival here. What is it you want? State your business and then be so kind as to leave!"

Longarm smiled. It did nothing to clear the air. She was adamant, her eyes cold and hostile. Longarm felt exasperation building in him and cleared his throat. Then he said, "Wanowi is a mite pleased to see me because I saved his life in Silver City. Him and three of his friends. I am not the marshal of Whipsaw. I am Deputy U.S. Marshal Custis Long and I am tracking a renegade army scout by the name of Ned Shortslef, who is not using that name, most likely, and was reported heading this way." Longarm felt his anger taking charge of his tongue. "Town marshals work for local townships and such. Deputy U.S. marshals work for the federal government and the office I work out of is in Denver. I am interested only in bringing in—"

"Enough, Marshal!" she said, smiling brilliantly. "My apologies! I am so glad you do not work for that cesspool of a town. Sit down! Relax!"

Longarm took a deep breath, and tried to hold off, but was unable not to return her smile. He followed her over to the table, held a chair for her, which astonished and delighted her, then sat down himself.

"One of the Indian women, Wahkeena, will be over soon to clear off this table and see to our supper. You will join me, I hope."

"Wouldn't think of missing it," he said, realizing suddenly that he was very hungry.

"You're amused by all this paraphernalia, I see. You think I should rough it, live as do the Indians I am studying?"

"What I think you should do is tell me who you are, since you now have the advantage of me."

"Of course. How boorish of me. My name is Barbara Spencer Tate. I am studying the Indian culture of the Great Basin before it is obliterated by lumber companies, mining interests, and rapacious settlers and cattlemen."

"You'd better get busy and move fast."

"Precisely. I have already accomplished much. These Paiute are most friendly and have already learned English with surprising speed. I only hope that somehow we can preserve this marvelous, almost purely Pleistocene culture."

Longarm scratched the back of his neck vehemently.

"You lost me some distance back, Miss Tate."

"Call me Barbara."

"And you can call me Longarm. But I still didn't get that part about Digger culture."

She took a deep breath. "Longarm, do not call these Indians 'Diggers.' It is a most crude and totally inaccurate appellation. These groups, or bunches, are members of the Uto-Aztecan family. Broadly speaking, most Great Basin Indians are either of the Shoshoni or Paiute linguistic affiliation. The Indians across that stream over there are definitely of the Paiute branch."

"I see. I'd better call them Paiutes."

"Well, that's much more accurate, certainly," she agreed.

"I guess you must read a lot, Barbara."

"Of course. Most anthropologists do."

"Then you must have read what Mark Twain wrote about these Indians."

The tall woman bristled noticeably. "Mark Twain is a humorist, not a scientist. I have only read one very crude and very vulgar and not at all informative reminiscence of his. It is called *Roughing It,* I believe. In it he calls these genuinely aboriginal people scrawny, lean, degraded, their faces and hands bearing dirt they have been accumulating for months and years. Silent,

144

treacherous, sneaking. Oh, yes. That funny Mr. Twain. What he saw, Longarm, were Goshute Indians who had been uprooted from their culture and left to beg for food and sustenance at the various stage depots, a scene he could have duplicated in any eastern city in this country, substituting Irish, Slavic, or Nordic affiliation for those poor Indians. Mr. Twain would be pleased to note, I am sure, that the Goshutes have embraced many of the white man's ways—they have become prostitutes and beggars."

"I guess I struck a sore spot."

"You did, I am afraid. But surely you do not feel as this Twain does. Didn't you tell me you saved Wanowi's life—and three of his friends?"

"I was just doing my job, Barbara. These Indians are wards of the federal government."

"I see. Do you want to tell me about it?"

He shrugged and told her what had happened, and when he was finished, her face was cold with fury—not at Longarm, but at what Bat Lawson's men and that crowd of loggers had been about to do to Wanowi and the others.

"Thank heavens you were there."

"Yes. But that's all behind me, Barbara. What I'm doing here, I told you before. If you could help me, I'd be much obliged."

"That deserter?"

"Yes. He's the man I'm after."

She nodded thoughtfully. "I understand. I know nothing at all about him."

"I haven't even described him to you yet. I admit you're smart, Barbara—but you ain't that smart, are you?"

She laughed. "Please forgive me. You're the first white man I've seen in months. Describe this desperado you're after."

"Well, maybe he passed through here on his way

145

north into Snake River country. If he did, there's a good chance one of your Paiutes might have seen him."

"They are not *mine*, Longarm," she corrected him. "But do go on. Describe this person to me."

"He's big. He was a Mountain Man once, before he joined up to scout for the army during the Indian Wars. Blue eyes. Lots of hair on the face. That's about all, I guess, except for the fact he's riding a grullo."

"That's not really much to go on, is it?" she asked, frowning.

"No, it purely isn't, at that. But I believe he killed a sheriff and I do want to bring him in."

"A sheriff?"

"Sheriff Tanner."

"Oh. That's dreadful," she said sadly. "On my last two trips to Silver City to use the telegraph, I met him. He was very nice. I am sorry to hear of his death."

"Maybe you could call over Wanowi. If he's the chief, he might be able to help me question the other Indians. Like I say, they might have caught sight of a big man like that moving north through these parts."

"Of course, Longarm."

She stood up and, with one imperious wave of her arm, brought one of the Paiute women across the stream almost on the run. Barbara told the Paiute what she wanted, and not long after, Wanowi made the trip across the stream, his small, wizened face solemn, his deference to Longarm still noticeable. Longarm realized suddenly that the Indian must be in his fifties. The smallness of their stature and the lack of tallow on their frames gave them all the appearance of little old children. It was unsettling.

Wanowi stopped before them and stood proudly, his shoulders back.

Longarm spoke first. "Wanowi, before I get down to why I'm here, I've got a question I'd like you to answer."

"Okay, Marshal."

"Call me Longarm, Wanowi. It means 'Long Arm of the Law.' Okay?"

"Okay."

"On my ride to Whipsaw, did you or any of your friends follow me?"

Wanowi glanced quickly at Barbara—then grinned broadly. "Yes, Marshal."

"And was it you or one of your friends who shot that poor cowboy in the back?"

"He was going to shoot you, Marshal. When Wanowi heard the shots, he climbed to where the cattle people was and he saw what you do. Very brave! You climb the mountain like fly. But you are not like the fly. You do not have large eyes that see behind and front, too. You not see that other cattle person. I shoot him high in the back. Miss heart. He be all right with white man's medicine."

Longarm smiled. "Thank you, Wanowi. You saved my life. We are even. And you are right. That fool cowboy'll be all right, soon enough. Now how about finding out for me, if you can, whether or not a big fellow on a grullo rode through this valley a few weeks back on his way north."

Wanowi shook his head decisively. "No big man riding grullo came north this way, I think."

"Will you ask around for me?"

"Yes, Longarm. Other bands." He pointed down-stream. "I will send to find out. You will stay with us?" he added hopefully.

"Yes. But not for long, Wanowi. I've got a lot of distance to travel."

"Rest here with the Paiute People. You are welcome. Wanowi and Longarm brothers."

"I'll buy that," Longarm said easily. "Do you want to shake on it?"

Delighted, Wanowi stepped forward and thrust out

his small brown hand. Longarm took it and was startled at the wiry strength it revealed as the Indian wrung his hand happily. Longarm finished the handshake barely on his feet and was rubbing his knuckles thoughtfully as he watched the Indian walk back to the encampment.

He turned to Barbara. "You said something about supper not long ago."

"Indeed I did. Relax and I will consult with my lady servant." She got up and walked down the slope and across the stream, moving in long, graceful strides. Longarm saw her talking to one very old, toothless squaw, who nodded happily and hurried off with two other younger Indian women. Barbara turned back around, saw him watching, and waved.

They ate in the cool summer dusk, with the Paiute women hovering like eager children about the table. Barbara had produced some wine from a trunk in the rear of the tent. She had it cooled in the stream and then insisted on wrapping it in damp cloths while she poured the wine into long-stemmed glasses. The meal was obviously of Indian manufacture and was delicious, though Longarm did not dare to ask what it was. The main course consisted of large meat patties of some kind, greasy and quite salty—but most tasty. He recognized one of the portions: carrot root, roasted in hot stone pits. It had a delicious, sweet potato-flavored flesh.

During the meal Barbara went on at some length about what she had recorded of the Paiute culture in the almost eight months she had spent with these people. It was obvious that she was more than anxious to share with Longarm all that she had found. It poured out in unabashed abundance and Longarm did his best to listen intelligently and nod at just the right times. To his surprise, however, he soon found himself fascinated.

Though everyone, it seemed, was determined to call

the Indians of the Great Basin 'Diggers,' implying that they should be regarded as little more than burrowing animals, Barbara felt that nothing could be further from the truth. To her the Paiute, Shoshone, and even the Washo had simply adapted with great skill to what she called a "desert culture." Where the white man would have perished, these Indians had found a home by a remarkable process of adaptation.

Longarm had trouble with all this. The words Barbara used with such fluency frequently made little sense to him. He insisted, therefore, on stopping her frequently and demanding an explanation. This only served to delight the woman. She said that in making her account simpler for him, she was helping herself see things much more clearly. And certainly her journals would benefit. As she continued speaking after every such interruption, Longarm found himself less and less confused.

She described the need for mobility on the part of the Paiute. The Indians had to be able to take advantage of short-lived opportunities for harvest and the hunt. Using only the bow and the net—and in some cases a throwing stick—they were able to obtain jackrabbits, cottontail rabbits, ground squirrels, tree squirrels, raccoons, wildcats, and groundhogs. Deer, she said, were taken by stalking. Frequently, when enough Indians could be brought together for the purpose, group drives and fire drives were organized to force antelope into large corrals, strong enough to hold a number of them at a time.

Because of the low availability of food, the Indians kept their bunches small, seldom more than thirty or forty people to a bunch. Wanowi was the 'captain' of this bunch, Barbara explained, but his leadership was tenuous. He had little more than advisory power. He could warn; he could suggest. But that was the extent of his control.

"Talk about a working democracy," she said, laughing. "It is pretty close to anarchy."

"Sounds like it. But if it works for them . . ." Longarm shrugged. "By the way, what else do these Indians eat?" He pushed aside his plate. "What kind of meat was that I just had? Jackrabbit?"

Her smile warned Longarm. "No," she said. "That wasn't jackrabbit."

"Raccoon?"

"Why do you think it was meat?" she asked, still smiling.

"It was salty, had a meat taste, that's why. Thunderation, woman! What was that you fed me?"

"Grasshoppers and large crickets, pounded up and mixed with animal grease, then cooked like pancakes over an open fire on a skillet I provided. I find it delicious, and I could tell you liked them as well."

"My God, woman," Longarm said hoarsely.

"You look a little green around the gills, Longarm," she teased, reaching over and filling his glass with more wine. "Drink that. You'll feel much better in a few moments. We could have served you fly larvae. Heaps of them are found on the shores of the lakes south of here, gathered up, dried, winnowed to get rid of the casings, then stored in those large willow baskets you see beside the wickiups. They are delicacies, Longarm, and Wahkeena was anxious to bring you some."

"Thank you. Now what were those small sweet balls? Or maybe I shouldn't ask."

"The women split open the cane they find in the few marshlands hereabouts, and lay the stalks in the sun until the sap has crystallized. Then they scrape it into those tasty, sugary balls you found so delicious. These Indians are very proud that you have come to visit them, Longarm. They are not holding back a thing in their efforts to make you feel at home. Nothing but the best for the marshal."

Longarm sipped the wine and glanced at her. "I see you don't mind if Wanowi and the rest of his friends go around with nothing on under those rabbit capes."

She shrugged. "And the women customarily wear nothing above their waists, while the babes at their breasts go naked. No, Longarm, I do not mind. I try to see beyond these surface indications of savagery to the heart beneath. I have come to love these people, Longarm. Can you understand that?"

"Not really. Don't get me wrong, now, Barbara. I don't mean to fault you. But it just appears to me like you look on them as happy, skillful children—something put here for you to study. Like they were some bugs under those spyglasses you people use."

"You mean microscopes, Longarm. You've heard of the work of Pasteur, have you?"

"Nope. Never heard tell of the man."

"It's not important." She frowned pensively. "But what you say—well, it has some merit, I am sure. I hope I am not in danger of looking upon these people simply as subjects for my studies. That would be—wrong, somehow—as you say."

"And if you really do care about them, you'll keep them away from those loggers. Do you mind if I smoke?"

"Not at all. I find the smell of tobacco pleasant." Longarm produced a cheroot as she continued, "The loggers are destroying their traditional pine groves, Longarm. The nut of the pinyon tree is an almost universal staple of these people. Their stores of these nuts carry them through the winter. That is what Wanowi and his people are doing in this valley now. Soon they will finish harvesting them and will move on to other pine groves. But already, vast areas have been taken from them as that infernal lumber company continues to rape this land." She blinked and started a bit as Longarm struck a match with his thumbnail.

151

"I know," he said, lighting the cheroot and shaking out the match. "You and the Indians and the cattlemen in the area all have a legitimate complaint. But there's nothing that can be done. This company has a perfect right to log this timber. So keep your Indian friends away from the loggers. One of them wounded a logger this afternoon, south of here. If this sort of thing continues, I'll have to alert the army—if Slade Desmond hasn't done it already. The army could make these Indians return to their reservations."

"Longarm, you wouldn't!" she said in a tremulous voice.

"I told you, I am a federal officer; this is federal land. Whoever breaks the law has to answer to me— or to someone like me. But I am not trying to run these Indians into a reservation, Barbara. I've got to find a deserter and it is turning into one hell of a job." He smiled at her. "I guess nothing is as simple as it looks to be at first."

"Then you'll be moving out tomorrow."

"That's right. North. Into Snake River country. There's a Cheyenne reservation there, and I've got a hunch that's where I'll find my ex-Mountain Man."

Mosquitoes and particularly devilish gnats were beginning to swarm about the table. The smoke from his cheroot kept them pretty well away from Longarm, and Barbara tried to ignore them, but it was getting to be a chore. Longarm stood up. "I guess you'll be wanting to get into that tent, away from these bugs."

She smiled and got up also. "Not only that, Longarm, but I have some notes to transcribe as well."

"You've got a lamp in there?"

"A camphene lamp. It does nicely."

"I'm sure."

"I'd . . . invite you in, Longarm. But that wouldn't be quite proper."

"No, it wouldn't," he said, then added, "It would be right nice of you, though."

She smiled a cool, intelligent smile, with all the passion she might have shown, all the warmth, tucked neatly behind it. An anthropologist, she was.

He touched his hat brim and started across the stream. "Thanks," he called back to her through the dusk, "for the grasshoppers and the crickets."

Her light laugh followed him all the way to where the Indian woman had set down his gear, and its musical ringing was still hanging about him in the darkness when he rolled into his soogan and closed his eyes.

He awoke well before dawn, in a cold sweat. Something was wrong. Not outside. Not anywhere in the Indian encampment. It was wrong inside of him. He glanced up at the night sky. By the position of Orion's belt, it was near one o'clock. Dawn was a long way off, but sleep now seemed impossible.

He had been dreaming of Terry Troy. She had been imploring him to do something about the loggers. He had promised he would do what he could, he remembered. But something in the dream—an urgency so strong it troubled Longarm deeply—would not let him sleep. There was nothing he could do. Nothing. And yet he had promised her. And she was dead now. It was almost as if she had extracted from him some kind of deathbed promise.

Well, now, old son—ain't that just about what she did?

Terry's death had affected him more than he had realized. Her pleas for him to do something for her land. Her wild, elemental abandon. It was downright unpleasant—ugly, even—to think of all that passion, all that life, dead. Of course he wanted to keep that promise to her.

Did she make Tanner promise, as well?

153

The thought startled him. He almost laughed aloud. Of course she did!

Something else bothered Longarm, too. It had only just come to the surface, as if it had been hiding down inside him all this time, waiting to hit him when his doubts and questions grew too ripe to ignore.

Restless, Longarm got to his feet and walked toward the stream. Barbara Spencer Tate's tent was dark. The wickiups behind him were silent, ugly little dwellings, all but lost in the brooding darkness. There was no wind. The night seemed to be waiting for him. He stopped beside the stream and listened to its passage. The clean, clear sound of the water comforted him, and brought his thoughts back to what had just started bothering him—the words of Fitz concerning Dodds.

Gus Dodds was a loner. He had no friends, Fitz had insisted. There was no trace of that big friend who had told Gus so much about himself. Sure, Gus had denied what Fitz had told Longarm. But why would Fitz lie to him? What could there possibly be in it for him? And if Gus *was* the loner Fitz described—if he had never buddied with this deserter during that fellow's stint as a logger—what did that do to Gus's credibility? How much could Longarm trust Gus to help him search out Ned Shortslef? And if Gus didn't really know this deserter, why had Sheriff Tanner gone to him first thing when he got to Whipsaw?

One more thing—the longer Longarm trailed this deserter, the more the feeling grew in him that he was chasing a phantom. Terry's description had matched Gus's, but Longarm could still not shake the feeling that something was wrong—very wrong. Ned Shortslef was not at all where Longarm was expecting him to be, or where Gus Dodds and Terry Troy had told him to look.

Longarm turned away from the stream. He was suddenly tired. *All that thinking,* he told himself ruefully.

His brain was beginning to smoke. But one thing he had settled—and he felt a damned sight better for having done so. He was not going north into Snake River Country for that phantom deserter.

He was going back to Whipsaw.

He had some questions to ask Dodds. And maybe—just maybe—he might try to get some relief for those ranchers while he was in Whipsaw. He would talk to Slade Desmond, and perhaps send someone to Silver City with a telegram to send off to the chief. Someone in Washington *had* to care about what was happening to this valley. It wouldn't count for much, probably, but perhaps then the ghost of Terry Troy would let him sleep again.

Chapter 8

When Longarm rode into Whipsaw the next day a little after noon, the loggers were all off on the slopes and ridges working, so that the town had a waiting, almost deserted look about it. The whine of the saw in the mill was more or less constant, and Longarm wondered how this must affect the girls' sleep. As he rode past the Paradise Valley, he heard the tinkle of the piano and short bursts of laughter—Bat Lawson's men killing a quiet afternoon.

He rode on past the saloon, dodging an occasional wagon piled high with fresh logs for the sawmill, and left the Morgan in the livery. He did not stop in the saloon as he walked from the livery to Ruby's hotel. He was given the same room he had had before, and he left to get a shave and a bath as soon as he had stowed his gear.

When he returned to the hotel, feeling a lot lighter, with a cloud of cheap cologne following him about, Ruby was waiting for him. She was sitting in an armchair when he entered the lobby, and got up to greet him as he started across it.

"Marshal, I didn't get the chance to greet you personally the last time you were here. I am so glad you are back with us! My, don't you smell nice!"

"I much prefer it to the smell of horse manure, ma'am."

"Of course! I quite understand. Marshal, could I

have a word with you? It won't take long, I promise you."

"I've got plenty of time. And you can call me Longarm."

She smiled. "Call me Ruby. Everybody does. I hate the name. Always have, but that's what my name is and that's my game, so I might as well live with it. Now, where were we?"

"You wanted a word with me," he reminded her.

"I have an office in here." With a wave of her pudgy hand, she indicated a room behind the front desk. "Would you mind if we went in there?"

Longarm shrugged and stepped back to let the madam lead the way into her office. When he followed her inside, he found the office quite cozy. It was decorated in red. With the light coming in through the window and reflecting the various shades of red from the rug, curtains, walls, sofas, and chairs, Longarm began to wonder whether he was in some antechamber of hell, with the flames of damnation reflected on the walls—a grim portent of what was to come.

Ruby sat in a large armchair and Longarm found a spot on a sofa across from her. No sooner had she sat down than a girl entered wearing a small, neat apron over her barmaid's uniform.

"What would you like?" Ruby asked Longarm.

"Nothing," he told her. "It's too early for me."

"My, what strength of character. Or is it devotion to duty?"

"A little of both, I suppose."

Ruby ordered a bourbon and water and turned to Longarm as the girl left. "It is about Alice," Ruby said. "She is very upset."

"I'm sorry to hear that."

"About you, and what you must think of her."

"And what *must* I think of her?"

157

"That the only reason she went to your room in Silver City was because I made her."

"Didn't you?"

"Yes, of course I did."

"Ruby, what's this all about?" he asked, a bit impatiently. "Alice is too intelligent a whore to have taken that business so much to heart. That's not why you wanted to talk to me, now is it?"

Ruby took a deep breath and settled herself higher in her chair. Her expansive bosom seemed to grow more massive. Her eyes gleamed in appreciation of Longarm's ability to cut through her strategems. "You do go right to the heart of things, don't you, Longarm?"

"As often as I can," he agreed. "You got something to tell me?"

"Only that I had no choice but to send in one of my girls. Bat insisted on it when he found out from that little constable that you were in town. I'm sure you can understand my position here. Bat and his men run this place, and that means they run me. The company gets a third of my gross. I'm lucky they don't take half. Slade has been very good to me that way. So I do what he says. It's as simple as that. But I don't like to get on the wrong side of the law—especially federal law."

"That's good to know. Maybe I can count on your help, then."

She grew wary. "Of course—as long as you know where my loyalties lie."

"With whichever side your bread is buttered on."

She smiled. "You put it so nicely."

"All I want is some information about a logger."

"Is that *all* you want, Longarm? After all, think about where you are. I have the best girls in this county —in this state, maybe. And Alice *would* like to make up to you for that unpleasantness in Silver City. It isn't often we extend such privileges on the house."

"For now, Ruby—and no offense intended—what I

want is information that only a woman in your position in Whipsaw would be able to give me. The man I am looking for is a very big, heavily bearded logger with blue eyes—a friend of Gus Dodds. And you know Gus, I'm sure."

"I know Gus. We have a lot of big loggers in this camp, Longarm. Hell's bells, most of them start at six feet and go on from there."

"I know that. But he was a good friend of Gus's. The two kept together, went places—maybe this place—together."

Ruby shook her head emphatically. "That's the funny thing about Gus. He's a loner. Keeps pretty much to himself. The girls like him at first, but after a while, they prefer others. They don't dislike him, you understand. It's just that he's kind of spooky—too quiet, if you know what I mean. And a loner. I was real surprised to see him with those other loggers in Silver City."

"So you've never seen Gus with this big fellow I mentioned."

"Never," she said flatly.

Longarm got up. "Guess I'll go up to my room, Ruby. Thanks."

Ruby pushed herself erect. She tried to do it with ease, but it was obviously a strain all the same. Her face momentarily beet-red, she managed a smile. "Why, it was a real pleasure, Longarm. Anytime I can help you, now, you just let me know."

"Just as long as I remember who your boss is."

She smiled, like a schoolteacher at a prize pupil. Longarm turned, left the office and went up to his room. He pulled off his boots and lay face up on the bedspread after rolling up some pieces of newspaper into balls and spreading them on the floor between the door and his bed.

It was still siesta time. The town was slumbering

below his window. Longarm slept with the whine of the sawmill in his ears.

The knock on his door awoke Longarm instantly. In the moment it took him to sit upright, he noted the increase in the level of sound coming from the street below the hotel. The loggers were already back in Whipsaw and skid row was coming alive.

"Who is it?" he called, as the person on the other side of the door knocked again.

"Ruby!" came the urgent response.

Reaching for his hat, he went to the door and pulled it open. As Ruby entered, bringing with her an aura of tinsel and cheap perfume, he went back for his boots and sat back down on the bed to tug them on. Glancing up, he saw Ruby standing in front of the closed door. There was a look on her face that gave him pause.

"What is it, Ruby? You look like the devil's got his hooks in pretty deep."

"He has, Longarm," she said seriously.

Longarm pulled on his boots and stood up. "Okay. What is it?"

"Fitz. They got Fitz."

"You'd better explain, Ruby." He reached out to her and drew her gently onto the edge of the bed. "Who's 'they'? And what's Fitz done?"

"He sent someone to tell me to come for you," she said, looking up at him hopelessly.

"Ruby, start at the beginning. What has Fitz done?"

She looked quickly around the room as if its corners were listening. Moistening her lips, she said, "He's a union man. He's been trying to organize the loggers!"

Longarm's eyebrows rose in disbelief. "Fitz? Hell, if I ever saw a good company man, he was it."

"He cares for the workers!" she protested with sudden emphasis. "Those loggers are treated terribly, Longarm. You ought to see how Slade cheats them out of a good fifth of their daily wages. He laughs about it, he does. And that stinking freight car they have to sleep in! It's crawling with rats and lice!"

"All right, Ruby. Go on. Where're they holding Fitz now?"

"In the Paradise Valley. There's a trial going on. Slade's the judge and Bat and his men are the jury."

"And the loggers?"

"They're outside, but some of them don't care what happens to Fitz. They're yelling in to Slade to string Fitz up!"

"But not all of them, Ruby."

"No. Not all of them."

"Let's go," Longarm said, inspecting his Colt and then returning it to its holster. "We can talk on the way."

Ruby heaved herself forward off the bed and left the room just ahead of Longarm. As she padded heavily down the hall before him, a few girls and their gentlemen friends poked their heads out of rooms to see what was going on. Ruby swept past them without a word, and this obviously worried the girls more than if she had reprimanded them. Doors were slammed shut hurriedly behind Longarm as they passed.

Once they were through the lobby and out the door of the hotel, Ruby turned to Longarm, and as they hurried toward the crowd of loggers in front of the Paradise Valley, she told him what had been going on. Fitz —a man she was obviously very close to—had been holding meetings in the hills with whatever loggers were willing to form a union. Better living conditions and higher wages were the issues. The problem of wages could be settled easily enough if Slade would simply stop gouging the loggers at his company store, and maybe even throw out the crooked roulette wheels and faro dealers he had brought in.

Slade had known meetings were going on, only he

161

hadn't known who was holding them and where they were being held. But a hired gun he had brought in the day before—Clyde Tigbee—had beat the information he wanted out of a logger, and Tigbee and Bat had gone after Fitz and brought him into the saloon for his "trial."

Longarm had heard all he needed to, and by this time they were on the fringes of the mob of loggers crowding about the saloon. Those men in Fitz's corner were raising their voices now, demanding that Slade let Fitz go. The few loggers who disagreed were being shouted down and some were being roughed up a little in the process. When those men in the back saw Ruby coming, with Longarm right beside her, they turned and shouted at those in front of them to make way.

"Hey!" a logger cried. "They got your man in there, Ruby!"

She nodded bitterly as she pushed into the crowd. Longarm had already had to swallow his surprise at Ruby's role in all this. Having seen her cozying up to Bat Lawson in Silver City, he had assumed she was Bat's woman. But then, as Ruby had reminded him earlier that day, she knew who her boss was. Fitz, from the extent of her concern at that moment, was obviously the only man in this place she really felt deeply about, a fact tacitly acknowledged by those loggers who pushed aside to let Ruby and Longarm pass.

Just as Longarm was pushing his way onto the wooden sidewalk in front of the saloon, there was a shot from inside. What sounded like Slade's voice shouted something as a warning, and the batwings burst open. Fitz stumbled out, his eyes wild, a gun in his hand. He saw Longarm and Ruby and made for them as the crowd of loggers let out a great cheer and started toward the man.

Before Longarm could reach the logger, two of Bat's men charged out after Fitz, their guns blazing. Fitz was hit high in the back once. As he twisted about in an attempt to fire at his attackers, another round appeared to catch him in the thigh, knocking him quickly to the ground. Longarm had drawn his Colt, and as the nearest of Bat's men aimed a second time at the already wounded Fitz, Longarm fired at the man. The slug caught him in his abdomen. The fellow dropped his gun and fell to his knees, his mouth opening and closing like a fish's.

The other gunman halted abruptly and dropped his gun. Slade and Bat—along with a long-nosed gent with a flamboyantly waxed mustache, a lean, cleft chin and black, unblinking eyes—pushed out through the batwings. They halted instantly at the sight of the two downed men. Longarm kept his Colt in sight and leveled it casually at Slade and the others.

"Just stand back nice and easy," Longarm suggested. "Nice and easy."

Longarm could feel the loggers behind him. Their silence at this sudden gunplay was awesome—almost frightening. It felt as if there were a great beast at Longarm's back, waiting to pounce.

"Help him to the hotel, Ruby!" a logger called out.

"Yeah," another piped up quickly. "Get Fitz away from here!"

Ruby had been bent over the sorely wounded Fitz. The man still clutched the revolver he had had in his hand when he broke from the saloon, but he no longer seemed conscious. Ruby looked up at Longarm.

"I'll need help," she said.

"Someone give her a hand!" Longarm called back over his shoulder at the crowd of loggers.

But no one stirred. Fitz was, after all, a man accused of starting a union—and there was ample evidence before all of them at that moment that such a twist in a fellow's thinking might bring him the same fate that had befallen Fitz.

163

"All right!" Longarm said sharply and irritably. "Which one of you fair-weather friends is going to help Ruby carry Fitz to the hotel?"

A big logger pushed through the crowd and up onto the wooden sidewalk. It was Gus Dodds. He nodded curtly to Longarm, moved past him, and bent down beside Ruby. The two spoke in quiet, urgent whispers, and then the one-eyed logger reached down and lifted Fitz in his arms. Turning, he started back through the crowd toward the hotel. Ruby moved just ahead of him, clearing a path.

The silent loggers—all of them somewhat shamed by their unwillingness to put themselves on the line for the foreman—moved back somberly, their eyes on the slack form in Gus's huge embrace. A few souls, braver than the rest, followed behind Gus and Ruby as they hurried down the street toward the hotel.

Longarm turned back to Slade. The fellow Longarm had wounded was moaning softly now, both hands clapped against his vitals. "Better get a doctor for your hired gun, Slade," the lawman suggested.

"I've already sent for the only sawbones we've got up here, thank you."

"Then I'll be warning you. Fitz will stay in the hotel under Ruby's care until he's out of danger. If any harm comes to him, I'll hold you responsible. I'm the law in Whipsaw, Slade. You'd do better remembering that."

"There isn't any law in this country that would allow foreign anarchists like Fitzpatrick to spread his doctrine," Slade said. "And no jury would convict anyone of murder for getting rid of some bomb-throwing anarchist."

"Is that what you call someone who just wants to start a union?"

Slade shook his head sadly at Longarm's stupidity. "Are you so busy riding that horse of yours up and down the backside of this country that you don't know about these anarchists? They're trying to take over our industry—our wealth! Hell, man, they don't believe in private property. They don't believe in *anything!*"

"Except maybe throwing bombs!" Bat put in. His voice was filled with outrage.

A doctor—judging from the threadbare black bag he carried—pushed up onto the boardwalk and began examining the fallen gunman's wound. He made unhappy noises and told Slade the fellow would have to be moved into the saloon, that he needed a table to work on.

Slade ordered two loggers to carry the wounded man into the saloon. As the loggers moved past Longarm to get to the fellow's side, the Marshal holstered his Colt and turned to go back to the hotel.

"You haven't heard the last of this, Longarm," Slade called after him. "Protecting a bomb-throwing anarchist is no business for a federal marshal!"

Longarm kept going through the dispersing, excited group of loggers without bothering to reply to Slade's strident outrage. Of course, maybe the damned fool was right. Maybe Longarm *did* spend entirely too much time riding up and down the backside of this country. Hell, maybe Fitz *was* doing more than just trying to start a union. Perhaps Ruby had fallen for an anarchist, and maybe Longarm had just put his badge on the line for one. But he couldn't help smiling at the next errant thought that came to him.

There's nothing wrong with this company town that a good bomb wouldn't cure.

The loggers who had followed Ruby and Gus to the hotel were crowded into the lobby. Some were standing in hushed groups, while others were sitting in the soft chairs along the walls. Longarm went to the desk clerk and asked where they had taken Fitz.

"Ruby's office," the man replied, his voice hushed. "There's her private bedroom just beyond."

Longarm nodded his thanks to the man and entered Ruby's office. A door was open on the other side of it, and through its frame, he could see Fitz lying on his back, face up on an immaculate white bedspread with his boots on. Gus Dodds moved his towering frame aside as Longarm entered the bedroom. Ruby was sitting by Fitz's head while a very competent-looking young lady was swiftly undressing the now barely conscious man. Alice was in a corner, watching unhappily. Longarm realized that she had by this time become Ruby's favorite.

Fitz's dark, handsome Irish mug was pale now, like polished ivory. Sweat stood out on his forehead. He was breathing in short, ragged gasps, his mouth slightly open, the tips of his white teeth barely visible. The girl working over him was dressed in a pink shift, her red hair in an untidy pile on top of her head. She was in the act of pulling off Fitz's heavy, blood-stiffened shirt. She had to cut off the top of Fitz's longjohns.

Something clattered to the floor. Longarm caught a glimpse of it as it rolled under a small table. He stepped over and picked it up. It was one of the slugs, battered and misshapen by its journey through Fitz's body. He showed it to the girl, ignoring Ruby, who was just sitting beside Fitz, searching his face with her eyes and occasionally dabbing at his perspiration with a perfumed handkerchief. The girl nodded and, without a word, showed Longarm the exit wound just under Fitz's right ribs. The hole was ragged and the blood was oozing out of it slowly, as if it were in no hurry to vacate Fitz's warmth.

The redhead had towels soaking in pans of hot water. She wrung out one of the towels and placed it securely against the wound, stanching the flow, and then, with deft skill, she placed a hand under his back and sat him

166

suddenly upright. Longarm moved quickly enough to see the entry wound. It was high on Fitz's left side. A considerably smaller hole than the exit wound. Placing another compress against this wound, she then swiftly wrapped a bandage around it and the other compress, then kept working until she had him wrapped about the chest like a mummy. After this, she let him back gently on his pillow.

She pulled off Fitz's pants and finished cutting off his longjohns, tossing them onto the pile of bloody garments on the floor beside her. The thigh wound was bleeding freely, darkening the bedspread ominously. The bullet was still inside, since there was only one discolored wound. The thigh—a greenish purple—had swollen monstrously.

The girl wrapped another hot towel around this wound as well, and when she had finished, another girl joined her and together they tugged the bloody bedspread and sheets out from under Fitz until they were down to the mattress. As the second girl left with an armful of bloody sheets and clothing, the redhead looked across the bed at Ruby.

"He needs a doctor, Ruby," she said. "He's still got a bullet in him and he's lost a lot of blood."

"We haven't got a doctor. You think Slade'll let that sawbones of his come over here? Get a blanket for Fitz! Don't leave him lying here like this, stark naked!"

Even as Ruby spoke, the second girl returned with a clean sheet and a blanket. She and the redhead quickly covered Fitz.

Longarm said to the redhead, "Clean off those scissors in good hot water and plenty of whiskey. I'll use the scissors to probe for the bullet. You can help."

The redhead looked at Ruby.

"Do as he says!" Ruby told her, her eyes never leaving Fitz's face.

"That's right," Gus said from behind Longarm. "You do as the marshal says. He knows what he's about."

The girl nodded, and snatched up the heavy scissors she had been using. As she started past Longarm, he took her arm. "Do you have longer, narrower scissors?"

"Barber scissors," Gus said.

"Yes," Longarm said to the girl. "Barber scissors. And hurry it up with that whiskey. If he comes to his senses, we'll need the whiskey to quiet him."

The redhead fled the room.

As Longarm took off his coat and gunbelt and began rolling up his sleeves, Gus stepped closer and started to roll up his sleeves as well.

"Maybe you could use some help," Gus said.

"I sure as hell could," Longarm admitted.

Then they stood silently, waiting for the redhead to return. Fitz still lay unconscious on his back, his breathing irregular. The only sound in the room was his ragged breathing. And then another sound joined it. Ruby, her face in her hands, was weeping softly.

Fitz came awake as soon as Longarm began probing for the bullet. Despite the quantities of raw whiskey they poured down his throat, he remained awake through it all. All of Gus's enormous strength was needed to keep the man on the bed. Only when the slug was in Longarm's palm, did the man rest his head back on the pillow and close his eyes. The redhead leaned over and gently took the rolled-up section of sheet from his mouth. The man had chewed almost through it, yet he had not uttered a single cry. Only the wrathful thrashing of his solid body testified to his pain.

As Longarm stepped back away from the bed, the redhead swiftly washed out the wound with soap and water—on Ruby's suggestion—and then bound the ragged hole securely to stanch, finally, the freshet of blood that poured from the man.

168

"He sure has lost a lot of blood," Gus said, speaking softly.

"There are some doctors who cure their patients by bleeding them, Gus," Longarm said.

"I know. There are damn fools everywhere. It ain't right. A man needs his blood—every bit of it. Look at Fitz's face, damn it."

The pallor had deepened alarmingly. Blue circles hung under his eyes, which had sunk deep into their sockets. Abruptly the man's eyes flickered open. He saw Longarm and Gus and smiled wanly. "Thanks, Longarm," he said softly. "Took you long enough, though. Where in blazes did you get a license to practice medicine?"

"Never mind that. How do you feel?"

"Empty. Light as a feather, as a matter of fact. But I'm glad that bullet is out." He began to cough, and had to turn his head away to clear his throat. Tiny flecks of blood appeared on his lips and dribbled onto the mattress. Ruby quickly reached out and wiped the blood from his mouth. He looked at her and smiled. His right hand came up and took hers and squeezed it.

She smiled stoutly back down at him. "You're going to be all right, you crazy Irishman," she said.

"Why, sure, an' there's little doubt of that! With Longarm here as me doctor and big Gus Dodds as me nurse!"

The effort required to express this optimism weakened the man alarmingly. He seemed to sink into the mattress as he let go of Ruby's hand. His eyes remained open, but he had the look of a man who is staring down a long, dark tunnel—with death waiting at the other end. Alice, who had seemed to melt into the wallpaper during all this, stepped closer to Ruby, now, and took her ha. d. The weary madam answered Alice's squeeze and then rested her head against Alice's breast. Alice wrapped her arm around Ruby's shoulder and held her silently. Catching Longarm's eyes, she shook her head sadly, in obvious concern for Ruby's state.

A commotion behind Longarm caused him and Gus to turn. A logger burst into Ruby's office and hurried toward the bedroom. When he saw Longarm, he halted, took a deep breath, and swallowed.

"Out with it," Longarm told him, moving toward him and out of the bedroom.

"That guy you shot—Bat's man. He's dead!"

"I'm sorry."

Gus came up beside the lawman. "I'll bet there's more to it, Longarm." He turned and addressed the logger. "Let's have the rest, Mike."

"That gunslinger Slade brought in is outside now. He's been appointed town marshal, and he told me to tell Longarm he wants him for aiding an escaped anarchist and killing what he calls 'an officer of the court.' " The logger took a deep breath. "He says if Longarm don't come out, he'll come in after him—and he'll make sure that damn anarchist don't get no better."

"That was a mouthful, Mike," Gus told him grimly. "Is that all he said?"

The fellow moistened his lips and nodded quickly. "That's all, Gus. That's what he told me to tell Longarm."

"You told me," Longarm said. "Go on back out. I won't be long."

As the logger bolted back out the door, fairly bursting with his sense of importance and the news he had to spread, Longarm turned to Gus and said, "You sure you want to hang in with me on this?"

"I'm already in," Gus said, his good eye glittering darkly.

"Stay here with Fitz, then, in case that jasper gets past me."

"I don't have a weapon."

"Get one," Longarm told him as he walked back into

the bedroom, strapped on his cross-draw rig, and shrugged into his coat. He patted the front of his vest, felt of the derringer, then lifted his hat off the bedpost and put it on.

"Ruby," Longarm said, "I'm going outside."

"I heard," she said, her voice hushed.

"Get Gus a gun."

Alice stepped away from Ruby. Ruby reached her hand up and let Alice help her onto her feet. She took a deep breath, squared her massive shoulders, then brushed past Longarm and headed for her desk to get a weapon for Gus. As Gus followed after her, Longarm looked back at Fitz.

Fitz still had that sunken, distant look about him, as though part of him had already gone on ahead. Longarm turned and walked out of Ruby's office.

Longarm did not find Tigbee waiting for him outside the hotel. Only the crowd of loggers was there, waiting not only for him to come out, but also as a vigil for Fitz. Their faces were grim as they stepped back to let Longarm through. Whatever loggers there were who thought Fitz should have been hung because he was a foreign anarchist were nowhere in evidence. This action of Slade's had, if anything, made a union almost a certainty now—either that or a work stoppage and the violence that usually accompanied such a course.

The logger named Mike who had told him the gunslinger was waiting for him dashed out of the Paradise Valley saloon and raced down the street toward Longarm. Longarm kept walking. As the man neared him, he glanced about. The sun was still pouring a heavy, golden light into the valley, but it wouldn't be hanging above the ridges much longer.

The logger pulled up. Longarm kept walking and the logger had to trot almost to keep up with him. "You said he was out here waiting," Longarm remarked.

"He's in the saloon."

The lawman nodded. Whoever the hell this Clyde Tigbee was—he still could not recall the name or reputation—he was evidently a jasper who drank his courage. Good. Longarm liked every advantage he could get when it came to using live ammunition.

"You tell this jasper I've been doing some thinking. Tell him I'm not so sure I want any of this to lead to violence. There's already been too much of that." Longarm looked sharply at the logger. "You got that, Mike?"

"I sure have, Marshal."

"Good. You go tell him that, and shake a leg, or I'll blow your goddamned head off." He smiled at Mike when he said this, but the logger paled and took off like a shot.

The batwing doors were still swinging slightly when Longarm pushed into the saloon after Mike. The logger was at the end of the bar and had just finished telling the hired gun what Longarm had said. Longarm stopped and looked around.

A crowd of Bat Lawson's men was gathered near a table, on top of which lay the covered body of the man Longarm had shot. The jasper who passed for a doctor in this pest hole was holding up the bar; a shotglass and a bottle stood at his elbow. Slade and Bat were standing with the new marshal of Whipsaw.

Longarm nodded a greeting to him. "You Clyde Tigbee, the new town marshal?"

The fellow glanced quickly at Slade and Bat, who then moved away from the bar toward Bat's men. Tigbee looked back at Longarm and nodded quickly. His uptwisted waxed mustache moved ever so slightly, his dark eyes lighting at the prospect of gunning down Longarm. The logger had evidently done another fine job of relaying a message. If Longarm didn't want any more bloodshed, if he wanted to talk, then he was

172

yellow. And that was just Clyde Tigbee's meat. Longarm read this clearly in the man's careless contempt.

Longarm thought, *Let the son of a bitch think what he wants. Let him think I'm as yellow as a canary and just as anxious to sing.*

"Mike says you don't want no more bloodshed, Marshal." Tigbee smiled expansively. "Well, no one's going to hurt you, as long as you let us have that anarchist. He's been inciting his men to revolution, and that's against the Constitution. Hell, you're a federal officer. You should know that's treason. You let us have Fitzpatrick and you can ride out of Whipsaw, proud you done the right thing."

"Well, he's hurt bad. He can't be moved."

Longarm moved away from the batwings and started toward that end of the bar closest to him. This way he was able to keep an eye on Bat's men and Tigbee at the same time. Behind him, Longarm heard a babble of voices as loggers flocked now to gather in the street in front of the saloon. The logger called Mike burst suddenly from the group around the table and dashed out through the batwings. Longarm could hear his breathless account of what he thought was going on inside.

As he reached the bar, the barkeep—a tall, swarthy fellow with three or four black strands of slicked hair brushed straight across a shining pate—hurried warily along the bar to him.

Longarm looked down the bar at Tigbee. "Join me in a drink? I've got to think on this some, and I think better with a little warmth in my belly."

"Watch him, Tigbee!" Slade called out suddenly. "He's up to something."

Tigbee threw a quick, almost contemptuous glance at his employer, as if to say, *Let me handle this. This is my line of work.* Looking back at Longarm, the man spoke sharply to the barkeep. "Sam, give us your best

173

whiskey and leave the bottle. Two civilized people is about to discuss an important matter."

"That's right," Longarm said quietly. "The security of the United States Constitution."

Moving down the bar toward him, Tigbee's eyes lit up. "That's it, Marshal. You put your finger right on it. I can see you're a man what understands these things."

The barkeep placed the two shotglasses down and stood the whiskey bottle next to them. Expansively, Tigbee poured for both of them, slapped the bottle down, and raised his own glass. Longarm picked up his drink. The two men tossed the liquor down. Smacking his lips, Tigbee glanced at Longarm.

"Now then," he said to Longarm. "You going back to that hotel with me to finish off that Irish son of a bitch?"

Longarm seemed to consider this for a moment, then turned casually, leaning his elbow on the bar. "I don't think I can do that. You might say he's a prisoner of the federal government."

Tigbee's dark eyes narrowed. "Maybe so. But I still got to take you in—for killing that poor man over there. He was a duly elected officer of the court."

"He came out that door shooting like a wild man. That's a hell of a way for an officer of the court to act."

"He was chasing a prisoner."

"He could have killed someone. The street was crowded with loggers."

"Loggers, shit!"

Tigbee, excited now by the argument, had taken a small step back from the bar, so intent was he on expressing his outrage that any concern need be felt for loggers. Had the gunslinger been a touch more sober, he might have been warned by the dangerous gun-metal-blue glint in Longarm's eyes, but as it happened, he was not ready when Longarm's hand reached in under his coat and drew his revolver. As the gleaming

174

weapon appeared in Longarm's hand, Tigbee flung himself away from the bar, his right hand slapping for his sixgun. Longarm fired. He missed, and the round blew a hole in a brass cuspidor, with a loud *whang*. Tigbee's legs tangled in a chair and he went down heavily.

Longarm's first shot had gone wild because the barkeep had nudged him quickly with a logger's peavey. Longarm swung at the man with his gun barrel, smashing him across the bridge of his nose, reducing it to a pulp of flesh and blood. The barkeep was stubborn, however. Recovering, he brought back the vicious, hooked instrument a second time. Longarm fired at the man point-blank.

The round entered the barkeep's chest just beside the breastbone, veered slightly, and severed the aorta. Since the man's heart was still pounding furiously, it sent a spray of blood bursting from the bullet hole with great force, as if through the nozzle of a hose. Longarm ducked and went down on one knee to escape the sudden spray just as Tigbee got off his first shot at him. The bullet tugged at the fabric of his frock coat, shearing the flesh just above his collarbone, leaving him with the sensation that a hot branding iron had rested momentarily on his shoulder. He forgot the discomfort at once, as another shot came at him from Bat's direction. The slug bit a clean chunk of paneling out from under the bar.

Longarm snapped off a shot in Bat's direction, just to set him thinking—then another quick one at Tigbee, who was still sprawled on the floor. The round missed the new town marshal, but sent splinters from the chair he was lying near into his face. He spun away. Longarm reached up, grabbed the edge of the bar, and vaulted over it, crunching down on the upper torso of the barkeep.

His shot into the crowd around Bat had produced the

desired effect—a bleat of pain and surprise, followed by a general stampede for the door. As soon as the men had cleared the room, Longarm poked his head up and saw that Slade and his crew had left Bat to handle things. The fellow was crouching down behind an overturned table. *Good,* he thought. *That makes it only two to one. Better odds than when I came in.*

Tigbee, too, had found an overturned table, Longarm noticed. But the man was still trying to dig splinters out of his eyes. Keeping well down, Longarm traveled the length of the bar and swung out from behind it, coming at Tigbee from an unprotected angle. Startled, Tigbee swung up his big Remington and fired. The round went high. The lawman heard it spiderweb the mirror behind him as he sighted deliberately on Tigbee's right eye and pulled the trigger. Longarm's slug instantly demolished Tigbee's eyeball. The eye socket appeared to expand miraculously, then deepen as a ragged triangle of bone and hair was lifted out at the exit wound. Tigbee's head snapped back so swiftly that as his body followed it, it seemed that it was his head that was pulling him over. He came to rest with his lower torso on an overturned chair, his shoulders and head out of sight on the other side.

Bat jumped up from his cover and fired quickly in Longarm's direction, then dashed for the door. Longarm aimed quickly and fired. His Colt's hammer snapped down futilely on the chamber Longarm always kept empty.

Spinning around at the door, Bat flung up his gun and covered Longarm. "Gawdamighty!" the man cried, "You're out of ammunition! Well, ain't that just terrible! Creeping Jesus! Deputy U.S. Marshal Long ain't got no more lead in his pencil!"

The man was fairly dancing with delight as he advanced on Longarm, his dark, hawklike face alight with deviltry.

"Drop it, Longarm!" he said menacingly. "Just drop that empty gun."

Longarm let it go. As the gun thudded heavily to the floor, Bat smiled. He was at peace with the world. All his prayers had been answered—and then some. This was the same man who had parted his hair with a gun barrel in front of his own men. Bat was really going to enjoy this.

Longarm smiled. "I'm an unarmed man, Bat. Don't do something you'll be sorry for."

"Hell, there ain't nothing I could do to you I'd be sorry for, lawman. This is going to be sweet."

Bat brought his sixgun back. Had the blow been allowed to land squarely, it could easily have crushed Longarm's skull. But the lawman ducked swiftly and the gun barrel whistled just overhead, taking Longarm's hat with it. Furious, Bat brought up his knee, catching Longarm just below his solar plexus. The pain that radiated out from that spot caused Longarm to gasp, then stagger back against the bar. Bat kicked him in the right side as Longarm twisted away, sending the marshal tumbling backward along the floor, his boots catching awkwardly in the brass rail.

Bat's bloodlust was thoroughly aroused by this time. He was tired of simply kicking the shit out of Longarm. Something more dramatic was what he craved now—something more final. He cocked his revolver and aimed coolly down at the figure still thrashing helplessly at his feet. Longarm had already palmed his derringer while Bat was busy indulging himself. Now he extended his right hand straight up and fired into Bat's stomach.

The muzzle of the derringer was only inches from its target. At that range the effect of the .44-caliber slug was massive. Longarm saw the man drop his revolver and clutch at his stomach; he watched him stagger back, buffeted by the awesome havoc wrought within

177

his gut. Bat collapsed to the floor, his eyes wide; he was unconscious before he hit, and dead not long after.

Longarm got to his feet and replaced the derringer in his vest pocket. He reloaded his Colt and placed it back in his holster. Buttoning his coat, he stepped over Bat Lawson's still body and picked up his hat. Squinting painfully in the smoke-heavy air, he made his way out of the saloon. As he emerged, the loggers cheered. Longarm looked around for some sign of Slade and his men. Finding none, he acknowledged the cheers of the loggers by touching the brim of his hat to them.

"Someone had better see to those men in there," he said, stepping off the boardwalk. "But there's no hurry. They ain't going anywhere."

He pushed free of the loggers, aware that the flesh wound in his shoulder had bled a bit, causing his shoulder to stiffen noticeably. He sucked in the clear air, appreciating it as Lazarus must have when he left his tomb. The sun was now just below the mountain ridge. As Longarm moved through the gathering dusk on his way back to Ruby's hotel, he could not shake the chill of death that clung to him.

He had come here to bring in an army deserter and had ridden into a charnel house.

Chapter 9

The vigil at Fitz's bedside was a grim one that night. Alice spelled Ruby occasionally, but Ruby slept on a cot that had been brought into her office, leaving word that she was to be awakened at the slightest change in Fitz's condition. Not knowing what Slade intended, Longarm and Gus took turns sitting in the office with a shotgun in their laps. It was a short-barreled Greener that Ruby's barkeep kept handy under the bar. Throughout it all, Fitz slept fitfully. His color improved steadily, though his condition remained precarious.

That next morning an odd thing happened—in fact, it was a remarkable occurrence for a company town. Only a handful of loggers left for the ridges. The majority of them refused to report to their crew chiefs. Instead, they spent the morning milling about ominously along skid row, giving the bars and the girls no rest. Their mood was ugly, as they kept a close tab on their wounded foreman's condition.

Surprisingly, Slade and his men made no move to force the loggers to return to work. One report had it that he had ridden out early with about ten riders, heading north into the wooded slopes. By midafternoon a strong wind began picking up the dust and debris that covered the main drag and the lots between the tents and shanties, filling the air with grit and eye-gouging alkali. Clouds rolled in over the valley as thunder muttered ominously. But the rain held off.

Slade rode into town not long after, and at once the

loggers realized what he had been doing. He and his ten riders were at the head of a sinister, scowling infantry of loggers—all those who had reported to work that morning. It was to be union loggers against those who disdained unions, a kind of civil war.

Watching from his window, Longarm saw Slade's loggers, many of them armed with tall pike poles, sweep down the main drag toward a hastily organized body of union loggers. Slade waited until he was within twenty or so yards of the union loggers. Then he and his riders opened up on the enemy. At once, his loggers broke into a run and closed with the union men. The union loggers outnumbered the others clearly, but they were disorganized and lacked the firepower Slade had just displayed. After a short, furious battle, the union loggers were in flight, scattering throughout the tents and shacks like ants from a ruined nest. In almost no time at all, Slade and his men had won back his town.

Longarm turned away from his window.

As the company's manager, this was indeed his town. Whipsaw existed solely to further the fortunes of the Western Lumber and Land Combine. Slade Desmond's job—purely and simply—was to see to it that this purpose was fulfilled. And that meant that nothing Slade did to further that end would ever be seriously challenged—certainly not by those bigwigs in Washington who owned stock in the company.

It sickened Longarm. There was no way to stop Slade.

A moment later he strode into Ruby's office. He found frightened loggers conversing with Gus, obviously telling him what had just happened outside. At Longarm's entrance, the loggers nodded curtly to him and darted from the office, obviously looking for a safe place to hole up until this trouble blew over. There seemed to be no doubt that all the loggers who could would report for work the next day and spend the following twelve hours working off their sullen rage.

"Were any loggers wounded seriously?" Longarm asked Gus.

"Three men were hurt. They'll live. I expect Slade will be in here next."

"Maybe. How's Fitz?"

"Better."

Longarm walked into the bedroom. It did seem a lot less grim. Alice was sitting in a corner knitting, while Ruby busied herself spoon-feeding Fitz, who had been propped up in a sitting position with the aid of several large pillows.

"Chicken soup!" Fitz cried as Longarm entered. "That's all she's given me. Sure, and I'm going to turn into a chicken before long!"

"How do you feel?"

"Why, this here foreman can run faster, jump higher, squat lower, move sideways quicker, and spit farther than any son of a bitch in camp!" He smiled up at Longarm. "But if I have to say all that again, I might have a relapse."

"Be quiet," said Ruby, "or you will."

"You heard what happened?" Longarm asked.

Fitz frowned. "Yup. I been told. Slade's taken back the town. Can't say as it's any surprise. He has the fire-power, sure enough. And a lot of those damn fools out there don't know what a union could do for them!"

"Look what it did for you!" Ruby said scornfully, poking a steaming spoonful of chicken broth at the man.

He opened his mouth hastily and swallowed quickly, his eyes bugging as the scalding broth boiled down his throat. "Easy, woman!" he cried. "You'll do me in faster than them bullet holes in my hide!"

Longarm shook his head, sighing. "Slade's within the law, you know. I can't see any court in this country going against a company man who's trying to save the country from the anarchists."

"No, Longarm. *Foreign* anarchists. That's what makes it so terrible, you see. After all, me bucko, there ain't a one of us here who didn't come from someplace else. And everyone's trying to hide the fact."

Longarm smiled at Fitz. He was glad the man was in such obviously better spirits. The strength of the man was astonishing. Nevertheless, he was still in great danger.

"I wish there was something I could do to stop Slade," Longarm said.

"You're the law, ain't you? Federal law. This here is federal land. You can stop him easy enough."

"In this country, for the next few days at least, the law is what Slade says it is. If he and his men break in here and kill us all, who's going to demand an investigation to find out what really happened? A union anarchist caused a riot and so many people were killed as a result. And my chief in Denver would just have to settle for that." Longarm took out a cheroot and lit it. "He'd raise more hell than a scalded cat, I reckon, but it wouldn't do him any more good than a fart in a windstorm—excuse me, Ruby."

Ruby placed her spoon down in the bowl of soup and looked nervously over at Fitz, then turned and looked up at Longarm. "You mean there's nothing you can do about Slade—legally, that is?"

"I guess that's about it."

"What do you think about the way this land's being torn up?" she asked.

"It ain't pretty." Longarm shrugged. "But it's legal."

"No, it isn't."

Fitz looked at Ruby in astonishment. Alice stopped knitting.

"What do you mean, Ruby?" Fitz demanded. "Of course it is! How else are we going to cut these trees?"

182

"That's not what I mean." Ruby looked back at Longarm. "I mean it isn't legal for him to be doing what he's doing."

"How do you know that, Ruby?" the marshal asked.

"I don't, for sure. But you let me tell you what happened a couple of months ago. Some men came up here all the way from Washington. They were all fat cats from the government, here to do a check on the operations, they said."

"What department were they from, Ruby? Do you remember?"

"Department of the—" She frowned.

"Interior?" Longarm prompted her.

"Yes, that's the one! The Bureau of Land Management was where one of them—a fine-looking lad—worked."

Longarm realized this could possibly be the survey team that Slade had told him had not yet sent back their report to him. So far, he saw nothing unusual in all this. But he was willing to listen. "Go on, Ruby."

"Well, sir, they came up here to check on this town's operation, no doubt, and they were supposed to check on how the land was being treated. That's what the young fellow told me. But Slade didn't let them out of Whipsaw."

"How do you mean?"

She smiled. "Well, you know what attractions a house like this provides. And they had plenty of everything—on Slade's orders. Pretty soon they drank so much and lost so freely at the gaming tables that all they wanted was comfort from our girls. I must say, the girls did a fine job. Those men never did get out of Whipsaw that week, and they were too drunk to know it when they started back to Silver City."

This was interesting, but hardly unusual. Slade was simply doing his best to keep these Washington bureaucrats in his debt by showing them a good time. "Is that all, Ruby? What's so unusual about that? The men probably had no intention of looking around. They were probably expecting just such a high old time."

"Not that young man from the Bureau of Land Management. He kept asking Slade to show him the survey map. He said he wanted to check it. And I could tell, Longarm, that he was disturbed about something. Well, sir, as soon as he mentioned that survey map, Slade went into action. All of a sudden he got my best girl and told her to stay with this fellow. Slade told her if he bothered him any more with talk about checking that survey map, he'd have her out of here on the first wagon back to Silver City." She smiled shrewdly. "This girl of mine did herself proud. She showed that young man every trick in her book and some I hadn't thought of myself—and the poor young fellow forgot all about Slade's survey map. Now, to my way of thinking, the only reason Slade would want to keep this young man from the government away from that map is because he's doing something that's illegal."

"Ruby, did you tell this to Sheriff Tanner?"

She looked at him strangely. "Why, yes, I did."

"When?"

"The last time he visited me. He was an old friend of mine, Longarm. He was on his way back to Silver City with a horse thief. Whenever he was up here on business, he stopped. He noticed how tired the girls were, so I told him what had happened earlier—like I just told you."

"What did he do when you told him?"

"Nothing much, except that he seemed interested—just like you are now," she said.

"But he didn't *do* anything?"

"No, he didn't. There wasn't much he could do anyway, was there?"

Longarm puffed pensively on his cheroot for a

moment, then said, "He returned to Whipsaw a few weeks later, didn't he?"

"Yes, but he didn't stop in here to see me," Ruby replied.

"Where did he stop?"

"I think he went in to see Slade about something. But then, I was busy getting ready for my trip to Silver City to pick up Alice here and the other new girls." She looked at him shrewdly. "This is important—what I told you—isn't it?"

"That depends, Ruby. Right now I've got to do some thinking. I expect you'd better finish feeding poor Fitz his chicken broth."

Longarm left the bedroom and walked past Gus to the window. It faced out onto the main street. A few of the loggers who had sided with Slade were apparently patrolling the street. They were for the most part old-timers, Longarm noticed. A lot of them carried pike poles, their mean-looking, spiked iron sockets about even with the men's heads as they stepped along. As Longarm watched, one of Slade's men rode into town, waved to the loyalists as he swept past, dismounted in front of the general store, and hurried inside to speak with Slade.

The wind had died down and rain was beginning to fall. It was not a sudden, roaring downpour, but a steady, light fall. The rainy season, as Wally had told him, was beginning finally. Soon, Longarm realized, Whipsaw would be one vast muddy slash pile. Still, this wasn't what was occupying his thoughts at that moment.

Slade had admitted himself that those men had come to Whipsaw to extend the area Slade could log. But they had been kept from seeing where the company was already logging. Slade had not wanted that one young man from the Bureau of Land Management to check his operations against the survey map. Ruby

185

was on to something, all right. Now Longarm remembered Terry's answer to a question of his. She had told him she had thought at first the company would be cutting timber on the other side of this range. Perhaps she had seen some of the original survey team members in that area—or had spoken to them as they rode through.

Longarm needed that survey map. It was probably in Slade's office files somewhere. If he could get hold of that—and it showed what Longarm thought it might show—he would be able to do a lot more than send a few futile telegrams. Hell, Slade would be in violation of federal law. He would have Slade by the short hair. Nothing would please Longarm more.

What about that deserter, old son? Ain't that why you're up here?

Longarm turned and looked at Gus Dodds. Gus saw the look on his face and got up from his chair and walked toward him.

"You see anything out there, Longarm?" the big man asked.

"Just rain and a few of Slade's loyalists marching up and down with their pike poles."

Gus nodded and peered past Longarm and out the window. "Looks like the rain's letting up some. You think Slade will try to rush us?"

"I don't know. How many loggers are holed up in here with us?"

Gus grinned at Longarm. "None. We're all Fitz's got right now—just you and me and Ruby—and the girls. They're out at the bar, enjoying their vacation."

"What's Ruby say about that?"

"Hell, she don't mind. She's finished here now, and she knows it. All she cares about is Fitz."

"And you?"

"I don't want to see no harm coming to that Alice," Gus said grimly.

186

Longarm nodded. "Is that why you threw in with Fitz and me?"

Gus scratched under his eyepatch with a grimy finger, and looked shrewdly at Longarm. "That's part of it, I guess. But I always liked Fitz, anyway. Best foreman I ever worked for."

"You helped me get away with that Troy kid, too. That couldn't have made you very popular with the other loggers."

"It didn't. But Fitz took my side. Like I said, Fitz and I got along."

Longarm looked closely at Gus. A curious, startling thought was taking form in his brain. "Goddamnit, Gus!" Longarm said softly. "Who the hell are you, anyway?"

"Now that's a foolish question, Longarm. You know who I am. I'm Gus Dodds."

"Are you now?"

Suddenly wary, Gus took a step back. "You feeling all right, Longarm? All this here trouble ain't made you soft upstairs, has it?"

"Maybe it has, at that, Gus. Maybe it has. But I wish you'd answer my question. I've got a strong feeling you ain't really done that yet."

"Well, maybe you'll have to wait a while before I do. Look out the window."

Longarm turned. Slade, at the head of a small crowd of loggers, was on his way down the street toward the hotel. It was showdown time, it seemed.

"Cover me from this window, Gus," Longarm said. "I'll go out and see if I can stall the son of a bitch."

Gus nodded grimly and moved closer to the window.

Slade held up his hand. The loggers behind him halted. He smiled at Longarm and walked to within a few feet of the hotel porch. The rain was sifting down gently.

"These loggers want the hotel back, Longarm. I understand you've got Fitz in there, with you and Gus Dodds standing guard. You let us back inside, nice and peaceful-like, and give these men back their girls—along with Ruby—and we won't have to do anything violent."

"No bloodshed," Longarm said.

"That's right," Slade replied easily. "No bloodshed. And you can tell Ruby I don't hold grudges. I didn't have any idea she was sweet on Fitz."

"You mean she can run the hotel—keep her girls —just like before?"

"Sure," Slade said with a smile.

"She'll be happy to hear that."

"I thought she would."

"What about Fitz?"

"Hell, you're a federal officer. Take him back with you. You can prosecute him for starting a riot, or let him go; I don't care which."

"You'll let me ride out of here with Fitz? And Gus?"

"Sure. Hell, you've done us enough damage already, Longarm. Let's say I know when I'm between a rock and a hard place. What I've got to think of now is cutting timber. It's beginning to rain now and that's going to make it a damned sight harder for me to meet my quota. Now that these loggers have learned their lesson and we've found the damned anarchist who was stirring them up, I can get back to work. That's all I want."

"Sounds reasonable, Slade."

"I'm a reasonable man," Slade replied, smiling thinly. "When I have to be."

Longarm paused, considering. Then he took a deep breath, and said, "All right, Slade. I'll take Fitz back with me. Your loggers can have their playpen back."

The man's tiny eyes narrowed shrewdly. "That's

188

fine, Longarm. You'll be moving out, then, with Fitz, back to Silver City?"

"Guess that's the best course, Slade."

The man appeared to take a deep breath. He took off his chocolate-brown derby, swung it to rid it of the rain, and brushed a quick hand over his gleaming skull. Then he slapped his hat back on. "How soon can my men move in?"

"Fitz is still hurt too bad to move tonight—especially with all this rain. You know that pretty stage you used to bring up Ruby's girls? Have it out here tomorrow morning, first light, and we'll take Fitz to Silver City."

"Tomorrow morning?"

"That's right, Slade. Tomorrow morning. The extra night's sleep will do all of us a heap of good."

The man wanted to protest, then thought better of it. He shrugged his broad shoulders and nodded, his buckshot eyes cool, appraising. "Tomorrow morning, then. First light. And you tell Fitz I said good riddance."

"I'll do that, Slade."

Longarm turned and walked back into the hotel. Inside the lobby, he glanced through a window and saw Slade and the loggers hurrying back to the general store through the rain. He watched them go for a minute or so, trying to determine from the way they carried themselves whether Slade really had accepted Longarm's proposal—whether they really intended to let Fitz and him have a good night's sleep.

Longarm told Fitz of his agreement with Slade.

"You don't believe him, do you, Longarm?" Fitz demanded.

"Of course not. But I do know one thing. He is anxious—he has been all along—to get me out of Whipsaw."

189

"Why do you think he wants that, Longarm?" Gus asked quietly.

"Ruby gave me the answer to that, I think. What I told Slade out there was just a stall to give me time to get into his office."

"Why?" Fitz asked.

"I want to look at that survey map Ruby tells me that young man from Washington was so anxious to see."

"What do you expect to find?" Gus said.

Longarm looked at him. "What I think Tanner found—and why he was murdered."

Gus's eyes narrowed. "You mean Slade killed—?"

Longarm held up a cautioning hand. "Don't jump to any conclusions. Let me check this out. First of all, I figure we'd all better lay low, get some shut-eye, and arm ourselves to the teeth. If Slade makes a move against us, he'll likely do it after it's dark."

"You think he will?" Ruby asked, frightened. "For sure?" Alice looked up at Longarm, her face showing alarm as well.

"It all depends on how bad he wants to get me out of Whipsaw without any more trouble. Ever since Silver City that man—or one of his coyotes—has been trying to prevent me from coming here." Longarm looked over at Alice. "That's why you were sent in to search through my wallet, Alice. Slade just had to know why I was riding to Whipsaw."

Alice paled, and almost lost the knitting resting in her lap. She swallowed nervously and nodded.

"I'm going up to my room now," Longarm said. "I'm beginning to stumble around a little, so I'd better get some sleep. You too, Gus."

Gus nodded.

Longarm left the bedroom and went upstairs to his room. He kicked off his boots, took out his Colt, dropped his hat over the bedpost, and fell back onto the bed. He was asleep almost at once, the Colt in his hand.

As Longarm made his way through the foggy night, his thoughts kept returning to the hotel. He had left Fitz asleep in Ruby's bedroom and Ruby was also sleeping, on the cot in her office. Gus said he had napped earlier that evening and seemed alert enough. Still, Longarm was worried. There was a loaded Peacemaker beside Fitz in bed; Ruby, too, was armed, and Gus's Greener was loaded with number-six buckshot. Nevertheless, Slade and his men could take them easily if they wanted to badly enough.

Longarm was banking on the fact that Slade wanted him out of Whipsaw so much that he would make no move against them either tonight or when they brought Fitz out in the morning. Of course, Ruby knew enough to realize that, no matter what, she was finished here in Whipsaw.

The rear of the general store loomed out of the night. The rain had stopped, but clouds hung heavy over the valley. There was no light from the moon or the stars. The wet darkness was oppressive, but provided perfect cover for what Longarm had in mind.

He found a small back porch, mounted it cautiously, and tried the door. It was not locked. He pushed it open, stepped swiftly inside, closed the door silently behind him, and found himself in a small corridor. He moved along it and came to a door, which opened as easily as had the first. Stepping inside, he found himself in Slade's office.

He closed the door and looked around the dim room. Since the office was in the rear of the building, Longarm decided to light a lamp. He had no choice, really. He couldn't find anything in such inky darkness. Locating a lamp, he lit it, then placed it on one of three massive file cabinets. It took him almost a half hour to go through the files. His problem was that he didn't know where such a map would be filed, if in fact it was filed at all. A dead giveaway like that would probably be hidden somewhere else, but he had to check the obvious places first. He found plenty of maps, reports on the amount of lumber cut and shipped, and so forth, but no survey map.

He went to Slade's desk, then, and ransacked it in less than five minutes. Nothing. He looked about and found himself staring unhappily at a wall safe tucked in a corner. If it was inside that . . .

He walked over and examined the safe carefully. It was small. A survey map was large; Longarm had examined quite a few in his time. It would be damned inconvenient to stuff a survey map inside this safe.

He went back to the lamp and lifted it high over his head. Immediately he spotted what appeared to be a draftsman's board in a far corner. He hurried over and saw a map tacked to the board. On closer inspection, however, he found it was only a tally map, showing what slopes and ridges had been cut and how much board feet each section had yielded.

Under the drafting board there was a wooden pocket, similar to a magazine rack. Longarm reached in and removed two large maps. One he discarded immediately. It was of the Whipsaw region exclusively, and simply showed how extensive the cutting had been in this area. The other map was a different matter entirely.

Swiftly he unfolded it and spread it out over the draftsman's board. It was the official geological survey map provided the company by the Bureau of Land Management. One quick glance told Longarm what he had by now pretty well suspected. The map was designed to indicate clearly just where on this range cutting would be allowed. Longarm found the river that ran past what was now Whipsaw. But Whipsaw was not inked in anywhere along that river. Opening the map farther, he found, enclosed by an irregular red line, those tracts that were to be cut. They were well over on the other side of the range. And there was Whipsaw, inked in at least sixty miles to the west of where it now stood, in a narrow valley that opened out onto the Black Rock Desert.

The Western Land and Lumber Combine was sure as hell operating illegally, just as Ruby had guessed. Slade was cutting on government land he had not been authorized to harvest. The company had been given vast tracts, easily as rich in timber as those it was now cutting, but there was no river for transporting the logs, and no railroad. In order to get the logs to the railroad, the loggers would have to skid the logs all the way across the range and then snake them down the mountainside to the railway.

Too much time. Too much labor. Too little profit that way. So they were cutting here—illegally.

Longarm began to fold the map. This made the cheese more binding. He had all he needed now to close down this operation and put Slade and his buddies away for a little rest. At that moment he wished Terry were beside him so she could see—as he now could—an end to the destruction of this valley and the ranchers who depended on it.

The door opened and Slade stood in the doorway, a gleaming Smith & Wesson in his hand. Stepping into the office, he closed the door behind him—and smiled. In that instant, Longarm remembered Tanner's last words:

Illegal! . . . Wrong place! Settlers—right. Stop him! Stop—!

For the first time Longarm knew who Tanner had wanted him to stop. It wasn't the deserter at all. It was Slade Desmond.

"You killed Tanner, didn't you, Desmond?" he said, though he already knew the answer.

"It's not going to do you any good to know that now," Slade replied.

"When Tanner returned to Whipsaw, he demanded that you show him this survey map," Longarm continued.

Slade took a step toward Longarm. "I can see now it must have been Ruby who alerted him to the possibility when he came through with that horse thief. You've got the map there. Too bad. Alice couldn't get away in time for me to stop you."

"Alice?" In that instant, Longarm realized his mistake in trusting her.

"She is confident she can do as good a job as Ruby. I was inclined to believe her. But she's too greedy. She insisted on a larger share." He took another step toward Longarm. "Give me that map, Longarm."

At that moment the night's heavy stillness was broken by the sound of sporadic firing from the direction of the hotel.

"You son of a bitch. Your men are going after Fitz."

Slade smiled. "And Ruby. She's too smart to be a whore."

The lantern was still where Longarm had placed it, within arm's reach on a table beside the draftsman's board. With one quick swipe of his hand, Longarm sent the lantern at Slade. Startled at the sight of the lantern coming at his head, Slade ducked away and tried to get off a shot at Longarm at the same time. But the shot went wild as Longarm flung himself at the man. He caught the small, blocky fellow in the midsection and sent him crashing to the floor under him. The lantern had struck the floor just beyond them a second before. With a tiny roar, flames erupted on the spot, and, following the kerosene, raced along the floor, sweeping in under Slade's bald head. With a terrified scream, Slade hurled Longarm's weight off him, scrambled to his feet, and dashed through what was now a low wall of flame and out the door into the night.

Choking from the acrid smoke and shielding his eyes from the flames, Longarm holstered his Colt and dashed through the flames and out into the night after Slade. It was raining steadily now. There was no sign of Slade. Longarm decided to forget about him, and raced through the slanting rain toward the hotel.

Soon he was close enough to the hotel to see a struggling mass of men just in front of it. Some were rolling in the mud, but most were still standing. A few of them were wielding peaveys, while others used the long pike poles. The sound of grunting, cursing loggers was loud enough to pierce the steady roar of the rain. Longarm saw heads snapping back and men staggering to the ground as they reeled out of the battling crowd.

And then he was pushing himself through the loggers. He narrowly escaped a couple of swinging peaveys, their iron spikes whistling close. Once inside the hotel lobby, he saw two weeping girls hovering over a bloodied and broken body that still had life in it as it tried to crawl past them toward the door.

Longarm halted and looked down. It was Tim Caulder. Half of his face and most of his shoulder were blown away. Any movement on his part now was just blind reflex. The man was as good as dead. Longarm left him and dashed into Ruby's office.

The carnage was awesome. Fitz, the Peacemaker in his right hand, was still propped up in bed with two pillows at his back. His fine, handsome Irish face was calm, even though the top of his head was missing. Two men, entangled half in and half out of the bedroom doorway, were sprawled in front of him.

195

Longarm recognized Jack Wilson and Ruel Tyson. Fitz had taken them both with him.

In the office, Ruby was lying on her side on the floor, a dark pool of blood under her. She looked like an oversized carnival doll, all lace and petticoats and long blonde hair. Beyond her on the floor was Gus. He was sprawled on his side, his smoking shotgun beside him on the floor, just out of reach of his right hand. Judging from the smell of gunpowder, both barrels must have been fired. That accounted for the man outside in the lobby and the other sitting against the the wall opposite Gus. The middle part of him was little more than a stain plastered against the wall behind him. His face was cold white, frozen into a mask of sudden dismay. Longarm did not know him by name, but had see him many times swaggering about the street with others of Bat's men.

Gus groaned as Longarm dropped beside him. Gently Longarm turned him over. Gus had suffered a head wound, ugly but superficial. The round had creased his skull just above his left brow, tracing a deep course on its way past his temple. His scalp was open and the bleeding was profuse, causing the wound to look far more extensive that it really was. But the slug had certainly knocked rather hard on the logger's head. Longarm shook Gus gently.

Gus opened his eyes. "I'm all right, Longarm. But I think they got Fitz."

"They got him. And Ruby."

"Jesus!" The man closed his eyes, then opened them. "Alice! Did they get Alice?"

"She must have got out in time."

"That's right. She wasn't here when they came."

Gus closed his eyes and took a deep breath.

"Stay low," Longarm told him. "I'll get one of the girls to clean you up. Just lie still."

"I ain't going nowhere," the big man said softly.

Longarm got the redhead and one of her chums to see to Gus, then walked out of the hotel. The rain had let up considerably. The fighting in front of the hotel had ceased also. Not a single long pike pole was in evidence. The union loggers had won this round. But what caught Longarm's gaze and the members of the crowd standing before him was the fire now consuming the general store. A roar went up from the loggers as they saw the flames envelop the front of the structure with a dull roar and begin swiftly to climb the false front. When the loggers discovered Longarm standing on the hotel porch, they soon grew silent and faced him, waiting.

"How's Fitz?" someone called out of the darkness.

"We came as soon as we heard the shooting," another man yelled. "Them scabs kept us out!"

Longarm cleared his throat and said, "Fitz is dead."

The silence in the crowd of loggers deepened.

"And so is Ruby."

The silence broke. Cries of rage and frustration broke from many throats. Someone dashed up onto the porch, stood beside Longarm, and cried, "Burn him out! Burn out that bastard, Slade!"

"The mill! Get the mill!" an angry voice shouted.

The logger left the porch in a bound and led the loggers toward the flaming general store. As Longarm watched, a groggy Gus Dodds appeared beside him on the porch.

"I heard them," Gus said. "That sounds like a great idea."

"I'd better get my horse," Longarm said, striding off the porch, "before they set fire to the livery stable."

"I'll go with you," Gus said, falling into step beside the marshal.

The general store was now a crackling shell of leaping flames and snapping boards. Occasional muffled explosions from within, like firecrackers under a tin can, indicated that the flames were reaching what stores of ammunition the place stocked. Longarm and Gus hurried past, ducking, as the detonating rounds increased in volume and frequency. The loggers, with flaming torches in their hands, were darting through the wet night firing every structure they could find upright, not missing the tents. The small shanties and the tents went quickly. The night was soon filled with lurid islands of dancing flames. It was surprising how quickly and easily the rain-dampened structures ignited.

Reaching the livery stable, Longarm found that the hostler had driven all the horses into the corrals and was busy quieting them down as more and more structures around him leaped into flames. Fortunately, the loggers had decided to spare the stable. Longarm saw that his Morgan was safe and gave the hostler a silver dollar to keep an especially good eye on it. The fellow's enthusiasm increased enormously.

The mill had not yet been fired. Loggers dashed past him, heading for it. A few stopped as they saw Longarm without a torch, held their flaming brands close to see who he was, then dashed off. Every one of the loggers with arson still on his mind was heading now for the mill.

Shots came from behind Longarm. He looked back and saw Slade and about six of his riders bearing down on him, with his regrouped loggers trotting right behind. The pro-union loggers were scattered and disorganized. Slade's orderly phalanx easily overmatched the isolated pockets of torch-bearing loggers. His armed riders found that the torches made excellent targets. Shots rang out in a steady fusillade. Longarm saw logger after logger stumble and fall, their torches guttering out on the rain-soaked ground.

Now the mill became a rallying point for the suddenly beleaguered loggers. Longarm and Gus also began to run toward the mill, through a rain that had begun to slant down with increased intensity. As Longarm ran, he turned occasionally and snapped off a shot at Slade. Gus, wielding Fitz's Peacemaker, fired a round or two also. Their combined effort was troublesome enough to cause Slade to pull back and regroup his riders.

In that time, Longarm and Gus reached the mill and dashed inside with loggers holding peaveys right on their heels. Soon the mill was swarming with loggers, as Slade and his own force surrounded it. The rain was now coming down with a ferocity that caused the metal roof of the mill to drum with an almost deafening clamor. Peering out of one of the windows, Longarm saw Slade on his horse, hunched under the force of the driving sheets of rain, directing his loggers to burn the mill.

"I know you're in there, Longarm!" Slade shouted above the rain's roar. "It's going to be a terrible fire!"

But his loggers were having trouble firing the mill in the rain. Flaming boards or beams that they snatched up from the burning shacks around the mill were either extinguished by the heavy rain or petered out and died before they could get the drenched mill to catch. Hurled peaveys from the besieged loggers took a steady toll of Slade's loggers as they attempted, again and again, to hurl burning brands into the mill. And·then Longarm saw a few loggers rolling barrels of what he presumed to be kerosene down the street toward the mill.

Thunder crashed overhead, further deafening them. Lightning crackled. As the forks of blue fire flickered overhead, Longarm and the loggers in the mill had no difficulty seeing Slade's loggers rolling the kerosene barrels closer toward them. They began to shout obscenities at the pro-union loggers, which only drew the fire of Slade and his riders. Longarm nudged Gus, then led him down to the second level of the mill and in under the saw's framing. The area was almost hip-deep in sawdust that had backed up from the huge pile outside.

Here, Longarm was sure, was where those loggers with the kerosene barrels were headed. He glanced at Gus. The man nodded, understanding perfectly. A second later, a long series of rippling tongues of lightning boiled above them in the sky. In that light, Longarm saw four loggers rolling their kerosene barrels in under the mill, directly toward them.

Above the pounding of the rain and the crackling of the thunder, Longarm yelled at them to pull back. They didn't hear him. Their heads were down as they rolled the barrels still closer. Then they let go and the barrels kept rolling, bumping finally to rest against the pilings the mill was resting on. Behind them appeared one of Slade's gunmen. His revolver gleamed in the night as he aimed at the barrels.

Longarm fired at the man, the slug catching him in the chest, spinning him back into the wet night to be replaced by another of Slade's men, this one armed with a Winchester. Before either Longarm or Gus could get off a shot, the man sent a rapid-fire volley at them. As Longarm ducked low, the slugs whining off the beams, Slade's man directed his fire at the four barrels.

One barrel would have been enough. Four was too much. The explosion flung Longarm completely out from beneath the pilings and up onto the huge sawdust pile behind the mill. A stunned Gus hurtled after him. At the same time, the exploding barrels—with a fierce series of detonations—sent out ribbons of flame that caught up Slade's rifleman before he could regain his feet. The man disappeared into the maw of fire and smoke without a sound. In almost the same instant, flames began consuming the pilings on which the mill

200

rested and started licking hungrily at the rough flooring above. Just below this, the waist-deep sawdust ignited with an explosive roar, the flames reaching out to the main pile, causing it to smolder despite the rain.

Screams and savage oaths came from within the mill. In the light of the fire, Longarm saw some loggers jumping from the mill to the ground, while others dove out of windows to land alongside Longarm and Gus on the sawdust pile. They promptly scrambled off and vanished into the darkness. It was the only course open to them now as the flames engulfed the mill. Some of the loggers remained trapped inside. Their screams infuriated and sickened Longarm.

Slade's riders appeared now out of the darkness, still on their horses, shooting up at those loggers hanging from windows or making ready to jump. One logger, perched on the steaming metal roof, hesitated before making such a jump. He was shot before he could make up his mind and plummeted to the ground. Slade's loggers began running down those loggers fleeing the mill, catching them in the back with their long pike poles.

Longarm and Gus were at the top of the sawdust pile. They kept to a prone position and were almost entirely concealed by the sawdust as they shot at carefully chosen targets. With some satisfaction, Longarm saw one rider he caught in the side tumble from his saddle to lie without moving in a flaming pool of mud. Another target, one of Slade's loggers, was busily impaling a wounded logger on the end of his pike pole. Longarm's slug caught him on the side of his head. The logger on the ground, the pole still in his side, crawled off as the first gray streak of dawn light filtered down into the drenched valley.

They had fought clear through the night and Longarm had only six rounds left in the pocket of his ruined frock coat. Fortunately, he had two cheroots left. He handed one to Gus and proceeded to reload his Colt.

"They're wet!" Gus complained.

"I know it. Chew on it. Smoking's a disgusting habit anyway."

"You ought to quit, then."

"I'm trying. Why do you think I gave you my last cheroot? Now shut up and let me reload. Slade's men are nosing around down there."

The mill crackled in the fire. The day brightened but the rain kept up.

Chapter 10

The mill collapsed, seemingly as much from the pressure of the pounding rain as from the flames. Scalding, billowing clouds of steam rose up as the walls of still-burning logs tumbled down onto the soaked ground. The loggers were gone from the mill area, most of the pro-union men undoubtedly forted up now in their vermin-infested railway bunkhouses, waiting for the storm to pass.

Slade had pulled his men back from the sawdust pile and now sat his horse alongside his four remaining riders, his derby pulled tightly down upon his bald skull, his bulldog chin set, as the rain slammed down onto him.

"I know you two are up there!" Slade cried suddenly, cupping his hands about his mouth. "You can't stay on that sawdust pile forever, Longarm! Not unless you aim to eat it!"

Dim, grudging laughter greeted this remark from the soaked riders beside Slade. The men had lost too many comrades this past night to be really loose. By this time it was light enough for Longarm to see Slade clearly—and for Slade and his men to see Longarm and Gus just as easily.

"Do you want to go down there and trust to the mercies of that crew?" Longarm asked Gus.

"Hell's bells, Longarm! There's only five of them. We can take 'em!"

"They're out of range of these sixguns."

"We'll trick 'em!"

"How?"

"We'll make like we're coming down peaceful. Then, when we get close enough, we can open up on them."

The plan was insane, of course. It gave them about as much of a chance as a hen at a coyote convention. Slade would not let either of them get that close while both men kept their weapons. And Longarm knew his derringer, carrying only two rounds, would not be enough. Not for five men, anyway. In addition, the flesh wound in his shoulder was beginning to ache fiercely, indicating to Longarm that he must have torn open the wound when he was sent flying ass-over-teakettle out onto this pile of wood shit.

Still, it *was* a plan. If there was little chance of its succeeding, at least it gave Gus and him something to do in the next fifteen minutes besides get rained on.

Abruptly, the rain's intensity increased. What had been a moderate, steady drizzle became almost instantly a solid, battering downpour. There was no mercy in it whatsoever. It felt like someone upstairs was emptying buckets; raindrops pounded like buckshot as they plastered Longarm's coat to his back, drummed furiously on his hat, then ran like minature waterfalls off the brim.

And it kept up. Through the sheets of rain Longarm could no longer make out Slade and his riders. *Now!* he thought. *Now!* This cloudburst could not last forever. He tugged on Gus's sleeve.

"Let's go!" he shouted into Gus's ear. "Head for the river!"

Gus nodded and began to paddle backward through the heavy sawdust. By now the pile was so completely saturated with water that Longarm felt at times that he was in danger of drowning in the stuff. At last he pulled himself free and the two men started racing through the almost blinding rain toward the tracks and the river beyond.

By the time they reached the tracks, the downpour had run its course, and the almost solid curtain of rain began to lift. Longarm glanced back. Slade and his men were still busy quieting their mounts. In a moment, however, the man would look over and spot them. From that time on it would be an uneven race to the river—Slade and his men riding horses, Longarm and Gus relying on shanks' mare.

A queer vibration seemed to fill the air and then sink into the ground beneath Longarm's feet. He glanced at Gus, who was himself looking quickly and nervously about. It felt like a heavy freight barrelassing down a steep grade—a *very* steep grade and a *very* heavy freight. Longarm looked up. Something strange was indeed happening. The mountainside beyond Whipsaw was changing its shape—rapidly. It appeared to be shrinking some, or perhaps settling. But, no, it wasn't just settling at all. *The whole mountainside was piling down on them!* The trembling was no longer confined to the ground; the very air itself was trembling, with a bone-rattling, buffeting force that beat on Longarm like a fierce wind.

Slade and his men were bent over their horses, trying to outride the mudslide. Some of the men began to cut toward the river. In a panic, Slade followed. The horses had broken from their corrals, and, like Slade and his men, were digging hard for the river. All of this Longarm watched, fascinated, as the entire side of the mountain—its broad slopes so recently plucked bare of its trees and grasses—swept down in a colossal tide of mud and debris. It had not yet struck the town, but Longarm realized that when it did, it would obliterate everything. A massive, thick, pudding-like soup, it carried on its crest a monstrous tangle of tree trunks and stumps, and a few boulders that shone in the rain like teeth in an old man's mouth.

The hotel crumbled, then was swept along, becoming a part of this monstrous mudslide that rushed over Whipsaw with an ease and speed that was awesome. The still-smoldering remains of the general store and the Paradise Valley went next. Longarm turned and headed for the river at a dead run. Gus was already well ahead of him. As Longarm reached the dark, swollen river, he paused to look back.

Loggers were streaming from the bunkhouse toward the river. Slade and his riders had almost reached it. The horses were already there, plunging in. Longarm thought he could see the hostler, well behind his horses—too far behind.

The tide of mud rolled and roared across the length of what had been Whipsaw's main drag. It absorbed everything in its path, advancing in a crescent shape that sent before it a forelip almost ten feet high, making a titanic hissing sound and nosing to the right and to the left as if it were on the spoor of still more buildings to devour—which, of course, it was. The mill's wreckage was swallowed up and the bunkhouses were lifted from their tracks and swept along.

Longarm turned and dove into the river. He was more than halfway across when he felt the water under him rise suddenly and begin to carry him with extraordinary speed to the opposite bank. Tumbling, he struck solid ground, remembering vaguely that he must keep going. Scrambling to his feet, he headed for the slope ahead of him. He might have made it if a very wet, gritty, heavy hand had not struck him down from behind. . . .

Incredibly, the sun was out. Its warmth poured down from a cloudless sky. Longarm groaned and turned his head away from it, then pushed himself to a sitting position. He found that every muscle in his body was singing a different tune. Some springs were missing and some bolts were loosened, but nothing was broken clean through.

He was covered from head to foot with a crust of dried mud. When he turned his head, he felt the dirt inside his collar grating against the skin of his neck. In a sudden burst of concern, he reached up for his hat.

"I got it right here," Gus drawled from behind him.

Longarm turned. Gus, sitting farther up the slope, handed him his hat.

"Been sitting here with nothing to do except listen to your godawful groaning. So I figured I might as well spend my time doing something helpful, and cleaned your hat. You'll have to clean the rest of yourself in the river. Your clothes, too. All that dried mud'll scratch you to death if you try walking in them now. You don't have to worry none about going naked. There ain't a girl left over there."

Longarm placed his hat gingerly on his head and eased himself up beside Gus. From where they were sitting, they could look across the river at what was left of Whipsaw. There wasn't much—only the burnt-out shells of two shacks, and a tent at the far end of town.

Longarm looked back at Gus. "*All* of the girls, Gus?"

Gus nodded gloomily. "They all went to the hotel when the fires and the rain started. And some of them was trapped in the Paradise Valley, I guess. Don't matter where they were, they're all gone now. Snuffed out."

"I'm sorry about Alice, Gus."

"She was a fine little chippy, Longarm. She wasn't one bit like them other girls. Kind and considerate, she was. That's why Ruby liked her so much. I liked her from the start, Longarm, the first time I seen her get off that train in Silver City."

"She was some girl, Gus, that's for sure." Longarm

found he could not look into Gus's eyes as he replied. "And you're right. Ruby did feel kind of partial to her." Longarm decided not to tell Gus of Slade's revelation to him concerning Alice.

"Well," Gus sighed, "there's no sense in crying over spilt milk. But I sure will miss her."

"I won't miss Whipsaw, Gus—and very few of the ranchers around here will, either."

"I guess you won't, at that. But them out-of-work loggers over there will. Some of them, anyway."

Gus was referring to a large contingent of loggers that had made it across the river and settled into a makeshift camp on this side. There were a few Digger-like shelters fashioned out of logs and slash, some fire pits, and that was about all. The river itself survived at this point only as a narrow channel, since the mudslide had almost completely blocked it. The new, narrower channel cut close to where Longarm and Gus were sitting. It looked as if a permanent and very wide meander in the river had been created, but the flow had not been interrupted, and for that the ranchers to the south could be grateful. The mountainside facing them from across the river looked raw—as if it were the carcass of some enormous animal whose hide had been ripped off, revealing the vital organs beneath.

Longarm stood up to get a better view of it, as well as of the valley that had been so ruthlessly stamped out. Gus stood up also, and pointed to the crest of the range.

"I'll bet it all started up there," he said. "There was a ridge along that crest. It's gone now. That was the first place we cut. I remember the deep fault behind it, some nice big fir was growing in it. We cut every one, first thing. The whole ridge must have just peeled right off."

Longarm nodded. That seemed likely. He'd been up there, he remembered, and seen for himself the condition of that slope. Of course, there was no way anyone was going to be able to find out for sure. The important thing was that Slade was stopped.

"Where's Slade?" Longarm asked.

"He's long gone. While you was having your little snooze, the loggers who made it across went after Slade. He only had four riders left when he hightailed it out of this valley, heading north just ahead of the loggers. Some followed him for a while on them horses that made it across—but they've all straggled back. Slade lost them in the desert."

Longarm immediately began to undress. "What happened to that hostler?"

"He never made it."

For some reason, that bothered Longarm. He shook his head, seeing in his mind's eye the lone figure running through the rain toward the river—so far behind the horses. "Go see if you can find that Morgan of mine, will you, Gus? I won't be long here. I can ride in wet clothes; this sun'll dry me fast enough. I don't want Slade to get too far ahead of me."

"You mean *us*, Longarm. I'm going too."

"Why?"

"Didn't he kill Tanner?"

Longarm considered this for a moment. "Yes, I'm pretty sure he did, Gus."

"I'm going with you. And I don't want no argument."

Longarm smiled and began peeling off his mud-encrusted pants. "I wasn't about to argue, Gus. Pick out a horse for yourself while you're at it. And see what gear you can rustle up."

As Longarm stepped out of his pants, he glanced around and saw that Gus was already halfway to the loggers' camp.

By the time the two men reached the desert, Longarm

was thoroughly baked into his clothes. He was pleased to be riding the Morgan once again. Gus had chosen a grullo. What gear they had been able to wheedle from the few remaining loggers amounted to little more than a couple of torn slickers and a total of four canteens. Gus had the Peacemaker and about ten rounds. Longarm still had only six rounds. He had cleaned his gun carefully before setting out.

Slade's tracks pointed due north across an ancient lakebed that was now only a baked alkali flat. A tumble of rocks gradually reared out of the heat haze, and it was toward this pile that Slade and his men seemed to have headed. The fierce, dry heat pounded down relentlessly. They kept their horses to a slow but steady pace. After what must have been an hour, they seemed no closer to the rocks. Longarm felt as if he were being drowned in light as the sun's rays slanted up from the table-salt whiteness of the alkali. Gus and he were moving through a brilliant emptiness without end, without hope—a kind of inspired, hellish punishment.

At last, as if some force had abruptly lifted the rocks and placed them hundreds of yards closer, they were able to see the stretch of badlands as solid reality, less than half a mile ahead of them.

"I didn't thank you," Longarm said, mildly surprised at the sound of his own voice.

"For what?" Gus didn't bother to turn his head.

"For pulling me out of that mudslide."

Gus shrugged. "I didn't want to leave you there. You looked like a beached catfish. When that slide hit the water, it was like a boot splashing into a puddle. You just got caught by a part of that puddle when it came back down. It was muddy, all right, and filled with slash, and it just about drowned you."

A canyon opened up before them. Leading the way, Longarm guided the Morgan into its blessed coolness. Once through the canyon, however, they found themselves lifting into a bleak, inhospitable graveyard of stone monoliths and spires. They passed under great, leaning gargoyles of stone.

"We better find some water," Gus said.

A shot rang out—from a revolver, judging by the sound of it. And then came another shot, the two echoes rolling frantically about them among the rocks. But no bullets whined close. Pulling up, Longarm looked at Gus.

Another shot sent its echo rolling after the others.

"Someone's in trouble," Longarm said, starting up again. "Off to our right here, I think."

Gus offered no contrary opinion, and followed Longarm into a narrow ravine. As they proceeded along the narrow trail between almost sheer cliffs, Longarm caught sight of a man propped against a boulder, his hat still on, his feet spread, a canteen resting in front of him in the sand. As they rode closer, the man raised his revolver heavenward and pulled the trigger. The man was too far gone to look up and see them approaching.

He began to tip over on his side. The gun fell from his hand and went clattering among the rocks, striking his canteen and sending it spinning away. By the time Longarm had reached the man and dismounted, the fellow was lying on his stomach. Gus dismounted, knelt quickly and pulled the man over. After one look at the swollen, greenish face, he turned to Longarm and shook his head.

"He's been drinking bad water—very bad water."

The man's eyes flickered open. He saw Gus leaning over and tried to talk to him. His eyes widened with the effort. Gus leaned close and Longarm knelt beside him.

" . . . water hole. I didn't believe them . . ." the dying man gasped. " . . . didn't believe!"

"Which way is Slade headed?" Longarm asked.

"North to the pines . . . get the Diggers . . . need food . . . water . . . "

211

Longarm stood up and went to his horse for the only canteen he had left with water in it. He was on his way back when he saw the man's eyes close and his head dip. Gus caught his head before it tumbled heavily down among the sharp rocks, then slowly lowered the man's body carefully onto the gravelly ground.

"That's one less to worry about," Longarm said, continuing to unscrew the canteen. He lifted the canteen to his mouth.

"Better go easy with that," Gus said, "until we find a spring or a water hole in this badland somewhere. And we better be more careful than he was."

Longarm nodded, took another swallow, and handed the canteen to Gus. He took a short swig, handed it back to Longarm, and said, "Let's go. The buzzards in this part of the world will be real pleased to see a fat meal like that frying on these stones." Gus looked skyward and called softly, "Dinner is served, you bastards!"

They didn't mount up again, but led their horses on through the ravine. Once they were beyond it, Longarm cut sign once again. He found he was following a trail that now led due west. To Digger country, of course. Longarm thought of Barbara Spencer Tate and became suddenly nervous. He knew he shouldn't be. Those Diggers—no, no, *Paiutes*—would take good care of the anthropologist. But still he worried . . . .

A water hole gleamed just before them. It was close in under the canyon wall, an overhanging ledge offering welcome shade. Longarm was out of his saddle before Gus, kneeling beside the still pool. The water was clear, but there was a faint sulfurous stink in the air. A few wild onions grew about it, but little else. Peering closer into the cool, icy, immaculate depths, he saw no bugs, no algae scum, no worms, grubs, or spiders. Nothing alive. The smell had warned him, and the lifeless look

212

of the water had convinced him. Gus, beside him, had seen what Longarm had. They both got to their feet.

"Looks so damn innocent and pure, don't it?" said Gus, shaking his head. "That's what fooled that poor bastard back there. The others likely warned him, but he let his eyes buffalo his good sense. He'd've been better off cutting his throat. I figure there's arsenic in that water—a good dose—along with a few other goodies."

Longarm turned back to his horse and mounted up. As Gus climbed up beside him, Longarm said, "We might as well follow those bastards as far as we can. There's water near the pine slopes. I know a spot."

Gus nodded. Longarm prodded the Morgan on. He didn't look back at the spring.

It was near sundown when they reached the barren, sage-dotted foothills of the range that still shimmered, a blue mirage, in the distance. There was not a drop of water left in their canteens, and the horses were beginning to stumble. They dismounted and led the horses through the foothills. It was a long trek, and by this time Longarm was more concerned with finding water than he was with staying on Slade's trail. He could pick that up later. The Paiutes would help. What they needed now—the horses, Gus, and himself—was water. Good old scummy, grubby, weed-infested water.

Out of nowhere, it seemed, clouds began to form over the range. They multiplied and merged, piling up like mashed potatoes, like sea foam—building upon one another like a second mountain range, greater than the one below it. The cloud forms seemed to jostle as they merged. As they walked wearily toward the building clouds, hope kindled in Longarm's breast. There was water in those clouds, plenty of it. The only question was, where would they let it down?

He heard thunder. More clouds seemed to form in the empty sky to merge with the others. The clouds began to shoot higher. Stratospheric winds began flattening their tops, giving them an anvil-like shape. Lightning glinted in their slate-gray bowels. The storm clouds began to spread rapidly now, taking over more of the sky. They were coming closer. The thunder was beginning to rock the hills around them.

Longarm stopped in his tracks. He could smell rain. Gus had pulled up also, and looked at him quizzically. They were both too dry to want to converse unless they had to.

"Dig holes," Longarm told Gus. "Line them with the slickers."

"You think we'll get it? That storm looks like it's on the other side of them mountains."

"Dig."

With a weary shrug, Gus followed Longarm's example and walked out to a flat expanse of alkali. Longarm broke the surface of the ground with his gun barrel, then scooped out the sand and gravel. Alkali dust soon covered his face and stung his eyes mercilessly. The sweat carried the alkali deep into the corners of his eyes, into his nostrils, and even into his grimly compressed mouth. But he kept digging, with his hands now, gouging out as deep a basin as he could.

When he had dug so deeply that his elbows were below the surface of the flat, he got up and untied the slicker from behind the cantle on the Morgan. He inspected it carefully, found no holes or rents in it, and then lined the hole with it. He stood back and looked over to see that Gus was about finished as well.

Then he glanced up at the sky. The storm was coming this way. Most of the sky was covered now with low, boiling clouds. Lightning stroked like gunfire through the clouds and Longarm caught himself remembering that ledge he had shared with Terry Troy not so long ago. He shook away the memory, saddened instantly by a sharp sense of loss, and felt volleys of thunder shake the air. He could smell ozone. The wind was rising. Longarm ducked his head and held onto his hat brim. When the horses began to drift back, he reached out for the Morgan's bridle and held it. Broad, dried streaks of lather covered the animal's chest and flanks.

Above them the clouds rolled in, thickening, then cracking and spitting with a roar that staggered them. Longarm clutched the horses's bridle tighter, not sure who was steadying whom. A flash of lightning—like a knife slashing open a belly—cut the clouds, and the rain came down.

Longarm took off his hat and held it out to fill for the Morgan. Then he tipped his head back and let the pounding drops clean out his eyes and face. His body absorbed the moisture hungrily, like a sponge. It took no time at all for his hat to fill. He placed it down carefully on its crown and walked over to the makeshift basins. His was full. While the rain still pounded down, he knelt by the basin and pushed his canteen under the roiling surface. The canteen was soon filled completely. He did the same with his second canteen, screwed the cap back on, then lay facedown on the soaked ground, ducked his head into the warm rainwater, and shook it.

Then he sat up, grinning over at Gus who was lying on his back, his face taking the full brunt of the downpour, his good eye closed tightly. Longarm took his canteens back to the horse and tied them to the saddle rings, then lifted the hatful of water to his horse's muzzle. She drank eagerly.

The rain began to trail off. The thunder and lightning passed over, and soon the rain diminished to a shower, then to a sprinkling, and finally to nothing at all. The clouds rumbled in the distance. A fresh, golden light broke through. Glancing up, Longarm saw a double rainbow, one foot of it lost on the pine slopes beyond the foothills.

The pine-clad mountains no longer looked so far away. They seemed invitingly close, fresh, and clear in the squeaky-clean air. Longarm glanced over at Gus, who was in the act of bringing his two canteens back to his horse, and said, "These horses need a rest. As soon as we get into those pines, we'll camp for the night. We can pick up Slade's trail tomorrow."

"You think the son of a bitch made it?" Gus asked.

Longarm nodded. "He's too goddamned mean not to have made it, I'm thinking."

Gus nodded and turned his attention to his horse. The animal wanted some more water. Gus picked up his hat and went back to his basin of rainwater. Longarm did the same.

Longarm woke from a sound sleep and turned his head. The bright white face of the moon was blocked entirely by the silhouette of an Indian. Longarm sat up. The Indian drove the end of his bow into the ground and hunkered down to face Longarm. In the bright moonlight Longarm recognized the face of Wanowi. The Paiute's bronzed, shiny countenance was troubled.

Longarm glanced across the dead campfire at Gus. The logger was sitting up warily, the Peacemaker gleaming dully in his hand.

"It's all right, Gus," Longarm said. "This Indian's a friend. His name is Wanowi."

"A Digger?"

"A Paiute. A member of a fast-declining Pleistocene culture."

"For Christ's sake, Longarm, speak plain."

Longarm smiled in the darkness and turned back to Wanowi. "What's wrong, Wanowi?" He didn't really have to ask. Evidently Slade had made his presence felt in the area already.

Wanowi gestured with his left arm and another Paiute slipped out of the pines and hurried toward them. This one dropped beside Wanowi and spoke rapidly in his own tongue to Wanowi, who listened intently, then turned back to Longarm.

"He say Miss Tate have trouble. Three riders in her camp. They go in her tent. Mr. Slade—Little Man With No Hair—is their leader. They have rifles. Shoot Indians, many."

Longarm threw back the slicker and stood up. "Where were you through all this, Wanowi?"

Wanowi pointed south. "My people gather nuts. It is our time—our grove. We spend week in harvest. Miss Tate stay near stream. She speak much to paper. She study many books. Busy."

"Okay. I understand." Longarm turned to Gus. "If Slade is still messing up the woman's camp, maybe we can catch up to him. I'm assuming this Indian scooted out of the place without being seen."

"Who the hell is this Miss Tate?" Gus asked.

"It's too difficult to explain, Gus. I don't rightly know, myself. She's a different kind of woman than I've been used to. Just get a move on. The horses are rested plenty. We should get there by sunup if this moon holds."

"Well, this dang moon ain't going to hold, and I just wish I could get a plain answer from you, *Mister* Longarm. I never heard there was a girl out here living with them Indians. Why the hell didn't anyone tell me?" He shook his head emphatically and knelt to roll up his slicker. "Never heard of such a crazy thing. Woman's probably tetched in the head . . . "

He was still grumbling when they mounted up and started north, the Paiutes trotting along beside them in the moon-dappled darkness.

It was past sunup when Longarm and Gus broke onto the meadow above the stream and started across it to the Indian encampment. A few of the wickiups had

217

been knocked aside, Longarm noted, but the tent was still sitting proudly on the grassy sward across the stream. For a moment Longarm had the absurd feeling that Wanowi—for some inexplicable reason—had lied to him, that he had invented the entire story.

And then he saw Barbara. She was in the midst of a small crowd of Indian women on the far side of the stream, spreading out blankets and sheets on the grass. The Paiute womens' hair seemed more than usually wild, Longarm thought. She was directing the operation with such intensity that she did not see Longarm and Gus at first. When she did glance up to see them, she stood up straight, looking as cool as he had remembered, still wearing her pith helmet, the golden bun of her hair resting on the nape of her neck, gleaming in the bright morning sunshine. She waved only once as Longarm and Gus rode closer.

"I see what you mean," Gus said grimly. "What in hell is that she's got on her head?"

"A sun helmet, favored by British soldiers fighting in the tropics. Keeps the head cool enough."

"Looks like a beehive."

Longarm had reached the stream by that time. He dismounted and left his horse with the same Indian woman who had taken her before. He told her to remove the Morgan's saddle, then led Gus across the stream to the waiting Barbara Spencer Tate.

"Meet Gus, Barbara," Longarm said.

"It is a pleasure, Gus," Barbara said.

"Gus, this is Barbara Spencer Tate, anthropologist."

"Howdy, Miss Tate." Gus was obviously as impressed by her jodhpurs and hunting outfit as by the steady gaze from her cool, hazel eyes.

Longarm turned back to Barbara. "Wanowi told us you had some visitors."

"Shall we make ourselves comfortable?" she asked him.

Longarm nodded, and with a quick wink at Gus, led him up the small slope to Barbara's tent. At once Longarm noticed that there were only four folding chairs where before there had been six. The table was gone as well. A small, ragged piece of canvas was lying some distance away near the pinyon grove. Without saying anything, Longarm sat down. Gus had some difficulty getting his huge frame comfortable in his chair. He seemed to be afraid it would collapse under him. Barbara ignored Gus's uneasiness and addressed Longarm.

"A small, defenseless little girl and two of the Indians left behind to guard this encampment were brutally murdered, Longarm. I shall never forget it. Never."

"How many men were there?"

"Three."

"And one of them was Slade Desmond?"

"Yes. The pig introduced himself to me. A small man, bald, wearing a ridiculous little derby."

Longarm glanced at Gus, then back at Barbara. "Wanowi said they entered your tent. I'm glad to see you're all right."

"They proposed to rape me, Longarm. Fortunately, they decided to do it one at a time. Unfortunately, Slade Desmond was outvoted by his hirelings—so he was not the first."

Longarm saw Gus's face go pale, and realized that he didn't feel so good himself. He swallowed, but his mouth had suddenly dried up.

"The first one—a pale, furtive slug—was foolish enough to be carried away by the sight of a naked woman waiting for him in a prone position. He dropped his gunbelt and hurried to me." She paused. Longarm saw her face whiten and her eyes grow bleak. "He did not see the knife I held at my side. . . ." She swallowed and went on. "Afterwards, as soon as I could, I snatched up his gun and managed to shoot the next in

219

line. But I missed Slade when the two of them rode out. . . ."

There was an awkward silence for a moment until Longarm cleared his throat nervously and asked, "You say you wounded one of them?"

"Yes. And killed the other. I . . . was not careful how I did it, I am afraid. At the moment I'm concerned primarily with cleaning the sheets and blankets. I only wish I could completely remove the stains from the cot." Her white teeth closed upon her upper lip. She bowed her head, her forehead resting in her palm.

Longarm saw her shoulders trembling as tears began to break through what had been an iron composure. He looked sharply at Gus and got to his feet. Gus stood up also. They left her and walked toward the trees. This gave her the opportunity she wanted, and she hurried into the tent.

Well into the pines, they came upon a fresh grave. There was no marker. There didn't need to be. Longarm knew who was under that fresh earth. The first eager rapist.

"She'll be all right in a little while," Gus said softly, hopefully.

"Yes," Longarm agreed.

"You were right, Longarm. She's a different kind of woman, all right."

Chapter 11

Four Paiutes with Wanowi leading them helped Longarm and Gus track Slade and his wounded sidekick. Late that same day they came to the end of the pine forests. Ahead of them lay treacherous, gullied badlands. Gaunt, shadowed buttes and mesas poked almost straight up. The entire, savage land seemed to possess neither grass nor water. Into this inhospitable land the tracks of the two horses led.

Longarm pulled up and looked at Gus. "Ambush country. They can fort up in there for as long as they need to."

"If they got water and food."

"They can shoot food, and there's probably water. They'll work their way through in about a week and be in Utah then."

Longarm dismounted for a conference with Wanowi. The Indian seemed eager to move into the badlands after the two men.

"Wanowi, let us go on. We can track these two ourselves, now. And we can go faster with our horses."

"Wanowi go, too," the small Indian insisted grimly.

"No. This is my business, Wanowi, my job. Remember, I'm a federal marshal. I represent the government."

The Indian wavered. "We can help, Longarm."

"You already have. Please go back and see to Miss Tate. She needs your help now."

The Indian drew himself up to his full five and a half feet, stared proudly back at Longarm for a moment, then nodded solemnly. "We go back to Miss Tate. Good luck, Longarm." He turned to Gus. "Good luck, Gus."

It was the first time Wanowi had spoken to Gus, since Gus, after all, was one of those loggers who had been tearing down their pine forests. Gus was pleased and, smiling slightly, he nodded curtly in response.

As the Paiutes trotted back into the timber, Longarm remounted and led the way down a narrow ravine.

They came to a sluggish, slimy little creek and forded it easily. The tracks of Slade and the other man were still deep in the soft sand beside the creek. A swarm of deerflies attacked them. One landed in Gus's hair and attached itself to his scalp. When Longarm noticed the blood flowing down the back of Gus's neck, he alerted the man, who slapped furiously at the fly, killing it. Longarm squashed another that had taken root on his own forearm. Only when they had gone a decent distance from the creek were they free of the little bastards.

They moved still deeper into the shadowed, gloomy country. The grass was scarce, the walls sheer and striated, so tall in places that they blocked out the sky for long stretches. The tracks of the two men, however, remained clear. Longarm was sure they were gaining.

Soon they turned into a dungeonlike defile that turned and twisted like a snake under overhanging and interlocking walls so high, so close, that this time Longarm found he could catch not even a glimpse of the sky. The floor of the cleft was irregular, wet, sandy, and in places rather soupy. The defile opened up at last and led onto a wide, flat rock serving as the floor of a broad canyon. The stream that had cut this canyon was only a thin, sluggish trickle as they approached it.

Longarm dismounted, and so did Gus. They let their

222

horses blow and get their fill of water. The two men silently filled their canteens, both of them looking idly about at the towering, forbidding walls. Slade's tracks had led out onto this canyon floor and then disappeared on the hard limestone. There were many exits from this canyon, any one of which could have been taken by the fleeing men.

But perhaps by this time Slade wasn't fleeing any more.

They mounted up and were riding down the canyon, both men keeping their eyes on the rocks above, watching for any glint of sunlight on metal, when they heard a faint and mournful wail. It did not seem to be coming from anything human. It appeared to emanate from abysmal depths far back in the bowels of this underworld of twisted canyons and hidden passageways.

Longarm pulled up, his head cocked, trying to locate the source of this weird cry. Both he and Gus decided on a dim, shadowed cleft in the canyon wall, and spurred cautiously toward it. As they rode into the narrow wash, the cry became slightly louder and seemed to be coming out of the very rock walls themselves. A terrifying caterwauling it was, multiplied and amplified by echoes piled on echoes, overlapping and reinforcing one another. Both Longarm and Gus found themselves nervously looking over their shoulders from time to time as they continued on down the snaking arroyo.

They broke out onto a small open space and saw at once the source of the awesome clamor. Not Slade, but a man who was obviously his wounded companion was slowly sinking into a patch of quicksand, while his horse calmly cropped some grama near a small stream only thirty or so feet away.

"Help me!" the man cried. "Get me out of here! I'm sinking!"

The two riders pulled up. The stricken man was up to his waist in the stuff. It was evident that he could not get out. On the other hand, he did not appear to be sinking. His hat was gone and one side of his vest was ripped away to reveal a bloodied cotton shirt. This was the one Barbara had wounded. So where was Slade?

Gus and Longarm exchanged glances as if the same thought had occurred to both of them simultaneously. Longarm looked back at the terrified man.

"Where's Slade?"

"The bastard left me here to die! He could have helped me, but he just rode off!"

Gus lifted off his hat and scratched his head. "How the hell did you get out there, mister? You picking flowers or something?"

"My horse! It stumbled in this muck and threw me. It got out all right, but it left me, the son of a bitch!"

The man was apparently beside himself. He began struggling again, which caused him to sink just a little farther. But Longarm was wary. He had never heard of a man buried completely in quicksand in his life. Most oldtimers he had talked to agreed that this was just an Eastern writer's fiction. Whenever animals and men were killed by quicksand, it was not through suffocation, but starvation or thirst. Quicksand could prevent an animal or a person from pulling free through his own frantic exertions. So Slade had left his friend trapped here to die by whichever came first—starvation or thirst.

"Shall we pull him out?" Gus asked reluctantly.

"Just hold it a minute," Longarm said. He looked around and up at the rock walls, searching for places where Slade could have settled himself while his live bait lured his pursuers into his trap. "That fellow ain't going anywhere in a hurry. Why don't we just look around?"

"Hey! You two ain't going to leave me here to die, are you?" the fellow cried in sudden panic. "You can't do that. Gus! You know me!"

Gus winced. "I *do* know the son of a bitch, Longarm," he admitted. "He was the only one of Bat's men who treated anyone decent. He wasn't exactly carrying a harp around with him, you understand."

"Pull him out if you want," Longarm said, "but I think you'd better let me look around first."

Gus paused to glance swiftly around him. "You think Slade's up there waiting somewhere?"

"What would you do if you were trying to shake two trackers hard on your tail?"

"Go ahead. Look around. I ain't anxious to get a bullet in my back."

Ignoring the frantic wails of the trapped man, Longarm and Gus rode back into the shadows of the arroyo and dismounted out of his sight. Gus winced as the fellow's cries became even more despairing and hopeless.

"Wait here," Longarm told Gus. "Two of us climbing around up there might warn Slade off, if that's where he is. Just stay in here out of sight. Let that jasper bleat all he wants."

Gus nodded and Longarm moved back into the arroyo, looking for a way up either side. He found a rough trail, clambered past the loose talus, and began climbing. It took him a long time to reach the rim of the canyon wall surrounding the small pocket where Slade's man was trapped.

As Longarm searched the rimrock, he could not escape the strident cries of the fellow so far below him. They echoed and reechoed among the rock walls and off the boulders. It was as if the screams had a life of their own. The trapped man was obviously convinced by this time that all hope was lost, that Longarm and Gus had abandoned him. This added such a keening note of terror to the man's cries that it was difficult for Longarm to push them out of his mind as he continued to pick his way over the rocks and crevasses along the canyon's rim.

Mercifully, the wild pleas for help ceased. The echoes died. Longarm straightened. *Good,* he thought. *That jasper is getting hold of himself. About time. At the rate he was bellowing, the devil himself would slam the door in his face.* As Longarm thought this, he was in the act of clambering over a particularly craggy outcropping. Suddenly he froze. He had spotted the glint of sunlight on metal on a ridge just ahead of him. Dropping lower, he started up again and moved closer to the ledge, taking his time, putting each foot down with infinite care. He had long since taken off his spurs. A large boulder blocked his path. He was moving around it cautiously when he heard Gus's voice coming from far below.

Gus! You stupid son of a bitch! I told you to let the bastard scream!

Beyond the boulder, a rifle cracked sharply. A cry of pain came from below, to mingle with the echoes of the shot. Drawing his Colt, Longarm darted around the boulder and ran openly for the ledge.

Slade was waiting. Levering swiftly, the man sent a withering fire at Longarm. The marshal flung himself to the ground, digging his elbows and knees painfully into the rocky soil. He rolled and kept rolling until he found cover. Slade's fire followed him relentlessly, the slugs whining off the rocks like hornets out of hell. .

The Winchester's rapid fire ceased. Longarm looked over the boulder behind which he was crouched. Slade had disappeared. He was probably reloading. Keeping low, Longarm raced toward the ledge. Before he reached it, he heard the sound of hooves. Turning, he followed the sound, looked down, and saw Slade galloping down a narrow trail just below him. Steadying his Colt's barrel on the top of a boulder, Longarm sighted and fired.

Slade's horse pitched forward, sending him headlong over its neck. Longarm clambered down the rocky slope, jumped the remaining ten feet, and raced along the ridge toward Slade, who was crawling slowly and groggily away from the thrashing horse, his gleaming Smith & Wesson still miraculously in his hand. As Longarm approached, Slade managed to twist and get off a shot. Longarm felt the round whistle past his cheek a second before he booted the revolver out of Slade's hand.

Slade flung up both hands. "I'm unarmed!" he cried. "You've got to arrest me! You've got to take me in, Marshal!"

Longarm holstered his Colt. "That's right," he said softly. "I do, don't I?"

"That's right! That's right! And you'll find I haven't done anything wrong! That was a mistake! A mistake! That damn foreman didn't know how to read the map!"

Longarm's blue-gray eyes were cold as he reached his hand down to assist Slade in getting up. Slade took the offered hand and pulled himself erect. On his feet, he began to brush himself off, a swagger already creeping into his manner.

"You're acting wisely, Longarm. Very wisely. I understand that your handling of me just a moment before was . . . done in the heat of the moment. You'll find I am a man who does not hold grudges. Indeed, I can do things for you. This whole business has just been an unfortunate mistake. And I'm glad to see you're not like that fool, Tanner." The man's cold, tiny, black eyes appraised Longarm shrewdly. "After all, you don't want to be a deputy U.S. marshal for the rest of your life, do you?"

"Wasn't Tanner sensible, Slade?" Longarm asked.

"Indeed he wasn't. He kept spouting nonsense about ruining the valley. He threatened to expose me."

"So you shot him."

"I had to."

"Like you had to shoot Gus down there. In the back, most likely."

Slade caught the deadly edge in Longarm's voice. He started to take a step back. Longarm reached out, grabbed him by the shirt front, and pulled him close. He slapped Slade once, twice, then repeated the punishment. The man's eyes rolled back into his head as he slumped toward Longarm. Longarm flung him over his shoulder, then turned and clawed his way back up onto the ledge.

Looking down, Longarm saw Gus sprawled facedown close to the arroyo, a dark stain on his back. The man he had pulled from the quicksand was gone, his horse with him. Slade began to squirm. Longarm stepped to the very edge and lifted Slade over his head. Slade was immediately awake, and in that one terrible instant he knew what Longarm intended.

"No!" he cried. "No, Longarm! For the love of Jesus!"

Longarm dipped his knees slightly, then straightened and hurled his twisting, screaming burden down into the canyon. He watched coldly. The scream was cut off abruptly. Longarm turned away.

Slade's horse was still alive, thrashing feebly below him. Longarm dropped back down to the trail and took out his Colt. He moved around to the front of the animal for a clearer shot and saw the Paiute arrow imbedded in the horse's chest. Astonished, he looked quickly around him. The Indians had followed him, anyway. It was one of their arrows, not his bullet, that had stopped Slade.

Longarm glanced back at the horse. The animal was completely still now, the big eyes fogged, lustreless. He left the dead animal to the buzzards and continued along the trail Slade had been using. It led back down to the narrow arroyo. When Longarm reached the canyon, he found that Gus was still alive. Slade's bullet had chewed a nice chunk out of his back, just under the shoulder blade, exiting from the side. Gus had bled furiously, but if luck and meanness counted for anything, he would live.

Gus groaned slightly and began to curse.

Slade had struck the quicksand headfirst. All that remained-visible of him was a good portion of his hind end, and it didn't appear to be sinking in any deeper. *The oldtimers are right,* Longarm thought, as he pulled the barely conscious Gus to his feet and helped him to where their horses were waiting.

When Longarm and a slack, grim-faced Gus rode into the Paiute encampment close to sundown, Longarm found the Indians gone and three burnt-out wickiups still smoldering. Barbara was standing in the entrance to her tent, and hurried down the slope toward them as they rode through the abandoned camp.

"Wanowi told me you were dead, Gus," Barbara said, as she helped him down out of his saddle.

"Maybe I am," Gus grunted painfully. "I just don't want to come right out and admit it. But give me time. I just might any minute now."

"Don't you dare," she said.

As the big man leaned on her, she quickly inspected the rough blood-soaked bandage Longarm had wrapped around Gus's torso with strips torn from his shirt. She looked at Longarm with sudden concern.

"We'll take him to my tent," she said.

The moon had not yet risen, and it was dark when Barbara stepped out of her tent, wiped the beads of perspiration from her high forehead with the back of her hand, and walked over to sit down in a camp chair beside Longarm. His long legs were stretched out, and he

229

was wishing fervently for a cheroot, all the while cursing himself for an unregenerate tobacco fiend.

"How is he?" the lawman asked.

Barbara sighed wearily. "He's comfortable now, I think. I washed the wound out thoroughly, despite his rather salty protests. If he can get some sleep now, he should be all right. I'll let him have the tent to himself tonight. I can sleep outside."

"Did you say you washed out the wound?"

"Yes, with soap and water—very warm water. That's what I was doing, heating all that water in the skillets. Of course, as you said, you have never heard of Pasteur —or Lister, either, I am sure—so you would not understand why I did that."

"Nope—not unless soap and water are better than whiskey for washing out wounds. You say Wanowi was here earlier, before we got back?"

"Yes. He returned to help his people leave here. The Paiutes regard death as vindictive. Every effort must be made to break the ties between the dead and their survivors. So they burned the dwellings of those who died and have moved permanently from this place. When Wanowi spoke to me, he was quite pleased with himself. He said he helped you again, but did not prevent you from using your own magic on Slade." She turned her head toward Longarm. In the darkness, he could not read her expression, but her voice contained a note of cold hopefulness as she asked, "Slade is dead, I presume?"

"Yes, Barbara. But the man with him escaped."

"No, Longarm. He didn't. Wanowi told me about that as well. But I suppose, since you're a federal officer, it would be best if I simply didn't mention it to you again."

Longarm nodded. "I'd appreciate that." He rose to his feet. "I'm going in to talk to Gus."

"He needs his sleep, Longarm."

"I've got a few questions. I won't be long."

He could sense her looking at him sharply. "Are you still searching for that deserter, Longarm? The one riding a grullo?"

He smiled faintly. "Yes."

She was silent for a moment before saying, "You tell Gus I'm sorry I hurt him so when I cleaned out his wound."

"I'll do that, Barbara," Longarm assured her.

Gus was tossing fitfully on the cot. His one eye cast a fiery glare at Longarm when he entered the tent. The lamp was sitting on a table, its flame turned low. Gus spoke first.

"That woman must have thought she lost something inside me, Longarm, she dug in so deep."

"She's sorry she hurt you. She just told me to tell you that."

"Hell's bells, Longarm. She can hurt me all she wants. I like that woman. I just enjoy blowing off steam once in a while."

Longarm pulled up a canvas stool and sat beside Gus's cot. "I've got a few questions, Gus. Shouldn't take long."

Gus looked at him and smiled through his pain. "I guess you *must* have a few questions, at that."

Longarm chewed on the untrimmed edge of his mustache, then shook his head and asked, "Who in blazes are you, Gus? You sure as hell ain't Gus Dodds."

The logger seemed unaccountably amused. "Who am I, then?"

"Ned Shortslef—with his beard shaved off and an eye lost somewhere along the line. You really *don't* have an eye under that patch, do you?"

The big man chuckled, and lifted the eyepatch to reveal a scarred eyelid closed over a hollow, obviously empty eye socket. "You going to bring me in?"

"I have to, Gus," the tall deputy said regretfully. "I don't want to, but that's my job. That's what I've been doing up here—looking for you. I'm glad you didn't kill Tanner, but that doesn't change anything. Sorry, old son."

"You're just bound and determined to bring in Ned Shortslef. Is that it?"

"You heard what I said, Gus."

"Well, you can do it if you want, Longarm—if you don't mind digging up a grave and hauling in a corpse. You buried Ned Shortslef when you buried Martin Tanner."

Longarm pushed his hat back on his head and leaned closer. "Tanner?"

"That's right."

The lawman scratched his square, unshaven jaw. "You better explain that, Gus."

"I was in the Rosebud campaign with Ned. I scouted with him. Sat around many a fire with him and his woman and that kid of his. Hell, Ned never did kill any soldiers. All he did was drive away a foraging party from the camp, then help his wife and her clan to clear out of there before the cavalry turned up. Someone recognized Ned, though, so he had to light out and leave his people. He didn't want to bring down any more trouble on them."

Longarm shook his head. "That description, Gus. It was in the folder we got from the army. Tanner was not as big a man as Ned was described as being—as you and all the others described him. He was tough enough, I grant you that, but not a very big man."

"After the Rosebud campaign I was told to give a description of Ned to a shavetail from army intelligence. Seems they needed one, since they didn't keep very good records on scouts in them days. So I gave the lieutenant that description to throw the army off his tail. Hell, Longarm, that little fuzzy-cheeked lieutenant *ex-*

pected me to say that Ned was as big as a bear with a fine crop of hair on his face. That's what he expected an ex-Mountain Man to look like. He went away happy, and Ned changed his name to Tanner."

"Then why in hell did he telegraph Washington that he'd seen Ned Shortslef up here?"

"To bring in federal marshals like you, Longarm. To stir things up for Slade. To stop him. That girl Terry from the Flying T, and the other ranchers and the Indians, too, were in a fix. He promised he'd do what he could." Gus looked at Longarm. "And it looks like you did it for him, Longarm."

"Terry knew about all this, didn't she—along with you?"

"Why do you say that?"

"She went along with me when I described Ned to her, and said he'd been to the Flying T looking for work." Longarm stood up.

"You going to put all this in your report?"

"I think it'll be a lot simpler to bury that big Mountain Man with all the others who got caught in that slide. Besides, it's what happened to Whipsaw—and why—that's going to attract all the attention."

Gus sighed deeply and rolled over onto his back. He seemed mightily relieved. So was Longarm, as a matter of fact.

"Good night, Gus. Get some sleep."

Gus was too tired to reply.

Longarm left the tent. By now the moon had risen, and the three burnt wickiups of the Paiute encampment across the stream were skeletal in its pale glow. He found that Barbara had picked a spot some distance from the tent and put down a very luxurious, roomy sleeping bag. She was sitting beside it in a camp chair, dressed in a long white nightgown, combing out her golden hair. She had placed a camp chair beside hers and Longarm sat in it.

"How is he?" she asked.

"Better. He should be asleep soon."

"You look tired yourself."

"It's been a long day—and a grim one, Barbara."

"For both of us," she murmured softly.

Longarm nodded, took a deep breath, and leaned himself back in the chair in an effort to relax the tension that still held him. Whether he believed Gus's strange story was not important. It made sense, when just about everything else about that spectral deserter he had been tracking so fruitlessly made little sense at all. But the important thing was that he *wanted* to believe Gus.

"Longarm," Barbara said, "my father and I were very close. And one thing he told me I've never forgotten."

"What's that?"

"When something bad happens, wipe it off the slate with something nice."

"Sounds like a good idea, at that."

"Let's make something nice happen. Out here. Tonight. Under this canopy of stars."

Longarm looked at Barbara. There was a quizzical smile on his face. Then he nodded quickly. "Sounds like a fine idea."

She stood up. "I'll go in to check on Gus."

As she headed through the night toward the tent—a tall, pale, willowy apparition, her golden hair a spike of light down her back—Longarm undressed quickly, ran for the creek, and dove in. The icy waters braced him and cleared away the cobwebs and the unpleasantness of the past days.

The light in the tent was out and Barbara was waiting for him in the sleeping bag when he returned, still tingling, to her. As he settled in beside her, her fingers warmed him, playing softly over his body. He felt himself growing toward her. She moved closer and pulled

234

him against her, the awesome warmth of her body replacing the chill in his soul, and filling it with wonder —and desire.

The canopy of stars Barbara had mentioned rolled well across the heavens that night before either of them thought to look up again. . . .

SPECIAL PREVIEW

Here are the opening scenes
from
LONGARM AND THE HIGHGRADERS
seventh novel in the bold new
LONGARM series from Jove/HBJ

Chapter 1

Longarm entered the Manzanita Saloon to the lilting strains of "Garryowen," being played very fast on what sounded like tin pans. Had he come through the front entrance, he'd have been able to see who or what was making all that racket an hour before noon. But when a shifty-eyed stranger tells a lawman that someone is waiting for him in a saloon, then darts away before he can be questioned further, common sense dictates a prudent avenue of approach. So Longarm came in the back door.

There was a pantry to his right. The kitchen to his left was deserted. Longarm nodded. Drawing the .44-caliber Colt Model T he carried for just such mysteries as these, he eased toward the barroom on the balls of his feet. He moved quietly for a man of his size, but the music out front was so loud that he probably could have ridden a horse along the corridor without being noticed. It was a noisy place, considering that it seemed to be empty.

That was something to ponder. August was hotter than the hinges of hell in the Sierra foothills, and the dusty streets of Manzanita were devoid of life as the siesta hour approached. He'd only been in town about a half hour, and hadn't climbed up on a soapbox to announce his arrival. Yet the rat-faced little cowhand had been waiting in the empty street as Longarm had come out of the livery after leaving his army issue gelding in a cool stall. The hand had just said something about Longarm's being wanted over at the saloon, and then had slithered away like a sidewinder seeking shade under a flat rock.

Who in thunder could know he was in Manzanita? They were expecting him up at the mine, and he'd intended to pay a courtesy call on the local law before beginning his investigation, but he'd deliberately arrived two days early. It was surprising what a lawman could stumble over that way. Yet he'd been spotted the moment he had ridden in. Someone probably had a reason for watching the trail from Angel's Camp.

There was a bead curtain across the doorway into the barroom. The tall deputy stood in the shadows behind it as he studied the barnlike space on the other side of the beads. There was no bartender behind the long oak bar to his right. The rinkytink music was coming from a coin-operated harmonium against the wall to his left. In the middle of the room, seated at a table with his back to Longarm, was a dark figure in a brocaded charro outfit. A black sombrero hung on his back between his shoulders. The exposed hair was dishwater-blonde. Some Anglo had apparently taken to the Old California style, which made no never-mind to Longarm, but he did think the double-barreled shotgun the stranger held trained on the swinging doors to the sunlit street was a proper thing for any lawman to take an interest in.

Training his .44 on the man at the table, Longarm said, "You just freeze in place and *listen*, friend. I've got the drop on you. A sudden sneeze could get you killed. You got that much of my message, old son?"

Without moving a muscle, the man in the charro costume asked, "Is that you, Longarm?"

"Deputy U.S. Marshal Custis Long, at your service. In a minute, we'll palaver about who *you* might be, and why you have a scatter gun trained on the doorway you invited me through. Right now I want you to slide your chair back away from that gun on the table. Then I reckon you'd best put both hands on top of your golden locks and stand up slow and easy. I'll tell you when I want you to turn around."

The man at the table didn't do as he was told. He crabbed sideways off his chair, shotgun and all, and pivoted on one knee to fire.

He didn't make it. The twin barrels were three-quarters of the way around when the Colt kicked in Longarm's palm and the lawman's first slug slammed into the man's chest. The shotgun went off, blowing a hole in the baseboard of a corner as Longarm fired again. Between the recoil of the 12-gauge and the .44 slug that caught him just under one eye, the would-be ambusher was thrown flat on his back to the sawdust-covered planks. A booted heel drummed mindlessly a few times, as if dancing to the music box, and then the corpse lay very still, staring up into the drifting blue gunsmoke with a bemused smile.

Longarm parted the beads and strode over to stare down at the man he'd just shot. He was a total stranger. Longarm reached into the side pocket of his Prince Albert coat for two fresh rounds as he studied the odd situation. The harmonium tinkled merrily on as he thumbed the spent brass from his cooling weapon, wondering how to go about shutting the infernal contraption off. He muttered to the dead stranger. "You likely thought you were as smart as an old he-coon in a hen-house when you put a penny in and cranked her up, huh? What was I supposed to think it was, a piano being played in a crowded saloon?"

Holding the Colt in his right hand, Longarm dropped to one knee, being careful not to get the spreading blood on his tobacco-brown tweed as he went through the dead man's pockets with his free hand. The man he'd shot was about thirty, with one of those uninteresting faces you see every day. He'd backed his shotgun with a brace of Smith & Wesson .45s in a silver-mounted gunbelt. Longarm noticed that one of the ivory grips had been notched four times. He sighed and muttered, "Jesus, you've been reading Buntline for sure. No calluses worth mention on your gun hand, so despite the vaquero outfit, you ain't a dally roper. You're tanned enough to have been out in the sun a few years, so you ain't some loco Easterner playing big bad cowboy, either. But those notches don't make you look like anyone with a lick of sense. Who were you trying to scare?"

At that moment a shadow appeared in the front doorway and a voice called out, "What's going on in here? You are talking to the law!"

Longarm looked up at the worried-looking newcomer in the doorway and replied, "I'm law, too. Just shot it out with this cuss for some fool reason. I'm still trying to find out why." He reached into an inside coat pocket. Producing his wallet, he flipped it open. His badge glittered dully in the dim light filtering in from the street. "Custis Long," he said. "Deputy U.S. marshal out of Denver. Now who the hell are you?"

The Manzanita lawman came in to join him, introducing himself as one Constable Lovejoy. As he got his first good look at the body, he said, "Oh, Jesus H. Christ! You've shot the Calico Kid!"

"Is that who he was? The name doesn't mean much to me, Constable. I pride myself on a tolerable memory, but if any wanted fliers on a so-called Calico Kid have ever come my way, I disremember seeing them."

Lovejoy said, "God, this is awful! We have a nice, quiet little town here, and I don't have deputy-one who'd go up against the Calico Kid and all."

Longarm got to his feet, dusting off his trousers and holstering his sixgun as he studied the concerned-looking smaller man. Lovejoy was gray around the edges and had a slight pot. He had the kind of politician's face that seemed to be made for smiling a lot. But right now he looked as if he were getting ready to burst out crying. Longarm said, "He did seem to think he was one mean fellow, but I doubt that he'll give anyone any more trouble. You reckon he really shot four men like he bragged?"

"Hell, it's more like a dozen. I'm going to have to do something about this mess, Longarm."

Longarm managed not to raise an eyebrow. He had no memory of having told the constable his nickname. Counting the dead man at his feet, that made at least three people in Manzanita who had been expecting him to ride in early.

Playing dumb, the tall deputy said, "Well, it was open-and-shut self-defense, even if I wasn't packing a federal badge. I'll make a statement for the county before I mosey on."

Lovejoy said flatly, "Longarm, you ain't going *nowhere* in *this* county! You just shot the Calico Kid!"

Longarm pushed his Stetson back from his forehead. "You keep saying that like it's important. Who was he, the bully of the town?"

"Damn it, he was a *killer*. Meanest son of a bitch we've had in these parts since Joaquin Murietta rode through in '53!"

"Well, don't get your balls in an uproar. His killing days are over."

"Hell, I'm talking about his *friends*, Longarm!"

Longarm looked down at the glassy-eyed corpse and shrugged as he mused, "He had friends? Well, anything's possible, I reckon. The way it seems to read right now is that he recognized me as I rode in and decided to build his rep some more with an easy murder. If his plan had worked, you'd likely be telling him right now what a serious thing he'd just done. I've got friends, too. They call themselves the U.S. Justice Department."

The constable was sweating profusely now. "Yeah, but *your* friends ain't likely to ride in shooting in the next hour or so. The Calico Kid's friends *are!* You take my meaning?"

"I'm not sure. Since I don't have the calling for raising folks from the dead, what is it you've got in mind?"

"I want you to *git*, damn it! If you've a lick of sense you'll fork that pony you have over at the livery and ride out sudden and far!"

Longarm shook his head and said, "Can't. My outfit sent me here to do a job and I don't aim to ride anywhere till it's done. I'll help you put what happened here on paper, then I've got to head up to the Lost Chinaman diggings. I was aiming to poke around here in town for a spell before I rode up for a look-see at the mine itself. But since everyone seems to know Uncle Sam has a man in the field already, I don't reckon it's worth my time to jaw with the local barber and such."

Lovejoy hesitated. Then he nodded and said, "I figured you were on that case. We'd best go over to my office. If you won't leave peaceable, we may as well take down your statement and at least get you out on the trail. Calico rode with a mean bunch and at least one of them knows you just killed him."

Longarm thought, *Strike two!* but didn't say anything aloud as he followed the constable out the door. Other men were standing in the street now, and Lovejoy called to one of them, "Hawkins, go fetch Doc Forbes and tell him we got a fellow who needs planting. Me and this deputy U.S. marshal will be at the jailhouse if you need us."

The little crowd parted as they crossed the street to the shady overhang of the opposing frame buildings. Longarm was now aware that the local law knew how he'd been set up. Yet he didn't remember having told

Lovejoy about the rat-faced hand by the livery. That could be taken several ways. Lovejoy might have heard it from the stable hands. It seemed a bit soon to conclude that he was in cahoots with the gang against a fellow lawman.

The Manzanita jail was a thick-walled adobe structure with a redwood-shingled roof. Lovejoy ushered him in and Longarm saw that it was a one-room building partitioned by iron bars. A morose-looking Indian sat crosslegged on the floor of the lockup. He didn't look at them as they entered.

The office was furnished with a rolltop desk and some bentwood chairs. There was a typewriter on the green blotter of the desk. Beside it stood a funny-looking contraption of a kind that Longarm had never seen before. He asked, "Is that one of Professor Bell's new-fangled talking telegraphs?"

"It sure is," Lovejoy said proudly. "We're up to date in California. Got us a line running all the way to Sacramento, now."

Longarm was impressed. "You must have some budget. My boss, Marshal Vail, has been trying to get him a telephone back in Denver. Washington keeps telling him it's a passing fad."

Lovejoy put a sheet of paper in the typewriter and began to hunt and peck, standing. Longarm snorted and said, "Hell, let me type it up for you. I ain't got all day."

"You know how to play a typewriter?" Lovejoy said incredulously.

"Some. I've been fooling with the one in the office in Denver."

He sat down at the desk and began to hunt and peck a bit faster than the constable had, but not much. For the life of him he couldn't see why everyone was in such an all-fired hurry to change things. He'd been writing his reports in longhand for six or eight years and nobody had ever said they couldn't read his Palmer penmanship.

He had typed out, *REPORT BY CUSTIS LONG, DEPUTY U.S. MARSHALL, DISTRICT COURT OF DENVER,* before Constable Lovejoy got up the nerve to place the muzzle of his revolver against the nape of Longarm's neck.

Longarm stopped typing. He asked, "Do you have a reason for whatever you're trying to pull, Lovejoy?"

The constable licked his lips and said, "You just keep them hands up there. I don't want no trouble, Longarm."

Longarm said, "Hell, old son, you've already *got* trouble." But he did as he was told. As Lovejoy held the muzzle of the revolver against the base of Longarm's skull with one hand, he frisked and disarmed him with the other. As Lovejoy took the derringer from Longarm's right-hand vest pocket, the lawman nodded and sighed, "Yeah, they gave you a pretty good run-down on me, didn't they? Not many folks know about the derringer on my watch chain. Who are you working for, those jaspers who've been stealing high-grade from the Lost Chinaman?"

"State of California," Lovejoy said, adding, "You could have rode out like I asked, but they said in Sacramento that you was a stubborn cuss. You get up, now, and move slow for the lockup. I don't want to shoot you, but . . ."

Longarm rose slowly to his feet, the gun pressing against his back, but he protested, "Lovejoy, you are starting to piss me off a mite. You can't lock me up."

Lovejoy cut him off. "You ain't the law in California. You're out of your jurisdiction, and Justice Field, down in Sacramento, says you have no call to mess in local matters."

246

As the constable opened the jail door and shoved him inside, Longarm snorted, "Hell, if you mean Justice Stephen Field, *he's* in trouble too! I wasn't ordered out here by the Denver office. I'm on a special assignment from Washington! It seems they've been wondering why the federal marshals out here can't seem to get a handle on those missing gold shipments." As the door slammed shut, he added, "We're talking about gold being sent to the U.S. Mint in San Francisco, Lovejoy. We're talking about Uncle Sam's money. Savvy?"

"Look, I just do my job as best I know how. Sacramento says your badge don't mean shit on this side of the Sierras and, damn it, it was your own idea to go and shoot the Calico Kid!"

"Come on, the silly son of a bitch was trying to murder me!"

"Maybe. We'll see about it at your trial."

"My *what?* What the hell charges are you holding me on, God damn it?"

The constable holstered his sixgun.

"Don't know. Maybe murder, maybe manslaughter. That'll be up to the district attorney, won't it?"

Longarm laughed, still more puzzled than alarmed, and said, "Lovejoy, this ain't going to work. I know you old boys up here in the Mother Lode play rough, but we're not talking about jumping some greenhorn's claim or robbing a Mexican. We're talking about over a dozen gold shipments sidetracked between here and the mint. You don't seem to grasp that it's federal gold we're talking about!"

Lovejoy shrugged and turned away. One of the townies came to the door and yelled in something about the undertaker. Lovejoy said, "I'll talk to him. Keep an eye on the jail, will you?"

As Lovejoy left, Longarm called out, "They'll send someone else, you damned fool! Even if you kill me, you're going to be combing U.S. deputies out of your hair until Justice finds out where all that ore's been shipped!"

And then the constable was gone. The man he'd deputized to take his place went over to the desk and sat down with his back to the lockup. He put his feet up on the desk and lit a smoke. Longarm asked, "You mind telling me something, friend?"

The man didn't answer. Longarm swore softly and turned away from the bars. The Indian on the floor said, "I am not a bad person. Don't hurt me."

Longarm went over to the fold-down bunk and sat down, saying, "I'm not a bad person, either. What are you in for?"

"My name is Bitter Water. I am a Miwok. What you Saltu call a Digger Indian."

Longarm had recently come to know and respect these groups of foraging Indians contemptuously called Diggers. They were peaceable, graceful, and intelligent people who were often ruthlessly exterminated or driven from their lands by avaricious whites. He had recently had occasion to help a group of Paiutes in eastern Nevada whose stores of their staple food— pinyon nuts—were being destroyed by uncontrolled, illegal logging. Longarm extended a large, calloused hand toward Bitter Water, and the small Indian shook it firmly.

"Well, I'm Custis Long," he said, "and I'll call you a Miwok. You didn't say why they arrested you."

"Yes, I did. I told you I was an Indian."

"Is that against the law?"

"In this county? Yes. Some Saltu came to the valley where my people have always gathered acorns. They said it was *their* valley now. They said they had a paper from Wa Sentan telling them they could keep cows there. When I asked to see the paper, they hit me. So I ran away."

"I'm sorry, Bitter Water. I hope you don't think all of my people are like that. But how'd you wind up in this jail if you got away?"

"You have a good heart, but you do not listen. I said I ran away. I did not say I *got* away. While I was running from the men with cows, I crossed some other Saltus' mining claim. They caught me with a rope and brought me here. They say I have been stealing gold. Someone has been stealing gold around here, and, as I said, I am an Indian." Bitter Water shrugged as he added, "I think they will hang both of us as soon as it gets dark."

Longarm shot a glance out front. Lovejoy had taken his watch along with his badge, gun, and last three smokes, but he could see it was still early afternoon. Turning back to the Indian, he said, "Lovejoy said something about a trial. How often does the circuit judge come over from the county seat?"

"I don't know. It does not matter. They will not hear of us over in San Andreas. The men in Manzanita who hang people call themselves vigilantes. It is said nobody knows who they are, but I think this is a lie."

Longarm frowned thoughtfully. Then he got up and went over to the bars again, calling out, "Hey, this fellow says you have a vigilance committee in this town. I thought that sort of thing went out with the forty-niners."

The deputy, if that was what he was, didn't answer. Longarm insisted, "Look, I don't know if Lovejoy told you boys the facts of life, but I am a federal officer. You just try lynching a federal man and you won't have to worry about the Justice Department; you'll have the U.S. Army up here asking all sorts of questions."

Again, there was no reply. Apparently the man at the desk knew how hard it is not to give anything away, once you start talking. The people behind this had their henchmen well-trained.

All right, he decided, *let's take as gloomy a look at this mess as possible and see where that leaves everyone.* His investigation had been nipped in the bud, either by some very clever plotting indeed or just a bit of quick thinking on the part of a skunk wearing a badge. It didn't matter whether the late Calico Kid had been in on it or not. By shooting the inept gunman, he'd delivered himself into their hands. The Indian's idea made sense, too, damn it. Longarm knew there was no way they'd ever hang a murder charge on him in open court. On the other hand, if he and Bitter Water were killed, by vigilantes, friends of the Calico Kid, or simply "trying to escape" . . .

"It still won't work," he called out, adding, "My office knows I'm here in Calaveras County. The Lost Chinaman is fixing to ship another carload of high-grade ore down to the stamping mills, and if I don't ride in with the gold, they'll send in another team."

No answer.

Longarm insisted, "Sure, you and your pals might steal at least one more shipment, but then what? You're spreading yourselves a mite thin already, you know. I figure even if we're talking about the highest grade of ore, it still can't run more than a few thousand dollars a trainload, before it's refined. I can see you've bought your own law all the way down to the state capital, but, like I said, there's only so much gold and there're a lot of palms to grease."

Hoping the silent man was at least listening, he insisted, "Look, you can bribe almost anyone to look the other way about a trainload of ore. But the rates go up as soon as you start killing folks, and a deputy U.S. marshal comes high as hell. I know you won't answer, but I want you to study on my words. Up to now, I don't have a thing on anyone. But once the government starts getting serious about you boys, it's all over. You have too many people in on it. One of you, only one, just has to get worried about his own hide, or maybe pissed off because he thinks he should have had a bigger share, and——"

The man at the desk swung his boots to the floor and turned around to snap, "You just *hush*, mister! You don't know what you're talking about!"

Longarm was a bit relieved to see that the man wasn't deaf. "The hell I don't. I'm talking about a U.S. deputy being hindered, or worse. You're not going to like it in Leavenworth, boy."

"God damn it, you got no call to say I'm a thief. I've never stole a penny in my born days. Me and every other honest man in the county is as riled as you are about them jaspers robbing the ore trains, and I'll not be tarred with the same brush as them!"

Longarm saw that the man was young and rather simple-looking. He smiled and asked, "Why are you holding me, then? Can't you see you're helping the high-graders, even if you're not in on it?"

The guard shook his head and said, "Don't fun with me, mister. You know you shot the Calico Kid."

"Then you must be one of *his* friends, right?" Longarm prodded him.

"Hell, I just said I was an honest man. I got no truck with them wild gunslicks Calico used to ride with."

Longarm shook his head wearily and marveled, "Loco. The whole bunch has busted out to nibble locoweed, unless I missed a turn a ways back. If you and Lovejoy ain't with the highgraders, and you ain't with the Calico Kid's bunch, what in thunder am I doing behind these bars?"

"You're in jail 'cause it's where you belong, damn it. You had no call to come here and stir up trouble."

"I'd say the trouble sort of came my way. I was only trying to do my job."

"No, you wasn't. You don't *belong* in these parts, mister. We got a town constable and a county sheriff.

We got our own federal marshals down to Sacramento. You're just a durned old carpetbagger! Nobody around here ever asked you to stick your nose into our business, did they?"

"I hate to call such an honest man a liar, but you are purely full of shit. I *was* asked to investigate those gold robberies. Uncle Sam asked me, real polite. Are you saying Calaveras County's not part of these United States?"

The youth hesitated. Then he said, "You're trying to mix me up," and turned away again. This time he meant it. Longarm tried reason. He tried argument. He tried saying mean things about the man's mother. Nothing worked. After a while he got tired of talking to the back of an obviously thick skull and went back to the bunk. As he sat down again, the Indian muttered, "We have nothing to worry about as long as they are guarding us."

Longarm started to ask what Bitter Water meant. Then he nodded in sick understanding. He'd investigated enough lynchings to know the form.

If that was indeed the plan, Constable Lovejoy would go through the motions for the rest of the day. A rural community like Manzanita went to bed early. Or at least, the honest elements did. Later, in the dark of the moon, Lovejoy would probably be called away from the jail on some obscure mission. That was when the night riders would arrive.

Later, some luckier lawman might put it all together and they'd know at last whether the late Custis Long had been lynched by men in the pay of the gold thieves, by pals of the Calico Kid, or by someone he hadn't figured out yet. Yeah, they'd get to the bottom of it, in time. You don't steal federal gold and murder federal marshals and hope to get away with it forever. But he didn't have forever. He had maybe eight or ten hours if he intended to crack the case himself. It wasn't a bit comforting to think some other lawmen might track down the answers, after he was dead.

The Indian's voice was soft as he asked, "Would you get mad at me if I made a suggestion?"

Longarm smiled and said, "No. I think it's a good idea."

Bitter Water looked puzzled as he asked, "Do you read my words before they are spoken?"

"Hell, if you're thinking about anything *but* busting out of here you must be loco, too. What's your plan?"

Bitter Water suddenly looked even more dejected. "I was hoping *you* had one. All I know is that we can't stay here overnight. Right after dark would be the best time, don't you think?"

Longarm shook his head and said, "That's when they'll be expecting us to try and bust out. One of the oldest tricks around is to leave a prisoner unguarded and sort of let him think he's escaping."

Morosely, Bitter Water studied the floor between his knees for a time before he sighed, "Heya! Waiting outside with rifles. Forgive me for being stupid. I have spent little time in Saltu jails. When do *you* think we should get away?"

"Right about now would suit me just fine. It's midafternoon and hot as hell out there. Half the town'll be taking a siesta, and the restless souls are likely holding a funeral for the cuss I just shot."

"I agree. But I don't see how we can get out of this place. If I had a knife, I could dig through the adobe wall, but—"

"It'd take too long," Longarm interrupted. "I think we'd better try an old trick and hope that jasper out front is as dumb as he looks. The old prison fight would never work on anyone who's worked as a guard for six weeks, but he might not have heard of it."

"He does look stupid," Bitter Water agreed. "But what is this trick you speak of?"

"Oh, you're going to start beating me up. I don't think he'd care if *I* started slapping *you* around, but—"

The suggestion caused a flicker of enthusiasm to brighten the Indian's features. "Yes. No Saltu is going to stand by and allow a brother to be bested by a dirty Indian. But what are we supposed to be fighting about?"

"Hmmm, we'll have to make it look a mite serious, won't we? Let's see now. What's a good old boy likely to have strong feelings about? I'll tell you what, Bitter Water. Take off your pants."

The Indian looked thunderstruck and muttered, "You are making a joke. What do you take me for?"

"That ain't important. It's what we want *him* to take you for. I want you to act like a wild, crazy Indian with a hard-on. Come on, old son, *I* know you ain't a jail-wolf."

Bitter Water shrugged and stood up, turning out to be taller than the lawman had expected. The Indian dropped his ragged britches and stepped out of them, naked from the waist down. Longarm shouted, "You ain't gonna do no such thing, you crazy red bastard!" and then he grabbed the startled Indian by the shirt and pulled him against his own frame, crying out, "Help! This crazy Digger's after my white ass!"

The guard swung around to stare openmouthed as the two men rolled over and over on the floor. Then he sprang to his feet and shouted, "Hey, what the hell kind of jail do you think we're *running* here? We don't *allow* that sort of thing in Manzanita, boys!"

Longarm whimpered, "Get him off me, then! He's as strong as a goddamned elephant and I reckon he'd fuck one, given the chance!"

The guard fished a key from his ring and fumbled with the lock, saying, "Hit *back,* damn it! You're a white man!"

254

"He's killing me! He must have been chewing that crazy Indian medicine they use to get riled up!"

The door was open and the guard stepped in, muttering, "Oh, for God's sake," as he drew his gun. Longarm saw what was coming and tried to shove Bitter Water out of the way, but the gun barrel slammed down against the side of the Miwok's head and Longarm felt him go limp. He rolled the Indian off, hooked a toe behind the guard's ankle, and kicked him hard in the kneecap with the other booted heel.

The guard went down, gasping in pain, but still holding on to the gun as Longarm rolled to his hands and knees and dove headfirst over his victim's thrashing legs. He landed with all his considerable weight on the man's chest and grabbed for the wrist of his gun hand as he kneed the guard viciously. The man gasped in pain. Longarm grabbed his hair and pounded his head on the floor until he lay limp and silent. Then Longarm hit him once for luck and got up with the other man's gun in his own hand.

He stood for a moment, listening. The sounds of the struggle didn't seem to be drawing any attention from the blazing furnace of the town outside. Both Bitter Water and the guard were breathing, but were obviously out of it for some time to come.

The Indian looked sort of silly lying there with no pants on, but his appearance was the least of Longarm's worries. He stuck the gun in his waistband and picked up the Indians discarded pants. As he knelt to fumble them on over Bitter Water's big feet, the Indian opened his eyes and asked, "What are you doing?"

"Trying to get you dressed and out of here."

Bitter Water sat up and said, "I can do that. Why didn't you run away as soon as you had the chance? Didn't you think he knocked me out?"

"You mean he didn't?" Longarm asked, astonished.

"No. I was only dazed. It came to me as I lay there

that I would be wise to let you run away and then leave myself. You are a good person, but you are Saltu."

"You mean you figured you could lose yourself in the timber easier without a white man tagging along?"

"Of course," Bitter Water replied with assurance. "No white man can track me in my native hills. But you did not run away. You stayed to help me. This is a new thing I must consider."

Longarm shrugged and said, "You light out on your own if you've a mind to. I've got to see if I can find my gun and badge."

But as he went out front to rummage through the constable's desk, the Indian, now dressed, took his arm and said, "Come, Saltu brother. The siesta will be ending and we must have at least an hour's start on them through the trees."

Longarm looked at Bitter Water with some surprise. "I thought you aimed to make it on your own, Bitter Water. Just let me find my stuff, and—"

"You are a good person, but a fool. You *had* your badge and they arrested you! When they find their friend unconscious, the whole town will be after us!"

"Us? All for one and one for all?"

The Miwok nodded. "You have me in your debt. Come with me and no Saltu will ever cut your trail."

"Well, maybe if I can get a few miles off and study my next move a spell . . . " Longarm speculated.

"Come. I will show you things no Saltu knows about these hills. Later, you can go back to Wa Sentan. Agreed?"

Longarm nodded, but then he said, "Not hardly. This case is just getting interesting."

"You mean to come back to this place? Without your badge? Without your gun? Without a friend in the county?"

"Hell, old son, I've *got* a gun. The other odds just promise to make the game a mite more interesting."